THE EYES OF AN ORPHAN

From JAR

J VIGH HERMAN . PHD,

Dedication / Author's Note

Christopher Reeve once said
"A hero is an ordinary individual who finds the strength to preserve
and endure in spite of overwhelming obstacles".

In my eyes, a hero doesn't need a cape or superpowers to help
people. Thank you to you all who were helping make this world a
better place.

Thank you for giving me the best life I could have ever imagined. I
want you to know that I'm glad that you two decided to adopt me.

CONTENTS

INTRODUCTION

The message of this book is birthed from the story of an amazing woman who changed the life of many children. She dedicated her life to a cause that changed the story of these children, who ended up moving to different parts of the world.

Life is a complicated journey and the fact that some people have it going great on one side of the earth does not mean it is not going horribly for some other people on another part of the earth. However, if you are on the lucky side, you may wonder why you should be bothered about the unlucky side of the circle.

You need to be bothered, because in the end, the earth is roughly a sphere and what goes around will probably come around, one way or the other. The truth is, we all need to help those who seem to be on the parts of the earth that are not as "lucky" or simply do not enjoy certain the benefits. However, it should not be because of our own selfish interests or from the standpoint of trying to avoid karma. It should be out of compassion. Many people in developed parts of the world have no idea about the menace being faced in third world countries. This book hopes to reveal that. It is a book that is bound to answer the question of "What should we do if things are going good for us?" and "How can we be of help to those going through tough times?"

Now, there are different people going through different things in the world, so the book picks out a certain subsection. The concern here are orphans. Many of the lucky ones end up getting housed by orphanages, so at every point, you would find orphans in an orphanage.

Now, let's talk about compassion. Compassion only portrays that you are human. It is a good quality. The entire theme of this interesting story is to spark up compassion and I hope you are moved to help those in need. You can start with those around you and stretch your hands to help those in parts of the world different from where you are.

Although this book and the different stories in it are purely fictional, they depict what several kids in our world go through from when they lose their parents to when they find an orphanage that serves as a safe space for them. Many of their stories start in an ugly manner and end up beautifully. You would love to see it.

Happy reading!

PROLOGUE

It was evening time. The kids were playing in the streets. The noise was something Julia had never understood, but seeing the kind of life many kids in Liberia lived, she had come to understand that they were having fun in their own way. They passed through the town's market and saw the kids running from corner to corner, hiding so their friends could not find them. Seeing them run, at first, she felt like bolting like something terrible had happened, but again, she remembered it was the way these kids had their fun; a way of living. Only few houses had televisions; the kids that were allowed to, gathered at these house at night to watch the television. Some even watched from the window. She often looked at the kids especially, with pity and wished she could somehow make their lives better.

In their one week stay as volunteers, they had visited areas in Grand Kru, River Gee and Bomi counties. They were now in Bomi. As their leader explained this and that about Liberia, she nodded but Julia was deep in thoughts. She wondered what it would had been like if she grew up in a place like that and she was thankful that she came to volunteer in Africa. Someone touched her shoulder and she jolted back to reality.

"Ohh…Maria" she said, realizing it was Maria. Maria gave her a peck, and then, a side hug.

"I am happy I have you right here, by my side. I was not sure you'd like to here, especially after everything you've been through."

She said, as searched Julia's eyes, to be sure of how her friend was really feeling. "But now, I'm glad you came." She concluded.

Julia smiled at Maria and returned her hug. "Thank you" she whispered.

Although many of the volunteers where black, they still stood out among the people in every town they visited. Julia and two other males were white. Maria, Julia's best friend was Hispanic. Unlike it did in many part of the world, their skin color and race differences did not matter much to the volunteers. They had a common goal; to help and that they did with no discrimination among themselves or the people they were helping.

They also got a lot of attention, especially when they had to share the relief materials they brought from England and they had to interact with the mothers of the children. Some of the women looked encouraged each time they queued to get the vaccine, others just looked sad; especially the teenagers among them. Julia reckoned that teenage pregnancy happened back in England too, but the standard of living there was a lot better, so the girls always received some form of support. However, here, it seemed as though there was little or no hope for support. Families did what they could, but they were living in poverty themselves. Hence, the extra burden of an unwanted pregnancy always brought frustration. The girls were sure to suffer the consequences of their actions.

As they continued to share the relief materials among the poor people of Bomi County, all of a sudden, Julia left the group. They were about to start educating some of the townspeople about polio, and Maria knew her friend had learnt so much about the subject and was also looking to teach the people about the little she knew. Now, she wondered why her friend was walking towards the small bush path. Julia's mother had called her aside to keep an eye on Julia while on the trip. She had been acting strange for months and everyone just wanted to make sure she was fine.

THE EYES OF AN ORPHAN

"Where are you headed?" asked Maria, who ran behind her friend. Julia wouldn't stop. Maria tried to catch up with her, but Julia was walking faster. She noticed that her friend would not stop following her and was also making her feel like she was acting like a psycho. So, she stopped and heaved a sigh.

"Okay Maria. Can't you hear a baby crying in a distance?"

"Yes, but babies cry all the time. It could be a baby struggling with its mother or just crying because they want something. This is common and should not be surprising to you, especially in a place like this."

"No, it's not surprising at all. It just sounds like that baby is in the woods."

"This bush." Maria laughed. "Why would anyone leave a baby in a bush?"

"Can't you see that the more we move into the woods, the more the cries become even louder?"

"That's because the child could just be on the other side of the woods."

"I say we keep looking. Let's just keep looking. Imagine a child being in here."

"Oh no, I do not want to imagine it."

"Then, let's keep following the sounds of the cry, close in on the child and get the necessary help."

"Okay, fine." Said Maria.

CHAPTER
ONE

"**W**ake me up." Said Sandra. "This must be a dream!" she said. She went from the kitchen, to the big dinner space and then, to the living room and the big fire place. Ever since their car stopped in front of the house, she could not stop admiring the beauty it was. It was a huge white house, with a nice garden, a big garage and enough space in the yard; just the way she had described her dream house to Joseph. He had told her that they did not have enough money to make such a purchase and looking through their accounts and the expenses to come, she agreed that they were not ready for such huge spending, and even agreed to get a smaller house.

They never liked the idea of a mortgage. They believed in the idea of saving and doing investments towards anything they wanted to get. They had done all that with the intention of getting a smaller house. So, coming to a big house like that was a shocking one for her. Joseph had been planning it all along. He wanted it to be a surprise, so he did not reveal it to her when the royalty for the discovery he made with a team of other scientists came through.

Instead, he showed Sandra the picture of a smaller house and its bill. After withdrawing the money for the purchase of the smaller house from their account, he added the massive royalty he had received and positioned himself for the next opportunity to buy their dream house. Although Sandra always talked about how much she wanted the house, he knew that the accountant in her was barely prepared to make a purchase as huge as that. It would shake their finances and they still had time to work towards getting that dream house, so left to her, there was no need to rush.

Joe had made contacts with the agent secretly and told her that he wanted to surprise his wife. So, really, they went ahead to check out a couple of smaller houses together with Sandra. They had agreed on a particular small house and the fact that it was good enough and bigger than the former one which they were ready to put up for sale.

When Joe changed routes while driving the house she thought they purchased, he promised he was only taking a shorter route, but once he pulled up in front of the white building and gave her a knowing look, it dawned on her. Her eyes lit up in the brightest way, as she looked at the sunshine on the building, which made it glow in her eyes. She could already imagine taking pictures around the house and making memories with the children who were still in their growing years. And oh, the garden. It was a good scenery for family photos and she even started daydreaming about inviting a few friends for a picnic from time to time, since they now had such a big garden and a large yard.

She hugged him tight. When she released him from her hold, "Baby, how??" she asked, surprised.

"Why not go in and see if you like it first? I bought it because of you, so this whole act is a total waste if it is not what you want."

Sandra smiled.

"Dad, will we live here?" asked Erica.

"Definitely baby."

Her eyes lit up. Erica and her brother, Leo, ran after their mother, who was excited and could not wait to see what the inside of the house looked like.

And oh, she was impressed! They made their way upstairs immediately. The living area was amazing and they just could not wait to see the bedrooms.

"This would be my room and I would paint it bright pink!" Erica shouted from one of the rooms loud enough for her mother and her brother to hear. Her mother laughed.

"Mum! I love it here" said Lionel. Are we staying today?

"No baby, we are moving in next week."

"Next week is so far away. Why not today?"

"Next week starts in three days, kiddo. Today is Thursday, remember." Joe and Sandra had gone ahead to pick the kids from school together, so they could see the new house. They had so many outdoor bonding activities that weekend and they had postponed for so long, that they weren't ready to call their planner to cancel yet again.

Leo did not exactly seem pleased at his parent's decision to move in the following week, but he always ended up realizing that he was only a kid and his parents called the shots. He loved the house and just wanted to move in the following day after school or maybe at least, on Saturday. He was not big on the outdoor activities his parents wanted them to have, he only liked to read his school books and get good grades and he had found perfect spots in the house for that purpose. His parents would say that those activities would form a part of their childhood they would always want to remember, but he never really cared.

Erica, seeing her brother was still not so happy about the moving time said to him, "We have forever to live in the house."

"Well, that is so true." He said, smiling as if his sister just reminded him of a good news he forgot.

"We would grow up here. I can invite my friends for a slumber party here." Said Erica.

"When I am a teenager, I can throw a night party when mum and dad are not home. Just imagine it Erica."

She smiled as she nodded. She was lost in her imagination, thinking of the many things that could happen in the new house and with all the space they had. Mum and dad will ensure the furnishing got finished and then, they would move into the place in the coming week.

Joe was smiling, seeing his family had been enjoying the view. They were yet to see the best part of it, so he called them, as he led them to the backyard area. And right there, was a nice pool for the family.

"What's better than a Sunday afternoon swimming with mummy, daddy and my darling brother?"

"Absolutely nothing baby." Said Sandra, who was now in tears. They were tears of Joy. She went ahead to hug Joe tightly. All she felt was pure joy. They were literally living a dream. Who ever thought they would get to this point in their lives? She would not let go and so, the children came and joined in on the hug.

Joe felt so happy. Nothing pleased him in the world than satisfying his wife and making his family happy.

"And that is how, my dears, you succeed in a hostile environment" Joseph said, as he brought his speech to a close.

"We would now move to the Q & A section" the moderator said, as they whisked Joseph Smith away to the inner room for a break.

"Urgh…" the crowd voiced out. They did not want his session to come to an end. They had come from different parts of the United States to hear him speak. While some people preferred to hear the speeches from these masterclasses in recorded versions, for Joseph Smith, the public opinion was a little different. It was usually said that there was a different kind of connection you got from looking at him as he spoke about his own life and work experiences. It was usually said that you had to be in the same room with him to experience that difference. Hence, people came from different states and some even from neighboring countries. As they expected, the experience was worth all their efforts. However, now, Joseph had be whisked away and the questions kept pouring in.

He thanked the staff as he got into the private room, catching his breath and wondering what he had just done once again. He knew he had experiences to talk about, but he wondered why the crowd could not get enough every time he talked. What was so special about his words? He could not figure it himself. Although he had worked on his speaking abilities by attending several helpful classes himself, but asides that, it was almost like he had a special gift of speaking that no one else seemed to have. He was grateful about the discoveries he had made as a virologist and how they had helped in helping health outcomes. However, above all, he was grateful for the experiences that were once bitter experiences while he experienced them. He was especially grateful for his childhood and wondered if he would be where he was today if he did not have those crazy childhood experiences. They formed his core and that core of his, was the secret ingredient, to his best knowledge.

He had been able to help several new scientists navigate their way in their careers and that was the mark of success for him. He remained a source of inspiration, yet he did not feel successful without being able to help people in need, because his own journey was laced with lots and lots of help from people on his way up; right from when he was a child. After answering the questions for the day, Joseph was on his way home. That was his best place to be. He loved family time and he loved being very available to the kids. He wanted them to be as happy as happy could be. He had taken the back door before the rest of the crowd could leave the hall. If he did not do that, the chances of getting home early in the evening was slim, as he would be too engrossed in answering questions one-on-one. The rest of the questions were going to be directed to his email and that was just fine.

It was about 4:30p.m. As he tried to drive out from the parking lot in his tinted vehicle that was sure to keep him from the kind of attention he did not want, a call came in from Sandra.

"I trust your masterclass was great as always."

"Sure babe."

Once again, he realized Sandra was the one and his life would never be what it was without her in it. It was not as though they had a perfect relationship, but in micro moments like that, he always just realized how blessed he was. It wasn't a question of what she had said for him; it was the way she said it, how she knew exactly how to use the right tone (in addition to words) to motivate him. He would have made a big mistake if he hadn't made the move to take their relationship to the next level. They would have remained good friends, and he would have continued to achieve a lot with them being friends, like he always had.

However, having her as his life partner was an entirely different level. He was sure that he wouldn't have achieved as much without her as his wife. Each time he heard her voice, he was constantly reminded that he had a great home, and a happy family. They had great kids; which gave him utmost fulfilment. Their kids always came out tops whenever they did anything; from school, to sports, to non-curricular activities. They were indeed happy and closely-knitted. For Joe and Sandra, this was a very important component of family; being closely knitted and having a place to run to when in utmost need. And they ensured to imbibe these beliefs in the kids too. The next generation needed this. Sandra had always been family to Joseph and vice-versa, it helped them through their life journey. They believed everyone needed that kind of support to attain all round success.

"Joe, would you please help get the kids from school today."

"I'll send the bill ma'am." He replied sharply before they both burst out in laughter. The couple was as determined as always to ensure they picked the kids from school by themselves. For them, it was yet another time to bond with the kids in spite of their busy schedules. They were always more than determined to put the kids first.

"What's up?" He asked.

"I have another emergency meeting with the board."

"Oh dear…you must be tired."

"Well, what can I do?"

"They need to let my wife breathe."

"Well, your wife happens to enjoy kicking ass."

They burst out laughing again.

"But that doesn't mean your wife isn't stressed. You can pick up some ice cream on your way home to make her feel better."

"Haha. That's a cute way of sending me to the mall."

"Tell me of the other things you'd like to get."

She wanted to laugh, but she tried to control it. However, she could not help but smile on the other end of the phone. "Joe, you know me too well. Thanks darling, I'll send the list to you right away."

"You know you can always count on me. When I say I have your back, believe me baby, I always mean it, every damn time."

"I know baby. I know you do. I have never doubted you for once. Always and forever."

"Always and forever."

With this, they dropped the phone with smiles on their faces. He was a blessing to her, and so was she to him. Through mutual efforts, they had achieved a lot together and they were dedicated to putting in those efforts, moving forward.

"Daddy!" Erica shouted as she ran to hug her father.

They had waited for an extra 30 minutes, as their mother's plan had changed.

"Sorry for keeping you waiting baby" he said, as he lifted her up into his arms.

"Daddy" Lionel said with a disappointed look on his face, as he walked up to his dad.

"Sorry my boy; your mother had an emergency and I had to come all the way from the other end of town to get you. I apologize on her behalf. You know we love you, right?"

"Yes daddy, we know." They chorused.

Lionel, 8 and Erica, 6, were just happy to see their dad come pick them. They had a good day at school, making new friends and Erica had so much to tell her dad.

"Dad, I made a new friend today."

"Tell me about this friend." he said, as he drove to their favorite ice-cream store.

"Ice cream!" Erica screamed, as her dad pulled over in the parking lot.

"You were trying to tell me something." Joe said, as he helped his beautiful daughter get off the car. "Daddy, I'll continue after having some blueberry"

He laughed. "As always" He said.

Lionel was so quiet the whole time. "What's the matter?" Joe said, as he put his hand over his son's shoulder.

"Dad, my grades…"

"Why not have some ice cream and then, we would talk about it." Joe interrupted his son. He had noticed that Lionel was always worrying about little things. He wanted his son to get a bit relaxed.

"…but Dad." Lionel argued.

"Son, let's have some ice cream." Said Joe. He was sure that his son was just going to tell him about some minor thing. Perhaps about the question that he did not answer as accurately as he wished he did or some kid who did not acknowledge his skills in some activity. As Lionel walked into the ice cream place, his father was watching him from the back, smiling because his son was exactly like his mother in her teenage years, just always trying to be number one at everything she did and worrying a lot whenever that did not happen. However, Sandra knew better now. Joe just needed to explain to him that he should always find a way to relax in spite of being a go-getter. There were so many other issues to worry about in life and he was determined to ensure that his child enjoyed his childhood even while striving to be the best. The mall was right beside the ice cream store and Joe knew he had to drop by to pick up everything on his wife's list before heading home.

Once the kids had taken half of their ice-cream, once again, they were back to wanting their father to hear everything from their day at school.

"Your brother seems very bothered. Erica, let's hear him out first."

The young brown skinned beauty folded her arms in disappointment. Her father always heard her out first, but turning her attention to Lionel today, he looked so troubled.

"Oh, he doesn't look happy" she said, turning her face back to her father.

"That's because I came second in the math test."

"Oh…you studied so hard for that test." Erica said. "I am so sorry Leo." She said, reaching for her brother's hand. Leo, as she often called him, just nodded his head. Yes, he studied all night for one week before that test. This was aside the fact that he worked his arithmetic every single day. He was really gunning for number one and nothing less.

Their father watched his kids all along. Honestly, Joseph knew how important this was for Leo, but he really wanted to burst out laughing. He felt like he was watching his wife in her younger years and it was just really funny to now see in their child that she had worried way too much back then.

"Look son" Joe started. "Here's the formula for not getting mad when someone else wins what you worked hard for: Do your best; your very best, and then, leave the rest."

"But if I did my best, then I deserved to win, right?"

"Not exactly son. This is real life; no one deserves anything. Remember, everyone was working for that same prize you think you deserve. Every other person who is working towards it thinks they deserve it. So, what if someone else gets it? The truth is, in the end, it is the person who wins the prize that deserved it all along. No one deserves a prize except its winner; it is that simple son."

Leo did not look happy about the response his father had, but it made a lot of sense to the eight-year-old.

"Trust me son. It is a lot of burden to go through life, thinking you deserve anything at all. Your life would be a lot easier if you can think this way. The best you can do is to study to be the best you can ever be and hope for the best, while visualizing your best self. But we humans tend to forget that this doesn't stop anyone else from studying to be the best they can be too. If their best beats your best, there is nothing you can really do. You can only study to become even better, but no one owns success. No one has the right to succeed. So, quit being angry dear son. Let it go and be happy for him."

"Dad, how can I be happy for him?"

"Clap for other when they succeed son. Then, wait your turn. This is the only way to live. Anything different from this is not a good way to live. Success easily locates those who are happy to see others succeed, as long as they keep working on getting better."

"Okay dad. I'll try my best to be happy for him and work on bettering my best."

Joe gave Leo a high-five. The rest of the evening was spent listening to Erica and her tales from making a new friend. When the talkative Erica had talked to her satisfaction, they headed over to the mall to get everything their mum needed. By the time they were done, Sandra was already on her way home. The kids were excited at this, they could not wait to get home and tell their mother their many stories too.

Sandra got into the house and made straight to the kitchen to make some macaroni and cheese. Joe helped the kids with their homework and a bit of study time, when they went over what they did in school for the day.

Dinner time was another time when the kids could tell their parents whatever they had in mind. Sandra called the family to the dinner table and once again, that night, Erica had something to tell the family. One day, she wanted to stand in front of cameras and take beautiful pictures that will be put up on billboards or be brought to the screens of individuals all over the world to see. She had seen a beautiful black woman on a billboard and ever since, the little girl had been dreaming of being that woman one day.

She had woken up several mornings, after having dreamt about seeing herself walk on runways and have a large crowd cheer. Prior to seeing that woman on the billboard, she had never really thought anyone could do that for a living, but she felt like being that kind of person was something that could give her joy. It was something she'd love to do and now wanted to ask her parents if it was a job a person could do for a living. She had talked about it in school and her friends had called it "modelling". The young wanted her family to know that she would like to be a model.

"I'd love to model for big companies." she said. It was not exactly the kind of news her parents were expecting to hear, but they were now pleasantly surprised. So was her brother.

Joe was the first to comment. "Oh, really. I would love to have a popular daughter. That's beautiful."

"Thanks daddy" said the six-year-old.

"Baby, that's beautiful, we could register you in an academy that prepares you for that and you could even start now. However, you have so much going on for you: Ballet, school work, all the extracurricular activities and parties you have to attend. Are you willing to do everything it takes to pull everything off or is there something you're willing to forsake?"

"Yes, let's hear your plan baby." Said Joe. "Apart from that, we would like you to have a profession. Modelling is not something you may want to take up fully with time and we want you to have options. Going to a college gives you options."

"Okay daddy. That's a lot. I think I like the idea of the academy."

Joe and Sandra had always planned to give their kids a chance to make their own decisions and defend them, all to an extent, to prepare them for the bigger picture that life always presented. They just wanted to make sure their kids were equipped enough to face life in every aspect, and they knew they had to infuse this into every single thing. This understanding is what always made them a joint force with the kids and the same applied today.

"First off, how do you plan to ensure you can keep up with your perfect grades?" Joe asked.

"Dad, now that I think of it, maybe I can cut some of my play time on the weekends and use them for trainings at the academy, if that can work with their plans. This way, my study plan would not be affected in any way." Erica was a smart girl. She read magazines and always listened on conversations adults were having. This way, she was a bit smarter than a regular six-year-old.

"That's a brilliant plan baby, but you'll have less time to spend with friends. You'll have less time to mix with your peer." Said Sandra. "What do you think about your sister's plan?"

"As long as she keeps her perfect scores, I think it's alright." Shrugged Leo.

"I already mix with my peers while doing ballet, in school and the birthday parties too. Cutting down on my playtime does not bother me in any way." She said.

"Alright baby." Said her mother. "Your own words and not mine and as long as you'll be happy, we'll support you."

It was surreal to Sandra that she was raising a child that was thinking so fast, beyond her peers and that knew enough to make good use of her time. She felt blessed indeed; a tear dropped from her eye, but she quickly wiped it off before the kids could notice. Joe expected this already, so he held her hand, and they looked into each other's eyes with so much passion, feeling happy and blessed.

"Leo, still thinking about basketball?" Joe chipped in, as he sipped pineapple juice.

"Until he's taller" said Erica. Even Leo could not help but laugh.

"Yeah. Between now and when I am taller, I'd like to focus on my academics."

His parents nodded in agreement. It wasn't so surprising; for Leo, it had always been about his studies. He just wanted to come out top of his class. He would replay clips from his cousin's graduation so often, clips of how he graduated with honors and the parts of the graduation speech that focused on excellent students. He watched it with rapt attention, so it was not difficult to figure out the direction of the young lad's mind.

He had been receiving awards ever since he was little and was more than determined to continue from what his parents could see. It was not as though he needed to do so much to assimilate, but the young man just read everything he could get his hands on.

"What about that summer trip dad?"

"Hmm...now, that's a tight corner." Said Joe, as he stood up to leave the dinner table.

"Dad.." The kids who were now doe eating called, as they ran after him. "You promised us a summer trip."

"Talk to your mother about it." Joe laughed as he made his way up the stairs.

Sandra chuckled. "Oh, Joe." She said.

CHAPTER
TWO

H ungry, grief-stricken, tired-looking, she ran towards the home of the white woman who she had been told accommodated young children. She was just six, but she had all sorts of marks all over her body. She ran as hard as she could, panting as the sun was setting. The townspeople looked at her, wondering what was going on with the girl and where she had come from. A few recognized her, but she had always been associated with trouble, so they turned back to their businesses, as though nothing was happening around them.

As she ran, blood dripped from parts of her body. She had been beaten to that point, and that was the last straw that made the six-year-old think to run for her life. Grief could make a child grow beyond her years and this was the case here. She had sat for many months, wishing that her life would be somewhat different soon, but she could ride if only wishes were horses. Rhonda's mum had died and she had found a new home with the white woman that provided a home for kids, so why not her? She could just pretend like she had no mother, because despite having one, it was so pointless. What was the use of a mother that could not protect her? What was the use of a mother who exposed her to danger and almost beat her to death every time she made mistake.

None—utterly of no use, she thought. It was hard to come to such a harsh conclusion, but despite being so young, she knew this. She was scared of dying too. At least, the kids that lived with the white woman were enrolled in the white woman's school and those who had progressed above basic education had been sent to secondary schools (high schools). At least she would be able to hold her head high in a uniform, like the other kids too, as opposed to distributing packages to criminals; packages from the one that was supposed to protect her—her mother. While she wondered what was in the packages, she had never asked. She didn't want to get beaten yet again.

All she ever really asked for was to deliver packages to people that were not scary; people that did not hold guns or stay in scary places, because they were hiding from the police. Instead of what she had asked for, what she received was beatings. She could not imagine why anyone would do that to her own daughter. There was usually no food in the house. Mama was always sleeping most of the time. When she was awake, she would listen to some reggae music while scratching her body. Then she would call her to bring her small box. Then she would sniff some stuff that would make her sleep again. She told her she loved her, but she never gave her food. Other times, she would tell her to go out to look for some food for both of them after she had taken in the stuff from her box. She would ask her to steal sometimes. She remembered that before Rhonda's mama died, there was food on their table every night and sometimes, they even invited her to join. So, how could her own mother not give her food? How could she have never seen mama make food right up to this point or even hardly care about if she ate? Once a while, mama would bring food to the house, but this happened only once a week.

Sometimes, when mama sniffed her stuff, she would say. "You won't be with me if not that my mama is dead. Taking care of a child is no easy thing to do. You would see this as you grow up. I do not know how I would have survived changing diapers. Thank God my mama was there to take care of you. I only had to breastfeed you, well sometimes." She did not think that was a nice thing to say, but she did not want beatings.

She had a faint memory of living with an old woman that died; perhaps that was the "grandma" mum talked about. She must have died around the time she was three years old. All the things her mother said frequently hurt her a lot, but what could she do? And now, she was sad that Rhonda, her best friend was gone. Girl just wanted to go meet Rhonda as soon as she could. Oh yes! Her mother called her "Girl". Grandma used to call her some other name, but since her mama called her girl all the time, she had a faint memory of the name. She was not like any other child with a good frame of mind, so it was not surprising that she did not remember the name her grandma used to call her. The only way girl fed while living with her own mother was by earning tips from the packages she delivered, but she was not interested in delivering packages to criminals anymore—not after everything that had happened to her. She could not imagine going to those dark corners to wait around for money again. Not even after she was whisked away and gang raped two months back. She had just clocked six. All the monies for the deliveries she made that day had been stolen. She staggered home in pains and bleeding. She tried to show mama her wounds and explain what had happened, but mama wouldn't even give her any audience. Instead, mama beat her some more. Mama beat her so much that Rhonda's mother heard her cries and ran in. She stopped mama from beating her and dragged girl away. It was then that she was able to explain what had happened to her. Rhonda's mama was moved to tears and rushed her to the hospital immediately and paid for all her treatments, including her stiches.

She also housed Girl for a while, till she was fine again. During those periods, mama would come knock the door of Rhonda's home to ask if Girl was still in the hospital. Rhonda's mama would say she was still there. However, not once did mama say she wanted to visit the hospital. Instead, she would complain about how she really needed Girl to run some errands for her. Girl would hear from inside and this would make her so sad. Why couldn't her mother be as kind as Rhonda's mother? What had she done so wrong to deserve such kind of punishments? When Rhonda's mama passed on, Girl cried a lot, just as much as Rhonda. The woman was a mother to her far more than her own mother. Rhonda's father had also died from a rare sickness, a year back. As for Girl, she had no idea who her father was. She never knew her father or even hear her mother talk about him. She also knew better than asking questions about him.

Girl continued to run. She was in pains, but this was the best she could do. She could not allow that woman catch up with her again. This was her chance at an escape and she was not going to lose it. She ran with all her strength, remembering how she had been beaten the last time she was raped and had lost money. After she got better and Rhonda's mama returned her to her mother, her mother complained that she had to pay off those she owed with their rent money, so they would have to live on the streets. She said Girl was bad and must have been showing off her body to the men she did deliveries too. She accused of causing her own rape. She said little girls like her deserved to live on the streets, especially now that the rent was due. Girl was literally living in misery all along. She had cried and cried until she finally decided that she would resolve to her fate. Then she went to bid Rhonda goodbye. It was at this point that Rhonda's mother saw her crying and asked what the matter was. She told her about the rent and the woman used some of her savings to pay the rent. Then, she went to Girl's mama and told her that the rent had been paid.

"You should really stick your nose only in your own business." She yelled at Rhonda's mama. "Girl ought to learn an important lesson that actions have consequences. Now, you've robbed her of that experience. She would go around, thinking life is this easy." She continued.

Rhonda's mama shook her head. They got into an argument where Rhonda's mama told mama that she was not taking care of

Girl well and if not that Girl shared some resemblance with her, she would not think she was her mother. Mama started crying and began to accuse Girl for being the reason why another person would come insult her. She told girl she hated her and even spat on her. Girl felt very bad and thought of herself like a bad child.

Turning to Girl, Rhonda's mum said, "This is not your fault baby." Then, turning to her mama, "you're a toxic parent." She said. She whisked Girl away, taking her into her own home. That night, she cried and cried, thinking she had put her mama in trouble. She wished she could be a better daughter the way her mum thought. She wished she had not been raped or stolen from, but now, what could she do about it. That night, Rhonda's mother told her that she deserved to know that her mum was not well and that was why she treated her that way. She told her that she had done absolutely nothing wrong and everything that had happened was not her fault. She reminded her that she was beautiful in spite of all that had happened and once her mama was feeling better, she would definitely treat her well, like other mothers did. Rhonda's mother had promised to get help for her mother's health, but now she was gone. Remembering these things made her cry every night—who would help her and her mama?

However, now that she got raped and stolen from again, with no one to turn to for help, she decided to go find help for herself. Her mama also needed help. She knew something was not right with her mama. Her young mind could not just figure out what it was. Staying at home after everything that happened would do them no good; she had to go. If she could find the home where Rhonda stayed, even better. She thought of all these as she ran, so her mother could not catch up with her.

The people in the town saw her mother and then realized who Girl was.

"She's the daughter of Sheila, the crackhead." They whispered as she stopped to ask for directions from time to time. It was as though her mother had also run through those areas in search of her, to punish her for the wrong she had done again. But Rhonda's mum had told her that situations like that was never the fault of a child; and she was just a child. So, she braced up and ignored everything people had to say, as she kept asking for directions. She had to run to safety; that was all that really mattered. She did not care that the people of Bomi County had to say that her mother was a crazy person or she was even crazier. Getting to safety was all that mattered to her.

She kept thinking as she ran; her thoughts served as the fuel that energized her to keep running. She hit a rock and fell to the ground, rolling in the dust of the untarred road. She yelled, but everyone was too busy to notice a young girl with no guardian, one they could not exactly recognize too, especially as more dust had covered her face and clothes. There was now blood running down her right knee. She stood up and staggered to run. She kept asking for the white woman's home all along and the people kept correcting her, saying the woman's home was called an "orphanage". Hence, when she saw the sign board of the turning that led to orphanage in a distance and jumped for joy. Finally, she was close to a new life; she did not know if it would be better, but if Rhonda was there, then she could definitely cope with living there and dealing with whatever came her way. At least her friend would be by her side and they could share their worries.

She got to where the white signboard stood with the name "THE SAFE PLACE ORPHANAGE". It was the turning to the orphanage and heaved a sigh of relief. She tried to run, but her left knee had a problem with that, it did not approve the idea of running. So, she continued staggering.

"Wait" she heard from a distance and saw her mama coming with a stick. "Where is my money?" she yelled.

Girl was disappointed. She thought her mama had been chasing after her because she could not afford to lose her. Now, she realized that mama really did not care about losing her; all she cared about was her money. And when she realized that she didn't have her money, she knew that she would force her to come back to do more deliveries or she could end up living on the streets. That was the last thing she wanted. So, she kept running.

She sighted the orphanage, a few blocks away and she knew she was not going to give up for sure. It looked good. The premises had several yellow buildings in it and she could hear the voices of happy kids. It was a quiet environment, so she could hear the voice of her mother coming behind her, but she was not about to look back. She got to the big gate of the orphanage. It was huge and she wondered if she would be heard, but she did not have enough time to think about that, she just had to knock. She had to try. So, she knocked on the big black gate, as hard as a girl of her age possibly could. The gate keeper peeked through a hole and looked at her for a second, but she knocked even harder.

"Help" she screamed.

The man realized the young was not safe and quickly let her in before her mother who had tripped earlier on, got the gate. The man asked no questions, he just let her in.

"Welcome to the safe place. You're safe here." He said to her with a smile. Seeing she was staggering, he tried to lift her up, but her experience with men had not been good, so she yanked off his hand. Understanding that she might had been through a lot and suspecting that she was being chased, based on his training, he locked the gate and then, he kept walking behind her, telling her where to turn, in a bid to lead her to the administration office.

As they were about to enter the office, another hard knock came on the gate.

"Please do not let her in" she said. "That is my mother and she may just drag me away. I do not want to go back to doing those horrible deliveries." Girl said, panting. Her worried mind raced and she thought of all the possible things that could happen to her.

"I do not want to live on the streets" she said. "I heard my friend, Rhonda is here. Let me just stay with her. Please, I beg." The man was too shocked to speak. Seeing the blood dripping from her right knee, he knew the girl had been through a lot.

"It's alright. We will ensure you are safe." He managed to say, gesturing to her to calm down.

Julia came out after hearing Girl speak. She looked shocked at Girl's state. Girl looked up and saw her. She ran to Julia and held her tight. "Rhonda's mama said my mama is sick and she needs help. Please help me, please her my mama." She said. Julia could smell a troubled child from miles away. She knew she needed to help Girl by all means.

Julia bent to her level and held her close. Then, she looked into her eyes as she said, "Everything will be alright. Rhonda is in; you are safe here, just like she is. I look after the kids her, you are with me now, you can trust me and I am sure you will feel better when you see Rhonda. We would also take care of your mama too." She sighed. "What is your name?"

"Girl."

"Girl" Julia chorused. The name was surprising, but Julia knew how sensitive the child already was, so it was not a time to question her name. The child just needed all the love and acceptance she could get.

One of the female workers then came along to whisk Girl away for thorough cleaning, like Julia had ordered. She helped her wash and in the process, she discovered that girl had been bleeding in different areas of her body and also felt pain in private areas of her body. Being ashamed, Girl tried to hide this pain, but the female worker who had been trained on issues like this, especially with children that were newly brought into the orphanage said to her, "You are now safe. You are safe here. I am a female like you and I am ready to listen to whatever might have happened to you, but only when you are ready to speak. I just want you to be fine. I also know that whatever has happened is not your fault. Girl, you are beautiful and there is even more beauty in your future. Opening up to me on whatever might have happened will make us ensure you get the right treatments and all the rest you need." Said the female worker called Janet. Janet knew that the girl had been abused in some way. She just needed Girl to speak out, especially so she could know the extent to which she had been abused. She was so sorry Girl had to go through all that and just wanted to help in the best way she could. She washed her carefully and with love.

"If I need treatments, does that mean you will have to tell everyone what has happened to me?"

"No, Girl. I would only tell Miss. Julia. Then, you will go to the hospital with her. However, the most important thing is that you know that even if any other person knows about whatever happened to you, you should not have any cause to be ashamed. It is whoever touched you inappropriately that needs to feel ashamed and in fact, run back into their shell. Definitely, not you, because you are a child and all that has happened is not your fault."

"They were three of them, the first time. They were three again this afternoon. I cried and cried, but they wouldn't stop." Girl said, looking into space, as though she was staring at the image of what had happened to her. Tears rolled down her cheeks as she talked.

Janet quickly hugged her. "You can always talk to me or Miss. Julia, please. You are really safe here and we are now in charge of caring for you. There is nothing to fear." She whispered into Girl's ear.

The hug was so warm and genuine that Girl began to feel at peace. She wiped her tears and tried. "Miss. Janet, can I see Rhonda now?" she asked, as Janet mopped her up.

"You are in pains."

"Seeing her will make me feel at home. I can manage. I need to see her."

"Sure, once you have some clothes on and look pretty. You want her to see you looking nice since you've not seen each other for a long time, don't you?"

Girl only nodded. Miss Janet was dolling her up. She looked into the mirror and saw the colorful ribbons used in tying her dark hair. She had a new dress on that just fitted perfectly. She had never worn anything that looked that pretty in her entire life. The only thing that came close was the dress Rhonda's mama got for her the last Christmas. She had so many lovely things to remember about that woman and she could not stop being so thankful for the gift of her. Now, she could not wait to see her friend. Girl felt pain, but she was determined to see her friend that she hid it. She still staggered as she walked, but it was easy for anyone to think it was because of the injury on her knee.

Janet took her to the class where Rhonda and other kids her age were learning. She helped excuse Rhonda out of the class. Rhonda, on sighting her friend, ran as fast as her leg could carry her to hug her friend. All the while she had been in the orphanage, she had been praying to God silently, to help her friend and if possible, make her come to her. She didn't know if her prayers would ever be answered, but she prayed anyway. Little did she know that her prayer would be answered that soon.

"I am so happy you are here." Said Rhonda. They hugged each other so tightly and after releasing the embrace, Rhonda began to tell Girl the one thousand things she had kept to herself because she was yet to find a friend like Girl in the orphanage. She talked about how she was enjoying her time in the orphanage and all the lovely things in there; from the food, to their guardians, to the games, friends and all the fun the orphanage had been. Rhonda talked about how she would have missed her mother more if she hadn't been brought to the orphanage by distant relatives who did not have the means to cater to her. She expressed how much she preferred being in the orphanage and promised Girl a wonderful time. Girl only nodded, thinking of the many possibilities and wondering if things were really going to be as beautiful as Rhonda kept saying they will get. However, she felt better and at home, as she had promised Miss Janet.

After allowing them enjoy each other's company for about ten minutes, Janet was back to ensure Rhonda was back in class, while she took girl away to the administration office, where Juliet was sitting.

All the while Girl was being washed up, Julia had let Sheila, her mother, in and entertained all her shenanigans. Sheila continually shouted about how her daughter had been taken away from her and while Julia did not answer the question of if Girl was with her or not, she told Girl's mother how she could be charged for child abuse with the way Girl looked at the time she entered the orphanage and how scared she was to be with her mother. The Justice system of their environment was not so great, but Julia knew that was her only chance at scaring Sheila off, especially so she could get the help she also needed. She became quiet at this point and was going to run out of the premises, shouting, "I do not want to have anything to do with the police."

The gateman caught up with her and Julia told her that she was willing to help her start over, as she saw that she needed help.

"How?" she kept asking. "I am so ruined."

"There is always a chance to get back on your feet, as soon as you are ready" said Julia. She nodded and Julia quickly called the government agency that helped in the rehabilitation of drug abusers. She knew they would come in no time to take Girl's mother away. As they took her away, she looked to Julia and said, "My girl has been through a lot and I wish I could really be better for her, but I am so damaged." She said. "I need to admit this. I don't even know how to help her or myself, but my baby," she continued. "…is strong. And I pray that one day, she would find a place in her heart to forgive me for the kind of childhood I let her lead, especially in the past two months. She has been through a lot and I am hoping this place is as safe as she thinks it is. She is a smart girl, so if she thinks this place is that safe for her, it probably is. It is probably safer than her being by my side. And I know that I have no rights and no money too, but please, do take care of my baby. She is really young and if this place would make her become a better woman than me, her mother, I am happy about that. I will try to stay strong and get better too." She said, as she entered the bus headed for the rehabilitation home. Sheila kept staring into Julia's eyes as they took her away. Julia knew that look. It was a mother telling another woman that she trusted her with her child. Moments like this were always like throwing a huge burden on Julia, but it was her calling; the kind of burden she enjoyed carrying.

By the time Girl was out and back to the administration office, her mother was gone. Julia liked it that way. She knew seeing each other might have triggered really bad responses from both ends, like she had seen in many cases. Girl would have been very scared and also definitely felt unsafe. Her mother, on the other hand, who just wanted her money that Julia had been so gracious to give her, would have her violent sides triggered. Julia did not want this to be the case. Once Julia gave her the money, which was hardly enough to buy lunch for a child, Sheila had become calm. The trainings she enrolled for (together with her staff), from time to time, had been very useful in handling the situation and for her, this was the kind of moment that made everything worth it.

As Girl walked into the office, Julia called the doctor to confirm their urgent appointment that afternoon, as Janet had given her all the necessary information about Girl's situation. She knew medical attention was supposed to be immediate, so had called the pediatrician that the organization used. On getting to the hospital, several tests were ran on Girl and treatment followed suit. She tested positive for some diseases, but they were treatable and the doctor assured them that there was no cause for alarm. Her treatment continued in the following weeks, including an appointment with a child psychologist once a week. Rhonda also made the process easier for her enough though she did not have all the details of what had happened to her friend. She just knew her friend was sick and Miss Julia asked her to stay by her side from time to time.

Janet also ensured Girl was taking her prescribed medication at the right time. Girl found out that she was in the perfect home, just like Rhonda had promised. The kids were warm and nice and Julia, who they called "mummy", encouraged them all the time and reminded them that they were very special too. She also made the kids feel special.

In the next week, Girl became bothered about her mother. She had been afraid to ask earlier on, but now summoned courage to ask what was going on with her mother. She also begged Julia to help her. It was then that Julia narrated how she had ensured that her mum was getting treatment and would probably come to say hi when she was in a better place. Girl's face lit up immediately and she even began to get more involved with other kids in the orphanage. She seemed freer to do everything and was even actively participating in classes, answering questions and showing a level of intelligence she never even knew she had in her.

She made new friends and her self-confidence improved on a general note. Girl, who used to bow her face down while walking when she just arrived the orphanage had developed better people and communication skills. She now walked around smiling and willing to talk to anyone who started a conversation with her, with no iota of fear. It was seeing kids like this that made Julia feel happy about what she had decided to do with her life. Kids like Girl made the process and all she had forsaken totally worth it. Once again, it had been proved by Girl's situation, that kids could do better once given better environments to live and function. Julia herself couldn't imagine growing up in a third world country. Perhaps, she would be nowhere near where the place she found herself at the moment. She was just happy about the progress Girl was making. Girl was happy too, but for her, one thing was missing.

She got really confused about her name. People called other younger females in the orphanage "Girl". Miss Julia always said every one of them was unique and special. Her name did not make her feel that way. She wanted another name. She had always found her name weird and was not comfortable with it anymore. She just wanted a name that people did not use to refer to any other young female.

"A name-changing process is usually a stressful and time-consuming process." Said Miss. Julia. "However, I understand how you feel, but your mother must have given you another name. You cannot change your name till you're up to the age of 18, so you must really think and remember if there's another name you already have, and you would like to be addressed as, especially before your full registration into the orphanage next month."

"She did not tell me about any, but my granny used to call me a name I cannot remember. My mama may just remember."

"Oh, really. That's not bad. Yesterday, I got a notification that she's better and you can now pay her a visit, but because of her situation, you may not have a lot of contact with her."

Girl was fine with that. In spite of all that had happened, she could still not wait to see the woman who bore her and was absolutely looking forward to paying her mother a visit.

It was a long ride to the rehab center. She rode in Miss. Julia's car. It was her first time in a car, she was so happy. She waved to the passers-by all the way up to the rehab center. She made Miss. Julia laugh the whole time.

Her mother was in a better place and was happy to see her girl.

"The name is Sandra" she said to Girl and Miss Julia.

And Sandra, they called her henceforth. *Girl Sandra Myles.* \

CHAPTER
THREE

The day dawned on both young and old, crisp and clear. The rays of the sunlight poured through the orphanage, lighting up the hopes and dreams of the kids once again. The voices of the kids enveloped the entire atmosphere; the innocence in their voice was refreshing to everyone who cared to hear. They sang their nursery rhymes and danced to the rhymes that required a bit of dance.

Those who were a bit older were already in their music class. They were kids, and as expected, they were happy for no particular reason. They were just being kids, clapping their hands where necessary and rubbing shoulders when the song required them to do so. The music was just to put everyone in the orphanage in a great mood and charge them up for the day.

"Their lives are not perfect, but are were happy. We need to learn from children." Celine had said under her breath subconsciously.

The orphanage preferred to start up the day with music in its various forms. It made the kids happy, so why not? Before those who were undergoing secondary education (in high schools), which the orphanage bus drove them to each morning, they also participated in the music classes. In about 15 minutes, the session was over and the bus was ready to take the older kids to school, while the younger kids hurried to settle in their classes. They had been thought to be orderly and so, they maintained decorum to a large extent, as they moved into their various classes.

As they settled in their classes, Celine decided to carry on with the warm-up exercises for the younger kids, as the day began.

"What would you like to do when you grow up?" asked Ms. Celine.

"I would like to fly planes" said Eddy.

"I would love to make people look more beautiful." Said Sylvia.

"I would like to treat sick people." Said Baron.

"I do not know what I'd like to do just yet." Said Kelvin.

"Oh Kelvin" said Ms. Celine and she then made sure to assure the kids that whatever they planned to do with their lives was valid. The kids always responded very happily. Who would ever know that these kids had their own struggles? Who would ever know they had no parents, seeing how beautiful they were now doing? Celine looked at all of them with this knowledge and her heart was full of joy.

She turned to the kids in the next row. They were the next set of kids to answer the question. Before she could ask, a girl already had her hand up. That girl was Sandra.

"What is your name?" she asked.

"Sandra."

"And what would you like do when you are grown?"

She paused for a moment and looked around.

"Come on, speak up. Don't be shy to say what you'd like to do as a grown up."

She looked around again, then looked straight into Celine's eyes, before she said "I don't know ma'am. I do not know if I can become anything nice like the others." She said, as a drop of tear fell from her eyes. Celine was moved to tears herself, to hear a child say such, but this was not the time for her to cry. She moved closer to Sandra, lifted her up and held her close. She was still shocked at the girl's words herself. It was definitely not the answer Celine was expecting, but now, she knew she had to act in the moment, and act fast too.

She hugged Sandra tight. As she had not been adequately trained on how a child gets taken into the orphanage, she was not involved in the whole Sandra's process. Sandra came in on the day she flew in from the United States and she had only watched from afar, thinking that the girl must have had some disease, but the girl had only been soaked in dirt from going through a whole lot that day. However, since she was there to help in any way she could, her sister had briefed her a little here and there about the kids. So she knew a little about Sandra's story, and now, it came to her remembrance in a split second. She now understood why the child will think of herself in that way. Sandra's story was a bit more unique, so it was easier for Celine to remember.

She now put her down and said to her, "Look into my eyes girl; you can be anything you want to become. You can be exactly whatever you plan to make out of your life. It starts by thinking of it, then saying it and then, believing it." Sandra nodded, but was obviously still not convinced.

"Say after me" said Celine, looking straight into her eyes, searching for where the remaining of the child's strength lied, "I CAN BE ANYTHING I WANT."

"I CAN BE ANYTHING I WANT" Sandra said faintly.

"No kiddo. No! I'll need you to gather all the strength in you and shout it as loud as you can."

"I CAN BE ANYTHING I WANT" Sandra said on the top of her voice.

"Roar it like a Lion kid!"

"I CAN BE ANYTHING I WANT" Sandra screamed with everything within her.

"Yes! That's it."

Then, she turned to the rest of the class and asked them to join in roaring.

"I CAN BE ANYTHING I WANT" the kids chorused as much as they could, in what sounded like a roar.

It broke Celine's heart to imagine that many of the kids were rejected at birth or in early childhood. She wondered what would have happened to them if they had not been found; what their future could have looked like. Although, the kids were living a life filled with routines, or basically ran by a routine, at least they now had shelter over their heads, as well as people who knew it was their responsibility to constantly show love to the kids, an essential component for their growth. The strict routines of the orphanage were put in place to keep the kids going and break the bad patterns they had learnt from their own peculiar situations.

Celine wondered what happened to orphans or abandoned kids on the streets, who were not lucky enough to find themselves in the orphanage, and had been born into a developing country like Liberia where a thing like child welfare was non-existent and resources were altogether lacking. She knew things would have been better in a developed country. It made her understand why her sister had refused to come back home after coming to volunteer in Liberia. The level of suffering was unimaginable. The stories of each of the kids were too heartbreaking. Sometimes, she wanted to shed a tear as Julia narrated the situation of a kid that passed by them, but she would just try as much as possible to hold herself back. She knew the implication of having the kids (who already had a lot on their plates), see her cry again. She understood Julia perfectly and she understood that this might indeed be the fulfilment of purpose for her sister. After everything Julia had gone through, she now had so many kids call her mummy. Maybe, just maybe, this was really it.

Their mother, who was aged, and simply could not understand why Julia had decided to stay back in such a country, had asked Celine to travel down to Liberia, to see what was going on with Julia and why she had chosen to abandon everything, including her engagement to David, all to come down to help some kids in Liberia. She thought black magic had a thing on her daughter. She had heard about black magic, but never really considered if it was a reality until this Julia's unique situation came up as a bother. Celine was almost on her mother's side and sometimes wondered if her sister had met another man who she was keeping a secret in Liberia. Julia was known for wanting to handle her own situations by herself, so it would not be surprising to her if her sister had made such a decision without consulting a single soul.

However, now, Celine understood better; more people existed in the world and the world was a lot more than their small bubble. Her imagination could have never fathomed the situation of things in Liberia, and the role her sister had chosen to single-handedly play. An explanation would not suffice either. It was something a person had to see for themselves. She brought along a camera and was making small clips from time to time, and taking pictures too, so she could show their mother. She realized that indeed many people needed their help and their resources, as Julia always explained in her letters and her brief phone calls. Celine's mind had just never pictured such a situation.

Back in the United Kingdom, their mother had demanded that Maria, Julia's best friend, explain whatever had happened and why Julia would not come back. After all, she was the one that suggested the trip. However, even Maria had not caught the vision Julia had caught. Julia had chosen to stay in Liberia since that time, and now, two years had passed. She always promised to visit, but she never did. It was about two years back and maybe seeing things now would make Maria understand why Julia wanted to stay back. While Maria thought it was important to reach out to less privileged areas of the world, she felt like volunteering was just the perfect way to do that. She had suggested the volunteering trip to Julia, but she never imagined it could come to Julia relocating to the place. It was just insane to her. And now, she did not even know how to explain to Julia's mother. Her explanations were just in bits and pieces; she had no concrete explanation for anything at all.

Celine seemed to understand her sister. The first day she walked into the orphanage, just before Sandra came and caught her attention (as she was bruised and tattered), she went into the place where the infants were laid. It was true beauty. Their cute cries moved her to tears herself, as she hugged her sister. She could not imagine the scenarios of a mother leaving a child that was less than a week old in some old carton in front of the orphanage gate. She heard that the rain had beaten some of the infants when they were found and the sun had scorched some, and how they survived only seemed like a miracle. She was moved to tears each time she heard a story and gradually, her attachment towards the kids developed.

"You are doing such a great job." She said to Julia occasionally, her look saying that she understood better now. In the past, she had begged and begged for her sister to return home, especially because of her relationship with David, a man that loved her so much. Everyone knew that David loved Julia a lot, going ahead to propose to her in spite of knowing that she would never be able to bear kids. However, Julia always felt like she would be a burden to David and had told him to move on a lot of times, but he never did. She just did not feel comfortable with the fact that he chose to be with a woman that could not bear kids, despite having the ability to bear kids himself. While it felt like a blessing to her family members, it was more like a burden to Julia; it was just too much. With him, she felt like she was carrying such a heavy weight, hence, she was never exactly very happy in their relationship. It was always basically him doing everything to possible to make her happy, while her on the other hand, was unhappy because she felt like a burden to him. She wondered why nobody else seemed to understand, and felt like they always made her look like the one who loved to sabotage something great.

She knew for sure that if she had decided to stay with David, something would have been off; the same thing that had been off all the while. Julia never really understood what was off, but being in Liberia from two years had given her all the clarity she needed. She clearly just needed to step back from everything and analyze what was wrong. She had been living in comfort all the while, but she was nowhere near her purpose. In Liberia, her living conditions where not perfect, but she always felt peace in her heart, like she was doing exactly what she was supposed to be doing. For her, she felt like this especially when the kids chorused her name, or she walked by the passage and received some warm hugs from those innocent hearts. It was always a beauty to behold.

The past two years had been the best two years of her life. She had tried to explain this to her mother over and over, but her mother never understood why Julia needed to be there in person. In her mother's opinion, people helped others from all over the world quite often, but did not have to stay there all the time. As for David, he came and stayed in Liberia for two days, trying to convince her to hand over things and leave without even waiting to understand why she wanted to be there at all. He obviously did not plan on seeing reason with her; she felt like he was treating her like she had lost her mind. If David had cared enough to understand her, he would have helped explain things to her mother. However, that would happen if only he understood her situation himself; but he didn't.

"Alright Julia, but you can legally adopt two or three kids from here, hand this wonderful place to someone who is originally from here and then, bring the kids over to the UK. You don't have to stay there all the time. You would not be handing over the orphanage fully; you will just have the person run it, get married to David and then pop in every once in a while. I get that you are trying to help, but you have done quite a lot. You have tried!" Her mother would say on phone, trying to proffer what seemed like a solution to her.

They had these conversations over the phone time after time, but there had been no coming to an agreement. Julia tried to explain things to her mum and send photographs to the UK from time to time, so her mother could see how wonderful the kids were and probably see reason with her why she could not leave the kids. While her mother agreed that she was doing a great job with the kids and was truly proud of her, she never just saw why Julia needed to put her life on hold to achieve all that. Her mother could not wrap her head around a purpose that would not make her daughter have her own family. What she did not understand was that left to Julia, the kids in the orphanage were family and the orphanage was the family she started.

"Mum, I am not putting my life on hold." Julia would say. "This is now my life. These kids are my family. This orphanage is the family I started."

David was ready to do anything to have her travel back. He had travelled down to see her yet the second time, but she had asked him to move on. She loved him and she was not trying to hurt, but truly wanted the best for him. She felt like she wasn't the best and he deserved better, even if he did not see it. They did not want the same thing from life; he could not see it, but she could see it. Her predicament had changed a lot about the way she saw things and David was not on board with that level of thinking just yet. As for Julia, there was something deep inside her that made her know she was exactly where she was supposed to be. She was fulfilled living in Liberia, even if it did not make sense to the people she loved. She knew it was going to be a long road and they would understand sooner or later.

The only thing that gave her worries was her mum's health. She suffered a recurrent stroke and had been through series of treatment. Hence, she couldn't come down to Liberia, as it was advised that she avoided stressful situations as much as possible. She just wished her mother would worry less about her and she determined in her heart to go and see her once she could get time away from the kids. However, she was glad Celine had come around to see the situation of things. Even though she figured that her mother probably wanted Celine to come convince her elder sister, for Julia, it was still a step forward.

She still did not like how David had come earlier, and focused on their relationship and nothing about her new interest. She did not like that and it was in that moment that she knew that they would not be happy together. David was a tall and good-looking blonde. He was also very successful. Any lady would beg to be with him. His family also always looked at them both and loved the idea of them because they were sure to make cute kids together, since Julia was a petite, but hour-glass shaped lady with black silky hair. She had nice blue eyes that anyone would fall for. As a pair, their looks always appeared like a match made in heaven. However, that was definitely no reason to get married; Julia could see this more clearly now because, now, she could not even make those cute kids. And what happened in situations like that? Did such scenarios make marriage pointless to some people? She could not stop wondering.

David just wanted them to get married, but after the marriage, what next? First off, she knew she would not be happy and again, she knew he would not be happy on the long run, as he chipped in adoption of some of the kids from the orphanage here and there, but the manner in which he said it made her realize that he would not be happy in the long run, he was only saying what he said because of the emotional attachment he could not get over. That was a personality problem he had to fix on his own, heal and then, move on.

The noise from the playground could not get past the notice of Julia and Celine that evening.

"What's happening out there?" asked Celine. It had been three days of staying in the orphanage, but even Celine could not stop her heart from loving the beautiful children. Why would anyone in the world want to abandon such beauties? That was one question she still could not answer. It broke her heart every time she looked at their faces and it dawned on her that many of them no longer had biological parents, or have biological parents who did not want them. She had grown attached to them; from their beautiful voices to their beautiful smiles and even to their noises. The first night of her stay in the orphanage staff quarters made her very pissed at the kids. They made a lot of noise even though the lights had already gone off.

However, spending more days with the kids had gotten her attached to the kids. She realized that they were just beautiful souls, trying to find expression in the best way they could. Now, each time they made noise, she smiled from the knowledge of the fact that kids that were once abandoned now had a safe space. They had somewhere they could fully express themselves without the fear of being harmed or being judged. So, she let them without judging them to be mischievous kids or anything like that. She now appreciated them and just learnt to enjoy the moments she had to experience their shenanigans.

The sisters went to see what was happening on the playground. They were surprised to see the kids fighting. The two boys did not look like they were going to let go anytime soon. It had been the sound of a punch they had heard and the boy that had been punched was now bleeding. Julia ordered them to report to her quarters immediately. They had both been fighting and blood was not exactly gushing out, so she decided that she could instill some indiscipline to them shortly before first aid was given. She loved the kids, but she wanted it to sink in that in the real world, actions, especially bad actions, had consequences.

Loosely spoken words had caused the fight. The boys had been arguing about who was uglier and one had said that no one would ever love the other. Those were the words that led to the punch.

Julia was pissed; not because the boys fought, but because of how lowly they thought of themselves. She looked out through the window and then, the passion that overwhelmed her the day she decided to stay back in Liberia and help abandoned kids enveloped her once again.

She had tears in her eyes, but they felt more like fire than the liquid that tears were supposed to be. "Why would you ever think you are ugly?" she shot at the boys. "How dare you think that about yourself?"

"You" she said, turning to the first boy, "Do you know how happy I was the first time I looked into your eyes? Very happy! It felt like I had won a jackpot."

"You!" she yelled at the other guy. "Do you know the kind of joy that filled my heart the day I found you at the gate of this building? Do you?!"

The kids looked down. They had never seen mum, as they all called her, so angry. They were little boys in the same grade. One was four years old, going on five. The other had just clocked five. She did not see why they had any cause to argue or fight. They were both good looking young lads.

"You are handsome boys; beautiful in and out. You are treasures and I would not let you see yourselves as less. You are handsome boys" She said angrily.

"And why would you let anyone call you ugly?" she said, turning to each boy from time to time. "Why? Why would you call yourselves ugly?" She yelled. "No one had the right to do so, but it hurts more than you both had accepted the fact that you were ugly and it was now a matter of who was uglier." She paused and paced. "Look at me kids! You are handsome boys!"

Ever since that incident, Julia talked to the kids about valuing themselves every night. She told them how important their opinion on themselves mattered. They chanted sayings every night that reminded them that they could face whatever the world presented them. Julia always told them to look into the mirror and affirm themselves. She told them how important it was that they knew that no one else could affirm them the way they did themselves. Every night, they sang songs that reminded them that people only had the power to put them down only if they chose to permit it.

Every night, Celine could hardly hold back her tears too. They were uninhibited tears of joy, which stemmed from seeing her sister achieve so much with the kids. It stemmed from seeing such beautiful souls being prompted to be even more beautiful. She could see the fact that Julia was planting seeds that would germinate into beautiful flowers. She was in awe of this and knew these kids had pure gold; her sister was that gold. She was happy to be related to such a change maker. She was proud and gradually became dedicated.

It was always a beautiful sight to watch; young kids affirming who they were. Julia always went to sleep each night after seeing the kids pumped up, constantly reminded why she started and smiling at the kind of progress she had attained. Again, it reminded her that she was doing exactly what she was supposed to be doing. She was convinced that this was her destiny. She wondered how different things would have been if she didn't follow Maria on her trip to Africa two years ago. It hit her how one simple decision could turn one's life around and how not making one decision could stand in one's way of attaining progress. This made her wonder if she should get on board with David and the marriage plans or if she was making a mistake by asking him to go. She rolled on her bed every night for the next week, wondering if she was on track with her decisions. However, she rested eventually, realizing that she was fulfilled and she had found peace in Liberia. The living conditions were not as amazing as that of Texas, Celine lived or Kent, United Kingdom, where she grew up, but she found peace and fulfilment in Liberia. She was happy too, and later came to the conclusion that wherever these kids were, was home to her.

CHAPTER
FOUR

It was a sunny afternoon in the orphanage, but the kids would not stop playing on the playground. They sang their rhymes, and danced to those that were used to the games they played. Sandra was happy. She made Rhonda her partner for every game and jumped for joy each time they won. She had never felt that level of joy in her entire life. She now felt happy and safe.

She had embraced her new life in the orphanage unlike some of the kids that cried when they were dropped off by relatives who claimed to be incapacitated to care for them. Some would cry for many days and even throw tantrums. It took months for such kids to adjust. It took only few days for Sandra to adjust; Rhonda's presence might have helped with that too.

She had spent three months in the orphanage and it told on her appearance. She looked a lot brighter and happier. Her wounds had healed up. Her skin was looking healthier. She was as active as any active person could be. She had her hand in every pie and had such a great deal of courage to try on new experiences. Additionally, at this point, she also knew the names of many of the kids in the orphanage. She could also say a thing or two about them if called upon to do so. She knew of Kira, the girl with the longest hair; Angie, the tallest girl; Amira; the girl who knew how to play the flute perfectly. There were also several other kids she was now familiar with including Nathaniel,

Martha, Sam, Chea and Rennie among others. Most of the kids in the orphanage had lost one or both parents in the Liberian war. Others had parents who were casualties of the war and only survived for a few more years before passing away. Some of the older kids had lost touch with their families and were brought to orphanage by those that found them. While some were brought hungry and reckless-looking, others were brought in after being abused or molested. There was also a small number of those who were found on the streets and dropped off at the gate of the orphanage almost dead. Additionally, some of the kids had been abandoned at the gate of the orphanage by teenage mothers who were incapacitated to treat them.

Among the kids was also John, quite a troublesome boy who was great at being in everyone's business and Joseph, another boy who was so quiet, but always failed every arithmetic test. Joseph and John were notable for getting into fights, because while John liked to be in other people's business, Joseph liked to keep to himself. John, who was a year older would try to pick on Joseph time after time and when Joseph could not take it anymore, they would have a full-blown fight. Since John was known for trouble, not only with Joseph, but also with other kids, it was not a surprising scene to see his clothes and his shoes look really dirty. Joseph was usually John's major target. He was a composed boy and only looked rough after getting into any confrontation with the troublesome John. Everyone knew of the way John used to trouble Joseph. It had happened time after time and Sandra had seen the situation play out herself. She usually pitied Joseph who was already struggling with school work, especially arithmetic, only to get extra trouble from having to deal with John. Each time the teachers complained about his grade, she always wondered if she could help the quiet boy study better. Perhaps, that way, he would even succeed at avoiding John's trouble.

Hence, this particular afternoon, when Sandra looked into one of the classes from the playground and saw Joseph in it, her attention was drawn to him, but she tried to focus on playing games with others. However, her mind kept going back to the boy in the class. Sandra wondered if it was a good time to offer help.

However, once more, she ignored the budge and continued the games. Each time she lost focus, she always made a mistake that made her lose points. Her points kept dropping till she lost. She was finally out of the game, but not sure of if Joseph would want any company. She kept looking back to see what was going on in the class until she saw him dozing. Each time he dozed, he ended up jolting back to reality and trying to focus on his books, only for him to doze off again. She watched the whole cycle like a movie over and over, and had a good laugh. She remembered that this was usually the punishment for failing a test twice. She figured that Joseph must really be doing poorly at arithmetic because she remembered that he was at the bottom of the class the week before. She did not pay attention to this week scores because she had been frustrated at the fact that she did not top the class in arithmetic in spite of loving it so much and even practicing really hard. She only paid attention to her scores and those of the two kids that did better than her by scoring extra two and three points respectively. She was only determined to do better, but did not pay attention to those that had scored far below her. Definitely, the last thing on her mind was paying attention to the kid who got the worst score.

"You're sleeping again" she said, as she took the seat in front of him. Joseph looked up, but did not look pleased to see her. He looked down again and continued to stare at the book full of various arithmetic problems the teacher had asked him to solve for an assignment.

"Can I help?" she asked.

His face lit up.

"Yes" That was the first word he ever said to her. It dawned on him that the girl in front of him could be his savior. He now remembered seeing her answer arithmetic questions in class. Hence, he became a bit more welcoming to her. "I find this whole thing difficult. I wish I would have someone to make it simple."

"Okay then. I will try my best" she said. With that, she kept trying her best to make him understand all afternoon. Joseph was such a slow learner at arithmetic, but promised he was better at reading. Sandra had to be patient to have him understand even simple arithmetic. It was frustrating that she was sacrificing all her playtime, as she thought she would only need to help him out for an hour or less. However, it turned out that she spent her entire playtime with him because he was such a slow learner. Sandra tried to be really patient with him all the while. Everyone knew him to be a fighter, but from what she could see, he just really liked to keep to himself, he was a peace-loving boy, just like she had guessed. It had been John all along; the hyperactive child looking for an outlet in a more reserved boy.

The part she did not know was that the young boy who was two years older than her, but in the same class as her had been through an experience that none of the kids in the orphanage would never understand. While they might have all seen him as a child who was not just as smart as the other kids, there was more to it. Joseph was a troubled child and there was a lot of depth to his troubles. Everything had compounded to the point that it now affected his academic performance and although he was getting therapy, he just never seemed to get good at school work, no matter how hard he tried.

Joseph had lived no simple life. His experience was no simple one. How would kids their age ever understand or even imagine that his father had killed his mother a year ago and Joseph, who was just seven years old at the time, had seen it all. He had always seen him hit her whenever he went into his anger fits, but hitting a kitchen stool on her head was too much for his young mind to process. As his mother fell down and gave up the ghost, he fainted on the spot. He woke up to the noise of neighbors trying to revive him. The noise of his mother hitting the ground with a big bang had alerted them all and they came to see what his violent father was up to again. Previously, when they came, despite being beaten, his mother would go to the door and pretend everything was fine. If need be, she would use a big scarf over her face to cover whatever new scar she had gotten for the day. She was such a sweet, hardworking woman who would ensure there was food on the table every single day, only for her husband to not only come home drunk, but also give her a fresh beating. Yet, she covered up for him and begged him to change. Well, he didn't change; he killed her instead. Her blood was still all over the place when they revived Joseph. The site was very shocking to him and left the young boy shivering. A neighbor quickly carried him away from the scene. He became scared of his father, who begged them not to take his son away.

"You plan to kill the boy too? You would rot in prison!" Screamed the woman who carried Joseph away. Her name was Comfort. Comfort took him to her home and covered him with a huge blanket and asked her kids to look after him, while she was out making sure the police got to the scene quickly, with the help of other influential women in the neighborhood. She had asked Joseph's mother time after time about the situation of things and begged her to speak up. Now, he had killed her, just like they all thought he would. She just thought that one day, Joseph's mother would be strong enough to speak up to her, being a fellow woman, and they would seek out her justice together, but the dead don't speak!

Now, the best Comfort could do was to ensure that the man rotted in prison for the rest of his life or even get a death sentence. He never deserved that woman in life and even now that she was dead, he did not deserve her giving him freedom to live his life like every other man. He was a woman beater, a monster, and monsters should not live together with humans.

After a while, the police was on the scene. He was arrested and when it became a court case, Joseph was called to testify against his own father, as a young child. He had to recount what he saw and with tears in his eyes, that he did. It was no interesting process. In spite of all the pain the man had caused him and his mother, he was still his father. Knowing that whatever he said could let the only parent he had in the world get killed or forever be separated from him, yet speaking that truth was indeed a hard thing to do. However, he knew in his heart that it was the right thing to do. And so, he did it for his mother. She deserved justice. She did not enjoy a good life, at least she deserved her honor being kept in death and that was the only way; just like comfort had said into the ears of Joseph. He knew it was the right thing to do too. His father had never been good to his mum. He had witnessed it and he did not deserve to go scot-free for killing her. The young boy still could not wrap his head around the fact that his mother was no more when he had to show up in court and speak of the evil his father had done. It was such a traumatic experience for him.

Being in a third world country, the custody for kids in a situation like his own had not been put into consideration by the government. Comfort knew he needed to see a child psychologist and maybe even undergo a mental assessment, but she did not have the financial capacity to give him all that help. She had five children of her own and her husband had died in the civil war. His parents had not introduced him to any extended family and his mother only kept Comfort as her friend in the neighborhood, all in a bid to keep her husband's vices a secret. Now, there was no one she could hand the young boy too.

This is why the moment she heard about a white woman who helped kids, she travelled from Nimba where Joseph grew up, to Bomi county, where the white woman's orphanage was situated to drop off Joseph and wished him the very best, as she handed him to Julia. She also explained his situation to her and signed all the necessary documents. Being a developing country, the paperwork was not as tedious and Joseph now had safe spaces as his home. The whole thing situation had happened one year ago, but Joseph still experienced the residue to a large extent, despite seeing a psychologist which had even helped him to become a lot better than he would have been.

He became one of the kids at the safe place at the age of seven. With open arms, the boy was welcomed into the orphanage and ever since, he received a lot of attention to ensure he was stable. Psychological evaluation, monitoring and counselling were also continually dished out for the young boy. The process continued for over a year and even up till the moment, Joseph had not stop seeing a psychologist. It was only not as frequent as before. He was now also in a better place, but everything that had happened had messed with the boy in ways he could not explain, but were visible to others.

There were stories of unwanted kids in the orphanage. There were all sorts of bad situations and there were actual orphans in the orphanage too. However, Joseph's story was certainly nothing like any of the kids' stories. Only Sandra's situation came close.

He chased her with a big club in his hands. She was running for her life yet again; she just had to escape this monster, for she was not ready to tell yet another tale of woes. She realized she was going to fall, her legs were betraying her or maybe it was the ground. She looked at the ground and realized the origin of the betrayal. She had come to a sloppy land, but had not even realized so in her quest to survive. She had been too busy running for her life. Now she had to thread with care.

"Thread with caution" came his huge voice from behind her; just as if he knew what was running through her mind. The sound of his voice made her little frame shiver. She wondered what was going to happen next, but all the same, she ran as fast as her legs could carry her. She only hoped that her legs would not betray her too. He did not stop chasing after her too, but since he had a bigger frame, he could not run in the clay mud as fast as she could. She was happy she had an advantage, but his huge shadow still enveloped her sight, forming an umbrella over her even as she ran for her life.

"Give up this chase." He yelled. "Let me have my way."

"No way" she shouted back. "I would rather keep running. I would rather die running than have you touch me."

She had gained distance from him, thanks to her little frame. She reached a spot with a tree and a small grass beneath it, a portion carved out of the muddy, sloppy land with no mud at all. She wanted to catch her breath.

"You couldn't escape me after all" came a voice from behind. How had he ran ahead of her? He was behind her, so why was he now coming from the other side of the road. She looked around, the mud seemed to have cleared out. She did not understand what was going on, so she tried to make sense of everything, all to no avail.

By now, he had lifted her up. In a flash, other men were with them. It was then that Sandra realized what was about to happen and began to scream.

"Leave me alone!" she screamed.

"H-E-E-E-L-L-P!!!" She screamed.

And her screams went on. She woke up, panting and screaming. Amira, Angie and Rhonda had surrounded her by now, and one of the other girls had gone to look for a staff. She almost jumped out of the bed, but the other girls held her. A sweat broke out from her forehead, then, she looked around and realized that she was in the orphanage—not in some forest she found herself in her dreams. Miss. Janet handed her a bottle of water, "You're safe here. You're safe with us." She said. "Look around, you are surrounded by your sisters. There is nothing to fear; we are all here for you. You have absolutely nothing to fear. You are safe here..." Miss Janet kept saying.

In the following weeks, the nightmares continued and Julia tried to make herself more available for Sandra. She could not begin to imagine being in her shoes, so she'd rather do everything to make Sandra comfortable than look for shortcuts. She knew that if she did not take drastic steps, the young girl may become paranoid about almost any and everything. This would affect her education and even her participation in social activities. Going back into her shell could be disastrous and leave her unprepared for any harm. It was a harsh world. Social skills and interactions with other humans definitely helped in preparing one for unforeseen circumstances. And she needed Sandra to be prepared, always, because life was no joke, no rehearsal.

For this reason, Sandra's therapy intensified. It was the necessary thing to do. She was now seeing a therapist thrice a week and it cost the orphanage a lot, but Julia knew that was the right thing to do. The young girl was not interacting as much with her friends at the orphanage, but if she was talking to her therapist really well, Julia knew that it would only be a matter of time before Sandra would begin to warm up to others.

Joseph was also yet to come out his shell fully as well. If he had come out of his shell, he would be using all his potential to their fullness. This meant doing better even at school work. The therapist advised that he came frequently too, so he had be visiting the therapist twice a week as well. Julia drove Joseph and Sandra to see the therapist each week and sometimes, they even stopped over for some ice cream. This usually brightened up the mood of the kids before they got to the therapist's office.

Gradually, Joseph and Sandra were talking more frequently with each other, as they spent extra time away from the other kids. Sandra started relating better with Joseph, and so did Joseph with Sandra. Julia saw this and her resolve was that it was going to be of help to them both. She alone knew that they had peculiar circumstances; having parents who were alive but not exactly the best for them at the moment.

Sandra, who had been helping Joseph with arithmetic all along, had stopped for a bit because of the nightmares she was having. She had also withdrawn herself from playing games and participating in class. Gradually, thanks to their therapy time, she began to find a friend in Joseph. She started talking to him about some things she had been through, as well as her current struggles. Joseph also began to feel comfortable enough to open up to her, being sure that he would not be judged. Finding Joseph as her best buddy and opening up to him made her more comfortable with everything around her and she was even willing to go back to the way things were.

She started by teaching Joseph once again and this time, his response was better. He was learning faster. As small as Sandra was, her mid was able to decipher that as long as a person could break through the walls Joseph had built around himself, teaching him and having him assimilate was going to only be a piece of cake. That was the little secret that seemed to unlock his assimilation level. That was the only that had changed between them and Sandra could tell that he did great because she had not only become his teacher, but she was a teacher he could trust. The more she got closer to him, the more she found it fun to teach him. He was also ever ready to learn and in no time, he was picking up. The teachers were impressed at his performance at test and even though his healing from all that happened to him was taking quite a while, his better scores served as a boost for his confidence. Hence, he was able to relate better in other kids and even participate in other activities too. Now, he was allowed to play as opposed to studying when other kids were playing. Joseph's life was gradually changing, all thanks to the fact that he had found a friend and a teacher that he could now trust.

The orphanage began to organize sporting activities for the kids. A sporting competition was coming up and the kids needed to practice, so they could have winners for each category. It was yet another extracurricular activity to boost the minds of the kids and Sandra could see it as a new start for herself. The sports master encouraged her when she signed up for short distance races. Rhonda, who had put on a bit of weight signed up to throw the discus for kids. Angie, who was the tallest of them, signed up for high jump and long jumps. John, who was also a tall kid, got involved in long jumps too and since he would always see Angie during practice, they got into a lot of arguments. John was such a trouble maker. As for Joseph, he would just sit out and watch. Left to him, sports was not just his thing. He would cheer the boys that participated in every activity until it came down to Sandra. He was always on her side if she was participating in any activity and this upset the boys, but he won't change where his loyalty lied. If the rest were family, then Sandra was his closest family member; she helped him become better at school work and he would be ever grateful. If she did not help him, he was too sure that he would have been asked to sit in and practice arithmetic, as opposed to watching the sporting activities.

"Sprinting is fun; you should give it a try." Said Sandra to Joseph, one afternoon after he congratulated her for winning a race.

"I don't think sporting activities are for me, and they just seem stressful."

"You have never tried. Just give it a try" she advised.

Joseph further expressed fear, so Sandra invited him to practice with her. The goal she gave him was to win her no matter what. In two weeks, he could run faster than her, and he now loved the idea of sprinting more than he ever imagined. He had speed, naturally and practicing for a bit had even made it better. It was like one of those hidden talents you never imagine you have until a need arises. He could almost not believe his ability himself, but gradually, he began to feel like he could do more with the discovery he just made about his sporting skills.

"I would like to compete for the prize too." He said to Sandra one afternoon.

"Then you should compete" she said without hesitation. "Why not talk to the sporting master?" she suggested. However, there were only three weeks left to the major sporting competition, so the master told him that he would have to prove himself to win a spot with others who had been practicing all the while. A competition kicked off and guess who came second? Joseph!

Nathaniel had won the first position. The sports master could not deny that Joseph had a lot of potential to be the best, so he took him in.

Meanwhile, they did not stop visiting the therapist, as Joseph still had to see the therapist and Sandra was still having her dreams every now and then. There was need to convert some of Sandra's sessions to a childhood counsellor's session for her, especially one who had a specialty in rape and abuse cases. The basis for this was that if Sandra felt somewhat empowered enough to take her life into her own hands and prevent herself from future instances of rape, perhaps, she would stop having bad dreams or stop being so scared of elderly male figures. Her mother had lost her father in the war and so, she never grew up to know him. Also, all the while she lived with her granny, she did not grow up around any male elderly figure. Her first real encounter with males was delivering drugs for her mum which ended in her being raped severally. Hence, she needed to know how to protect herself if such situations came up.

First off, the counsellor reminded her that the rape instances were never her fault, but she had to learn protect herself to avoid future instances of it, thanks to the society in which they found themselves. She was taught to take her own safety into her hands at all times, whether she was alone or not. She was told to avoid being found in very private situations with strangers and asked any stranger that approached her (with her voice raised), to show their identity. Raising her voice was to make the stranger know that people around her had been alerted about him being with her and if he had planned to do anything negative from being with her, it was unsafe for him. She was also taught that she could use any sharp object around her to attack her attacker; be it her key, a spray or even her pen. Plunging her pen into his eyes or any other sensitive area was an example. Gradually, Sandra was beginning to feel empowered. She was not as scared as she used to be because she felt like she could now protect herself. Hence, she was now having less of those dreams. She always went to bed, ready to injure whoever wanted to harm her in any way in her dream. However, the dreams did not come anymore. They went away totally and Sandra did not need to use any of her new skills or her new knowledge. She hoped not to get into those kinds of situations anymore. Now, she just needed to confident enough with elderly male figures. She literally jittered around them. Hence, she kept seeing her counsellor and her therapist, but now, less often.

All the while, Julia had been using a lot of money to cover for the therapy and counselling sessions for Sandra. She was also using so much money for Joseph's therapy too, which had already lasted for over a year. She had applied for funding, but hardly got funding. It was a non-governmental organization, so getting money from the government was not exactly a feasible option. They got donations from individuals, but they came whenever the individuals could afford it and did not come in the months when those individuals did not have spare cash for charity. She had sold all her valuables in the United Kingdom and had been using all that money to run the orphanage. Her family, as well as David, had also donated some money to the orphanage, but she had spent so much. She was now applying for international funds, but they were yet to come through. She was indeed in a fix.

CHAPTER
FIVE

"**H**ey!" Let the child come through" Kira said to the guard, who was shielding the crowd from crossing over to the demarcated side of the room where she was, as she shook her fans and signed autographs. A demarcation had been made to ensure the excited fans did not jump on their favorite model. There were so many black girls in the front row, waiting to get an autograph. She was the first model of color to have modeled for one of the best hair lines in the world, as they had just launched products which were specifically for people of color. As she signed autographs, she was almost in tears, knowing that these black girls now looked up to her as symbol of hope. She did not have so many people to look up to in her industry while trying to climb up, so it meant a lot for her to be someone the girls could look up to, especially in the modelling industry.

She smiled as the guard now let the young girl come through. The girl ran to her and gave her a tight hug. Kira wasted no time in lifting her up.

"What would you like to do for work when you are grown?"

The girl looked down, now shy? Kira smiled.

"How old are you?" she asked.

"I am ten years old." Kira smiled again, but this time, a tear dropped and she quickly wiped it before anyone could capture it on camera. It was about the time Julia had taken her into the orphanage.

In a split second, she tried to imagine what her life would have been like if she did not get adopted into the orphanage. She wondered where the others from her childhood were or how their lives had turned out. It hurt her to even think that the kids she grew up with may still be somewhere, wallowing in lack and poverty in their adult lives. She tried to hope that those thoughts were not true; she tried to take her mind off that way of thinking because it stung her to even think that way at all.

She turned back to the ten year old black girl in her arms and said, "You have to start by thinking and then, saying what you want to become baby. So, be bold and think of something you would love to do when you grow old and tell me right now. I'm waiting."

They were conversing in whispers and the body guards looked at each other, wondering what was going on, but they had been given instructions on things that could possibly happen by the brand she represented and how they had to be patient. The brand had explained that a moment as that was an important one for black women and they really deserved to take all the time they wanted and enjoy their moment. Kira caught the young girl looked at her mother who was somewhere in the crowd, cheering her on with gesticulations and expressing joy that her daughter was now with Kira. Kira waved to the girl's mother. The woman waved back happily.

"I would love to be on television one day." The young girl said. Kira finally understood the joy on the face of the girl's mother. She was really someone her daughter could look up to for what she planned to do with her life.

"That's so lovely" said Kira. "Now that you know, make sure you do everything you can to get to that height. Never give up, because it is really up to you to become that which you desire and no one can stop you except you. I would be looking forward to watching you on TV." She said, as she signed an autograph for the young girl. She hugged her tight and then, she let her go.

She remembered that Miss. Celine had been encouraging the younger kids the same way that day in class, and she had been peeking through a window. She had been ill on that day and was in their small clinic, which was very close to that class. Although, she did not get the chance to tell the rest of the class that she wanted to be like a model like Naomi Campbell (since that was not her class), she had held on to the things Miss Celine had told the kids. She had stumbled on Naomi's picture, her profile and a short story of her life on a small piece of newspaper that had flown into the orphanage the month before. As if it were destiny, the page of the newspaper that had been torn from the entire thing had flown all the way, just to land just in front of Kira. She had been immediately fascinated to see a woman with exactly the same skin as hers in the midst of many other beautiful women with different skin colors. She had decided ever since, that one day, she wanted to be that woman that represented women with her skin color on newspapers. She wanted to represent everything they stood for; if someone had to be there to do that, it really had to be her and she was ready to climb up to that feat; by working as hard as she could to achieve her dreams.

She signed more autographs and even allowed a couple of people to take pictures with her. The entire thing was indeed a huge blessing and she was more than happy to represent her people. She looked straight to the back of the room, her eyes searching, like she was searching for someone or maybe more than one person. And she found them! Her parents were right there, at the back of the room, waiting for their only child. Just like every other event, they were there once again to give her all the moral support she would ever need. They had been there this same way for every single audition and every casting that did not yield much success. Here they were again, not minding that she was now a 30-year-old woman. She loved it too! Their presence reminded her of the time she dared to say to her new parents that brought her along with them to California, United States that she wanted to model.

Their joy was boundless that day and they promised to support her all the way to success. She had only been 16 years old at the time, but what they did not know was that the road would not be as easy. In fact, the road would be a very difficult one. However, like they had promised from the start, they had been there every step of the way. She was ever grateful for them. She knew she was an amazing kid, but so were all the kids in the orphanage, but she was glad that they chose her 16 years ago. They could have picked a younger kid, but they chose her. She had tried to find out many times why they had chosen her, but her father had answered exactly like her mother, that it was love at first sight. This response always got her speechless and left with no other question to ask. She asked these questions because she had been in the orphanage for six years, before she got adopted. Year in, year out; Kira would see her friends get a scholarship, get chosen by an organization or adopted, but she still remained the orphanage. She wondered if it was because she was the oldest kid in the orphanage, but another boy who was brought into the orphanage when he was about 14 years old got adopted in the following year. Once more, it made Kira wonder if she was less desirable because she was a girl. She would check her features in the mirror from time to time and find herself wondering if there was something about her that people just hated altogether. Every last Saturday of the month, when couples came to check for kids they could adopt, she would stretch her neck from whatever activity they were engaged in to see if there were people driving into the orphanage and if those people looked like they would like to have an older child.

She got disappointed time after time. She would cry to sleep and even Miss. Julia would not notice as Kira had been in the orphanage for a long time and Julia's focus was now on newer kids. Kira could bet that none of the staff even imagined that she was hurt, as kids usually found it hard to say goodbye when they got adopted. She figured that they felt like she was enjoying her time in the orphanage and she had no worries. Additionally, Kira was not a child that bothered anyone;

she hated it. For that reason, she bottled up her feelings and kept them to herself. The bad part of that was the fact that she felt she was an undesirable child. She felt unwanted. It was after she got adopted by her present parents that she was glad all that delay happened. She understood it; she got the very best and their support confirmed that.

And now, he numerous auditions, through which they supported her, had finally paid off. They had been so supportive and seeing them backstage yet again almost made her burst into tears. They were tears of joy. She wondered what she would ever have achieved without them. She did not know there was a life as good as the one they provided for her, right until when they did. They supported every of her interests and even sent her to a fashion school in London when she indicated her interest in fashion. This further boosted her style, and her love for the beauty industry. She had signed so many autographs, so her manager had them call it a night, as she went to meet her parents backstage.

She wiped her tears as she got close to them, but she could not hide the fact that she had been crying. By the time she got there, there was a moment of silence between Kira and her parents. It was a long pause and the silence was deafening. She kept turning her eyes from her father to her mother. Then, the trio quickly moved towards each other and hugged as they all cried. They understood her journey and knew there was so much to be thankful for. Her fashion business had been going well, with the launch of a great fashion line, but she had decided to have people manage the business for her, using the blueprint she had made, while she went on to squarely face her modelling career. When she said she would model at 16, the truth is that her parents also wondered how it would play out, considering her skin color, but they chose to be positive. She modeled on the side, on a small scale while learning about fashion. When she had left her business to face modeling full time four years ago, they felt it was crazy, but they chose to trust their child's ability and instincts. They chose to support her; in spite of the fact that they wondered if everything would truly work out. The journey had not been easy for them too, but they only chose to trust the process and support her with everything they could. The journey of being her parent was not easy on them too, but they loved her with everything in them and did not look back for once. People of color would wonder what white folks were doing with a black teenager. They usually looked at them like they kidnapped her or planned to hurt her in some way. They could not explain their ordeal to everyone in the world, so they knew they had to toughen up. And so they did; they toughened up for her.

As for Kira, this big break meant a lot for her in a saturated industry. Now, she had a name and something solid to add to her portfolio, to make her even more marketable. Her very long, black, coarse hair had given her an edge. It was exactly what was needed for the role. She had thought of cutting off her hair two months back, but had been reminded by her mum that it was a pointer to where she came from. Now, she felt so fulfilled doing the job. Strangely, getting that role took her mind back to the time when she was about four years old and her biological mother would threaten to cut her hair each time she complained that she did not want to make it into cornrows because of the pain she felt each time she sat for a weave. Her biological mother would then tell her that if she tried to make her hair in spite of her pain, it would grow long and beautifully, as the hairstyle was a protective one. However, if she left it, she may stand a risk of breakage.

Remembering this short story from her life and how her life played drew her attention to a very important lesson in life; that if she gave up that easily from the initial hardship she faced once as a kid and also in her modelling career, she would not have gotten the opportunity to see the beautiful outcome she now had at the point she was in her life.

Her hair had also grown long, full and beautiful after enduring all the hardship that came with came with making it back in the days. This story from her own life experience was the one she narrated during her audition that gave her an extra advantage that made those in charge decide that the role was hers. Hers was an original story and it appeared to be a story could sell their product to their target consumers. To the brand Kira represented, they had given her a job. However, to her, it was her destiny.

As she strut on the red carpet that night in her natural hair, she felt like herself. She felt like she was "Kira unrestricted" and she had no reason to hide any part of her. She was bare, she was herself, she was confident in who she was and she wanted women that looked like to feel the same way. She wanted them to aspire to be the same way. She wanted them to have someone to look up to, as they dreamt; just the way she had looked up to Naomi Campbell. She was exactly where she wanted to be, achieving what she had hoped to achieve as a kid. She now understood that delay is not denial. Yet, she knew there was more to do. She was only at her starting point.

Summer came early for the Kira and the other models she worked with on the branding of the hair line she represented, as the company decided to sponsor them on a trip to Jamaica. The trip tickets came with VIP acccss cards to several exclusive parties where they were going to represent the brand. Kira was excited, as she was planning to go to Jamaica the following year, so she saw the fact that it came earlier as a blessing. She planned to spend some of the money she had kept aside for a summer trip on exotic shopping, asides the shopping vouchers the brand she had represented had provided.

The next day, she started her shopping day with black coffee as she was tired from one of the parties she attended the night before. Since her endorsement, she had been continually invited for numerous parties, some thrown in her honor and some which she got invited to, as a way of representing her people. She was also paid to show up to some parties.

She had attended yet another party and was feeling drowsy, but she liked doing her shopping herself, as opposed to employing the services of a personal shopper. Shopping was how she cooled off, so the last thing she wanted was anyone shopping for her. For this reason, she decided that she needed her black coffee to stay alert and not make shopping choices that she would end up regretting. As she drank her coffee, she watched the morning news.

It was then that she stumbled upon the news of a girl in Africa that survived a fire she started in one of the building in her villages. Yes, the girl had indeed started the fire, but hers was a unique case. It was a story of self-defense. She was an orphan and she did it because she had to protect herself from some rapists that had been found culpable among the people in her community, but had become so powerful that the authorities in the community could not touch them. They were known faces, they had raped several young girls, yet they had gone scot-free. The people in the community could do nothing about them, until that day when they decided that it was the turn of this young girl that hawked food for sale. They rounded her up in a desolate building and were going to rape her when she remembered that there was a lighter in her pocket. She had also seen that the building, especially the angle the men were coming from were made of flammable wood. Hence, she had lit up the building by throwing the fire directly at the men. The wood caught fire immediately. It spread fast and there was no escape route for them, since she had carefully tricked them to an angle of the building without one. The people in the community only noticed the building burning and she was the only one who came out alive. After a while, she was calm enough to narrate her story of self-defense. She said she threw the lighter directly on a spot with plenty of flammable wood, and the fire started quickly and surrounded the men. It came as a shock to them and their bodies caught fire before they could think up an escape plan.

The major point of the story was that the girl was out of school, hawking and that was why she was an easy target for the men. She had lost her parents for many years, yet continued to cook and hawk food for survival. The reporter mentioned that an account had been opened for a donation to her schooling. However, more than anyone, Kira knew that without seeing a psychologist, schooling was not going to work out well for the girl in question. She remembered her own life and how things kept going downhill for her before Julia had realized that she needed to see a psychologist. The people donating did not really understand he depth of what the young girl had been through. Her story was indeed one that Kira deeply resonated with. She knew she had to do something different. Hence, she called her assistant to make enquiries on a psychologist the girl could see in that area of her country. She would foot the bill and in fact, she was going to donate the exact worth of the shopping voucher the brand had given her into helping the girl in question.

As much as Kira did not want this act of hers to go viral, because of her peculiarity and her resent deals, she became a subject of discussion and she was quite an interesting subject to many. People at large loved what she did, while a small amount of people still thought she did that for publicity. Kira knew better; her celebrity status had both the good and the bad. Little did these people know that the story had resonated with her and her background so well. Kira felt like that girl could have been her. She felt totally blessed and honored to be at the position she was in life and apart from a sense of duty, she also felt really happy to be giving back.

It was as though more brands could see through the fact that her acts were genuine, so almost every single day, she got yet another offer to be the brand ambassador for a new brand, all with various benefits. At the end of the week, she realized that the singular act of setting out to shop had set her up for blessings she never imagined could come her way. She now had an array of companies and NGOs to choose to represent based on the best deals, as well as her own personal values. Her mother had always taught her that personal values were important even in business and she was not about to take that for granted. Her life was taking a turn she had hardly expected and she was just full of gratitude.

Her trip still stood, so she set out with other models for the Jamaica trip. Jamaica was all the fun she thought it would be and more. The atmosphere was welcoming to all and sundry and there were people from all walks of life out there, just looking to have fun. And fun they did have. The VIP treatment for Kira and the other models was almost unbelievable. They had called it a vacation, but it was almost like living the dream, especially with all the massages she was getting. They were treated as princesses. Kira could hardly believe her own life. She had never imagined that a time like this in her life would come, when she would be someone the rest of the country would talk about or someone that would get such kinds of treatments.

Meanwhile, the kind of attention Kira had gotten from the media in the past few weeks had made her even more popular. More people than she expected now knew her and wanted to either sign autographs, take pictures or include her in their video. While signing autographs at an all-white party, a female voice came calling Kira's name with so much confidence.

"Kira!" she had called out. It was then Kira turned around to see that the lady had familiar eyes and oh…her chin. Her features really looked like those of someone she had known, but had not seen in such a long time. She was a beautiful black lady, who was curvaceous yet petite. Kira rounded her up to not be more than a size eight.

"The flute girl in Liberia, remember me?"

With this, Kira wasted no time in wrapping her arms around her. There was only one flute girl; the one who played so well, who always insisted that Kira bathed for her every morning. She was Amira and her black skin was glowing even better than it did back then. Kira could not believe her eyes. Amira also confessed that she could not believe her ears at first, but seeing the "highly-spoken of" Kira was such a great moment for her.

"I kept telling my friends that we grew up together and you used to bath me every morning, but they saw me as a joke. I am so proud of everything you have achieved." She said to Kira. "At least, now I can take pictures with you for reference purposes."

Kira on the other hand was also happy to be with someone that knew her life from her early years. Her fame was a bit too much for her in that moment and she was glad that she had found someone who had just always known her and who she could be fully herself with. They ended up sitting at one of the lounges at their resort and talking about their lives over drinks and to be honest, the ladies were proud at their own achievements. They had indeed done so well for themselves.

Amira was now an investment banker and she had risen to a high point in her career quite early. She worked in New York. She had been fortunate to be raised by parents who were descents of royal families in the United Kingdom. She had enjoyed a great life and was on the overall, a happy and polished lady. However, the fortunes of her parents did not make her lazy at any point. She had always been driven and it showed in her career. Kira was glad to listen to the tales of Amira's progress. She had seen Amira as her younger sister back then and she still did right now. So, it was more like she was happy to regain a long lost sibling and to hear that the sibling was also excelling in their field.

"Miss Julia was right." Said Amira.

"Miss Celine was also right" said Kira. "Indeed, we could be anything we set out to be. We are living proofs of that."

"Just look at us." Amira responded. Kira had retired from taking photos for the night. It felt like home with Amira and she just wanted to continue to enjoy what that felt like. She chose to stay in Amira's room for the night, as opposed to staying in the suite where she was lodged. She just needed that child in her to come alive again. She needed to go back to those days and smell the air once again; the air of possibilities, which was all they hand and was the same air that had carried them right unto this point in their lives.

Kira had found a friend she could share drinks with every night in the resort. It was one night over drinks that Amira sold her the idea of starting a skin line. Apart from being an investment banker, as a matter of passion, Amira always wanted to own a skin care line for black people. However, it took a lot to do that and also reach out to people effectively, especially with the publicity and brand representation aspect. Amira also had a career. She had to make it all work and had always thought about having a business career.

Now, Amira had begun to see how Kira would fit in. She wanted to bring Kira on board as a partner. All she really needed Kira to handle was the publicity and brand representation areas, as Amira was not big even being in the forefront of a brand. She just preferred to do her work behind the scenes and let the products speak. However, the brand needed a face their target audience would love; not just as a model, but also as a promoter that would sit well with the culture of the target audience.

Amira was fine with only representing her clients as an investment banker. She did want anything else that would bring her out of her shell and was definitely not cut out for representing a brand. They both agreed over drinks that the new brand indeed needed a great representation and Kira fitted perfectly into the picture, especially with the recent waves she had made.

Once the vacation was over, Kira and Amira swung into action concerning the skin line. The production phase was the major thing at first and it all came out beautifully. The aim of the product was to boost the confidence of black queens, so they could afford to walk into any room, own their looks and achieve their goals on the overall. It was a lot of work, but they had been built to never give up, right from when they were kids and this was the exact kind of energy the ladies brought on board to achieve their goals. It took several months of work to perfect the products Amira had already worked on. Being a beauty expert herself and having gotten some beauty certifications, Kira could bring in creative juices for some modifications to be made.

In the end, it turned out beautifully. As a result of the image Kira had developed, people trusted the brand and bought their products only to realize that the products were indeed perfect for black women, just like the adverts and other mediums had described them. They made massive sales. Amira and Kira could not stop being grateful that the universe somehow aligned to help in bringing them back together, not just at any point in their lives, but at that point where they really needed each other to launch into the next phase of their life.

When things began to fall in place for them, they could not help, but just look back and come to the conclusion that their lives played out exactly how it was supposed to. They had indeed gone through bitter experiences that had brought them together; however, everything had still worked out for their good. If they hadn't known each other, there would have been no deal between them and no massive returns made. Additionally, if Kira had no reason to leave her community, she might have never seen that newspaper page, she would never have gotten adopted or even had the access her present society provided her to succeed the way she had done.

Kira had to do a lot of healing from her childhood hurt and losing her family while at the orphanage. It was no easy feets for any child or teenager. Now, she was not happy all that had happened, but she realized that everything had worked together to bring her to where she was. After all these years, she hardly looked back in regret anymore; only gratitude, as she kept praying for the souls of the loved ones she had lost.

CHAPTER
SIX

Kira had a long hair and was so beautiful. She always looked out for the other kids. She even helped in bathing some of the four-year-old girls. However, none of the kids could ever imagine what she had to go through. Being older than most of the kids, she had been a direct casualty of the Liberian war. Her father fought in the war. The war was said to be for the greater good of the country, so why not? He was proud to fight and alas, he was proud to lose his life for his country. So, the rumors said. For him, it was a matter of honor and duty, but for his family, the tale was different. It was about the saddest thing to ever happen to his family at the time. Her mother would not stop wailing. She wished life would be better, but there were no answers and no one to console them. Others were also fighting in the war. About every family had a man fighting and they lost their people over and again.

However, they were too sunken in their grief to realize what was coming for them. They did not envisage any impending doom. They were trying to get their lives in order. Kira had just started basic schooling. She had been through a lot, but was also a resilient child who wanted her mother to smile, so she was trying to give her best to school work. Because of the war, they could not continue going to school, but one of their teachers who lived in the neighborhood and was also searching for something to distract at her from the war decided to take a couple of kids under her wings and teach them in her home. Her husband was also fighting in the war. At the time, Kira had two brothers; King, the older one and Klint, the younger. They mother had them in the house all day, just to shield them from everything going on during the war. The young boys in their community were being given guns once they were up to five. Kira's mother did not want her sons to see the sight of that.

She was only trying to protect her sons by not letting them step out of the house. She was not certain of what the future held for them, but she wanted to be with her children when the war was declared over. She also wanted their view about life to be intact. She did not want the psychology of her kids to be damaged—young boys should not carry guns or learn how to shoot other humans.

Kira was a girl, so all that was needed was to ensure she did not stay out late; not even in the evenings. One fateful day, as it almost clocked four, Kira began to run home as fast as she could. Her mother wanted her home latest by 4p.m, but they were having so much fun with their favorite and only teacher that they failed to realize that it was almost 4p.m. The teacher's home was her only place of escape from the things happening in their community; from the bad news that came in on a daily. She always enjoyed her time away from home—she got to spend time with her friends and escaped how she really felt about her father's death. She was little and the war had been on for only a week, before she had lost her father. However, the fact that she was six did not mean that she would feel its effect. Her mother was always sad and she did not like to see it. The house had a gloomy feel. That explained how the girl that was used to lively home felt. Everything was happening so fast.

It was yet to dawn on Kira what losing her father really meant. It had been two months and it had just felt like he had travelled. On that day, she ran home as she realized it was almost 4p.m. She did not want to be her mother's source of worry. Little did she know that she would never get the chance to be a source of worry to her mother again; not even once more.

As she approached their home, she could smell the smoke, but it formed a fog over her sight as tears rolled down her eyes. She could not stop herself from crying, yet she could not believe her own eyes. Everything was still confusing for the six year old. She needed to understand why the crowd that had gathered in front of her house were now running away, everyone to their houses. Their house, which was at the entrance to their community had been burnt down to ashes along with the houses of a couple of their neighbors. There were no cries, no shouts from inside any of the houses and the fire was gradually dying down. She could see many buckets; it was obvious that the people had tried to quench the fire to no avail.

"Mama! King! Clint!"

"Mama! King! Clint!"

"Mama! King! Clint!"

"Mama! King! Clint!"

"Mama! King! Clint!"

She shouted repeatedly, as she rolled in the sand, feeling helpless. If there was something her young mind could pick, it was the fact that she was now alone in this world. There was so much noise around her, but she was also in too much pain, to realize that people were running helter-skelter around her. Whoever started the fire had extended it to the all the houses around them and in fact, to the whole of the community. There was so much noise, so much grief, so much crying all over the place. There was confusion too; people could not make sense of what had happened. However, if there was something that made sense, it was definitely the fact that the fire was no mistake. It was intentionally started, and it did not take just a single person to burn down a community; it had to be a group of people. They were not prepared to save people from the fire which started in no particular direction. It just happened anyway.

"Get up! Run!" A woman said to her.

"No! My mama, King, and Klint! They were in there. I need them to come out. I need them to come with me." The little Kira said.

"They don't exist anymore. You need to save yourself now."

She tried to turn around to see who was talking to her, but instead, it dawned on her that the whole village was running. Kira started to run in the direction which the rest of the crowd started running to. They didn't know where it led to, but Kira and others at the back followed. At least, the area was free from fire.

However, it was too late. Their captors were all set to take them away. They had purposely left that area fire-free. They had no time for discussions. They were armed and so, they captured the people from Kira's village. The women and children were not expecting to be captured. They had all their belongings including anything they would have used for self-defense in their homes that were now burning to ashes.

The captors put them in chains; one person attached to the other, and they set out to move to the community of their captors. As they walked in their chains, they realized that their captors were members of the neighboring communities, especially from how they spoke. They spat at them as they walked, telling Kira and her people that they were suffering for the sins of their men who had turned against their own men on the war front. They told them that this was revenge and they just got started with them. The neighboring community had hidden some of their own teenage boys and a few young adult men and had now used them in carrying out this act of theirs.

Members of the neighboring community had never been peaceful, but Kira's people never imagined that the day would come when they would try to kill the women and children in their community and take the survivors hostage. However, no war is ever totally predictable. When it comes to human violence, no one ever knows how far it could go. They walked slowly because of their chains, but were quickly reminded that the chains were not an excuse to delay their agenda. The people were grouped. Kira and some of the other young girls were tied together. They did not know that their lives were about to go from bad to worst!

As they settled into their new community, they settled in as slaves and quickly assumed different roles. The woman and children that survived the fire were taken to work the fields of the other community. They were constantly reminded that they were paying for what their men had done on the war front. Kira and other young girls were quickly thought to cook and clean for their captors the way they liked. Irrespective of how young the girls were, they were always cooking or cleaning and only got two hours of sleep every day. However, that was not the worst to happen to them.

The worst thing the girls experienced was seeing their mothers or the mothers of their friends being raped by young men that could be their own sons; all because they were in chains. In addition to their chains, the women had worked hard on the fields to the point that they were too weak to resist when their captors tried to rape them. The captors took turns on the women, and the women also had the duty of going to offer themselves to the captors based on a roaster that had been made for them. The situation made Kira cry, but the women would say in whispers from time to time, "We are at least glad that they are not doing this to our daughters." This saying gave Kira a bit of encouragement to have an ounce of gratefulness; that was her first coping strategy. The coping strategies of Kira and her people got better over the next few months, as the war continued. Now, their captors were beginning to experience their own share of grief too with more deaths being announced by the day. Hence, their grip on the people reduced and they slept for more hours in the coming months.

By time three years and eighth month since their capture, grief had eaten Kira up and she had cried as she worked, with reality steadily hitting her that all she had was herself. Her father, her mother and her brothers were dead. She was the only surviving member of her family and she instantly knew that she had to take her life into her own hands. She knew her people had given up and resolved to their new life, their women now even willingly surrendering themselves to their captors. Listening in on the conversation of one of their captors one day, she realized that their captors were talking of how they were getting tired of sleeping with the older women and ladies. One of them suggested sleeping with the younger girls, and the others agreed. According to them, the girls were now older. It was at this point that Kira knew she had to run. Her mother always told her to stay strong and never give up without a fight, especially during the war. When the war started, her mother being a brutally honest woman, had told her what rape was and how she should never allow any man rape her without a fight. She knew the only way to fight in this situation, was to run as fast as her legs could carry her.

"Do you think there's something better out there?" she asked the girls one day as they did the dishes.

"Life would only be miserable outside this camp."

"Imagine going for days without food."

"I'd rather keep living this way."

These were the responses the girl had to give and at this point, Kira knew that she had to carry out her plans alone. The girls were not ready for the life she had been thinking of. Even before she heard the conversations of those men, she had considered running away from Liberia. She just wanted a life that was not what she was currently experiencing. When she saw that the other girls were not thinking in the direction which she was thinking, she knew she had to make a move and even though it would be a crazy one, she just had to do it. She knew she might go hungry sometimes, so she did not want to force anyone into her plan. After all, everyone was now relaxed; their captors and her people alike.

While they were all asleep that night, Kira escaped from the camp and the next day, the captors who had relaxed their hold on them, did not notice that they were short of a girl. It dawned on the girls that she had left by the time they woke up the following morning. It was then that her questions made sense to them. When the captors discovered that she had left, they went searching the neighboring woods and since they could not find her, they assumed she had fallen into a big ditch or had been torn apart by a wild animal. They were too torn apart by their own grief and wearied by the war to put much effort into searching for a girl that did not mean much to them.

Kira had a hard time finding her way through the woods. She was almost ten at the time. She cried severally, but knew she was fighting in her own little way. She had ran all night, far from where her captors would search and into the woods of another nearby community. She peeked into the community the next day, and so they seemed more peaceful. However, in the next one month, she lived in a shed she had found in the woods, eating nuts and hiding from the view of anyone. It was crazy, but she hoped for something better. When things got tough, she would come out and beg for food before going back into hiding. Luckily for her, people were too concerned with their own grief to care about a shed in the woods. She had cold nights and sunny days, but she found a big cloth under the shed which she used to cover herself. It seemed as if someone had once lived in that shed. She was grateful to whoever that person was, at least she had a hiding place. Thanks to the war, the people in the community had killed most of the animals in the woods and there was hardly any to scare the young girl. All she had to worry about was insects and with time, she learnt to eat those too.

After four unbelievable months of hiding under the shed, the war was declared over and a new president of Liberia emerged. There was peace and it was then that she freely moved around, looking malnourished. Being a wandering child, she encountered the volunteer group that Maria and Julia had come with to Liberia and after receiving a relief package, she monitored them. Although she knew that they would leave pretty soon, she saw that they were good people and she could trust them. She also wondered if they could help her, and thought to try anyway.

She followed them on foot, by running from place to place. Whenever she lost them, she asked people around for the route their bus had followed and just made sure she found them. However, she was sleeping behind a tree by the time they left. This was hurtful to her, especially after she had put in all that effort. When she decided to turn back and figure out what to do with her life, she sighted Julia and walked up to her. As she was about to open her mouth, she fainted!

Julia saw that the girl was malnourished and simply needed all the help she can get. She had asked Maria to send money and a couple of other valuables when she got back to the United Kingdom. Hence, she started spending all her savings which she had brought in cash for the trip. At the point, she had just been told that she would never be able to have her own kids and it was not a problem that money could fix. Hence, Julia had resolved that money was nothing and was willing to spend it on whatever made another human's life better.

To some, Kira just looked like another helpless child, but to Julia, she was a sign. She was also a motivation to have her stay in Liberia. She watched the child till her health improved; she learned what do, what to say and how to act with children in that situation, all while taking care of Kira. And when it was time to start up her orphanage which she started in her small apartment, Kira was the very first child in the orphanage and her first goal was to get the child to look healthy again.

Lydia groaned. Every single part of her body hurt, especially her insides. Was this the punishment for running away from home? She groaned and then, looked at her baby girl which she had wrapped in all the warm clothes those in the neighborhood gave her when they found her roaming around in the cold with a little baby girl. She smiled at her beautiful baby; her only consolation that everything she had done was worth it. However, her insides still hurt. Who would she tell that she needed some medicine? She did not want to be bothered. Those in the neighborhood were already kind enough to her. They had shown her this warm place that was left without an owner after the war. The owners were quite old and their sons did not survive the civil war, an event Lydia did not exactly like to think about.

She groaned yet again as she thought of her siblings. Phillips would be so grown by now, probably a teenager growing muscles. She hoped they survived the war; she had heard of communities in their region that were burnt down and she really hoped that no one in her family was a casualty. When she thought of them, she thought of everyone seated to eat on a mat like they always did, with their father taking the first morsel. Home was always such a happy place for her, and she had enjoyed everything her family did together, especially their dinner time. She hoped her father had returned from the war to make the family complete once more, but without her? Her family must had definitely remained incomplete and it was all her fault. Her father must have been thoroughly heartbroken when he returned from the war and did not see his first daughter. But she had done what she had to do. She'd rather have him heartbroken that having to give her that look of disappointment. It was really the last thing she wanted. She had thought of going back, but again, it felt like she had ran too far away and there was no going back now. Perhaps her family now considered her dead. She sobbed.

She was in a lot of pain and it felt like she was in her last days, but how would any of the people in the neighborhood want to help a woman that smelt so horrible. She always beckoned to them to throw clothes, foods or any other item they were willing to give at her. To them, it definitely sounded like something a mentally deranged person would ask for, but she knew that the moment that had an idea of what she smelt like, they would want nothing to do with her. She had experienced a person's reaction once. At the time, she didn't know she smelt that horrible, but from that reaction, she could tell she always had to keep her distance from people. She could see the look in that man's eyes; he was utterly disgusted!

And how would she explain to anyone at all that what she suffered was coming from her privates? They would consider her a slut and say she got exactly what she deserved. No one would want to associate with her. Once upon a time, it was only her privates that smelt bad, but now, she also felt pain on her insides. Her stomach area hurt so much; everything hurt! Once upon a time, she had been another innocent girl who hid at home and hoped her father would return safely from the war. She had been that girl that wanted peace, so everything would go back to the way they used to be. However, her life changed before her own eyes one afternoon when she ran a quick errand for her mother to make a delicacy. She was the oldest daughter and she was the one who could run that errand perfectly, given their family setting. Unfortunately, on her way back home, she was captured and carried away by some unfamiliar faces. She was raped and raped. It was such a nasty experience for a fifteen year old girl. She was naïve and had never been introduced to the idea of sex. So, for her, she felt like a person had perpetually punctured through her muscles till there was blood. She walked home, in shame and pain, after stopping at a public tap to clean her legs which had blood running down from it. They had left her helpless and hopeless and she had been there for twenty minutes, doing nothing else but crying. She felt like she was now a disgrace to her family and she had the biggest secret to hide. She went home and told her mother a story of how she had slipped and fell at a point where a lot of water had been poured. Her mother who was busy tending to her younger ones advised her to rest before starting her other chores for the evening. She was in pains, but was happy that her mother had been distracted enough not to notice what was going on with her; her new secret. At least, she was safe and would not break her mother's heart.

Everything was fine until she felt nauseated one morning. Her mother had been off to the only local market in her community to sell the knitted clothes she usually made. She remembered once seeing Brenda, their neighbor's eldest daughter vomiting and her mama beating her like she had done something wrong. She could remember being confused and asking her own mother what was happening, only to learn that Brenda was going to have a baby and she did not even know who the father was. She remembered hearing that Brenda had brought shame upon her family. Remembering all these things, she did not want that to be her. She did not want to be the girl that made her mother that unhappy.

So, with nothing, that morning, Lydia looked at her brothers, kissed each of them on their foreheads and was off to a destination she wasn't certain of. She sneaked out of the house from behind, with a small bag, and kept running without looking back. She had taken the golden earrings her grandmother had given her. She was going to sell it and use it for her journey to a place she did not know. Left to Lydia, anywhere far away from home will be fine.

She was lucky enough to find a truck driver who only cared about what she had to offer than why her parents had left her alone on a journey to the community he was going. She did not know where it was, but from the unhappy look of the passengers who fitted into the small spaces in between the goods he was going to deliver, she could tell that their journey was still far away. While that fact was not one that excited them, for her, it was bliss. She really needed to go as far away from home as she possibly could. The rest of the trip entailed her puking to the irritation of other passengers who could not wait for her to get off the truck, only to realize that she was going nowhere. She was going to follow them right until the trip was over, her golden earrings had fetched her that.

Carrying heavy woods while she was pregnant was certainly no happy thing to do. However, she needed a place to lay her head at night and if that was what it cost, so be it. She had settled into living with one of the passengers from the truck. The woman used her for manual labor, but she resolved that this was better than being unsafe once again. The woman had confirmed she was pregnant and promised to house her till she had her baby. She couldn't promise her anything after the child, as she could not imagine housing two extra life beings, just as she had said. All she had to do was to work for her safety and get the only thing she cared about now—safety for her baby.

As young as she is, as her baby grew in her, she became more careful. She would rather have a log of wood hit her leg heavily than have it come anywhere close to the new life that was growing in her. The woman with who she lived was only a business woman who did not have any family. She was just trying to survive through the harsh times and helped Lydia to the best of her ability, as far as she did her work. The time came when her benefactor was looking to move to another community where she was sure her wood business would boom. However, Lydia was already in her ninth month of pregnancy, so she decided to wait just a bit to see the young girl put to bed just before she left.

Truly, once she helped Lydia to the point where she could hear the cry of a child, and as the child made her way out through Lydia's body, Sylvia prepared to go.

Sylvia herself had been through trying times, losing all her children to a disease, including an infant. As a result of that experience, she found it hard to be with infants. Immediately Lydia's child was out, Sylvia wanted to leave. There was the placenta in there to be cut, but Sylvia could not even stand it. She just really wanted to go. The placenta made its way out slowly and Lydia, being weak and unexperienced, cut it badly. As a result, she healed quite poorly through the period after which she gave birth. She had no one to look after her and she kept feeling pain, but she had her baby's face to look upon—her very reward for everything she had to put up with. Lydia had given birth to a baby girl and from the moment she looked at her face, she knew the name she wanted to give her child—Amira, the name of a curious Arabian woman who had come to Liberia out of curiosity and had shown kindness to her as a kid.

Over the next few days following the birth of her child, she began to feel pain the lower part of her abdomen. This was something she thought was normal, considering the fact that she had just given birth. However, the next week, she developed a fever and then, her privates stunk. She tried to ignore it like she did in the days when she had morning sickness and also in her third trimester, when she had to work regardless. Once again, she went around trying to work and make some money. However, now, she had a baby she had to keep an eye on from time to time.

Another difference was also the fact that now, she smelled from her insides and those she worked with did not fail to make that obvious. She knew she did too, she did not just know how to handle it or what to do about it. She left her manual labor out of shame and got to wooden house Sylvia had left behind, still feeling more pain from her insides. Her birthing process had not been properly handled and her baby had only been lucky to be seen by her neighbors. They were the ones that taught how to properly clean up the child.

Lydia still felt her pain, but only one thing now mattered to her— Amira. Amira just had to be fine. As the months went by, Lydia did not get any better. It did not take so long for her to figure out the fact that her day was close. Who would take care of her daughter? She had heard of the women in the next building, gossiping about some white woman who cared for homeless kids. She had an inkling that she had found an answer to what worried her so much. If she took care of kids, she hoped that she would be willing to take care of her daughter too. When she found the orphanage, her joy knew no bounds. She put her daughter in a carton, waited and watched from the woods on the corner of the street. She waited till late in the afternoon. At around 4:30p.m, the white lady who was going about her daily business, came to the front of gate, screamed at the sight of the baby in the carton. Then, she lifted the baby up and carried her into the orphanage. "Amira" had been inscribed on a thin leaf and dropped into the carton.

Lydia saw Amira hold up the leaf and read what was there as she carried the child in. She found peace in that. Left to her, at least if she could not give her child anything else in the world, she had at least given her a beautiful name.

CHAPTER
SEVEN

Julia looked through her email just like she did every night. There had to be something for the kids; someone must at least be looking to help kids. There was a lot to do for the kids, many of the kids still had to go for therapy at least twice a week for their own balance. Julia was hardly someone who could look away from doing things the perfect way. She wanted the best for the kids, but it always cost so much money. It had been a year since Celine came yet she sent some money to the orphanage every month. That was a major source of funding for the orphanage. However, Celine's wedding was now coming up and Julia did not like the idea of collecting money from Celine at such a time.

Celine had always wanted a big wedding. Finding the perfect groom was the task on the top of her to-do list at first, but she was lucky enough to fall in love with the perfect guy and have him fall right back for her. Celine absolutely loved Craig and could not wait to be his wife. Ever since they were kids, Celine had always fantasized about her kind of wedding. It had to be grand; not in the number of guests, but in terms of quality. She had saved for the moment for many, many years. Julia knew this herself and had suspected that the money she had been sending to the orphanage must have been part of the money she had set aside for her grand wedding. The thought of this was not something Julia liked, but she had kept collecting the money because she really needed it; the orphanage really needed it.

She sat up, thinking; there had to be a way—some way. She could not keep making her sister go out of her way to do her favors. She was not comfortable with the whole situation. She felt like she had been too relaxed based on the fact that people came in to give to the orphanage from time to time. However, it was an unpredictable source of income and in fact, not one to be depended upon.

After a while of coming up with nothing, a thought struck Julia. Africa was a portion of the world people pitied. She remembered being in her sophomore college year and seeing some students solicit for donations that were going to Africa. She remembered that people always talked about giving to Africa. She knew that if she surfed the net with the computer Celine had brought for her, for just a bit, she would find organizations willing to give to Africa. It sounded brilliant to her, and even if it didn't sound brilliant, she was going to check out those organizations any way, as she could not come up with any other idea for funding.

Julia resolved to do more research on organizations looking to help kids in Africa, especially those directed at countries just recovering from the effect of a war or even those for war-torn countries. She found a couple of them and started constructing letters specifically directed at each of them. At this time, it was already 5.a.m. She was tired, but she had a goal and she just needed to achieve it. She wanted to do only what the kids wanted and at this moment, the kids would definitely want her to send out those letters, so they do not go hungry.

Once it was 6.a.m, she knew the kids had to start their day. Thinking of it alone made her feel weary, even as she typed those letters. She was just tired of everything. She loved the kids so much, but the love was not all that was required to run the orphanage, it was only the basis. She needed funding as soon as she could get it. She did not want the kids to ever realize that anything was amiss in terms of provision, she always wanted them to be provided for. She knew how much of a burden it usually was for kids to think there was no money for the things they needed. Once kids know that things are amiss financially, they would join adults subconsciously, to carry the financial burden. Julia knew that kids did not deserve that; they only deserve to live happily and get every necessary chance to grow the right way. She knew this because provision was one of the things that made her comfortable as a child. She had always wanted her kids to have more than she had. Now that the kids in the orphanage were her kids, Julia wanted to give them that good life too.

She was weary, yet she had to launch into another day for various activities with the kids. Although she had teachers and other staff that helped with the kids, they still depended on her for the running of the orphanage. She was the mastermind behind it. With only thirty minutes left, Julia began to wonder if it was about time she used her accounting degree to do something that could fetch her income. However, she knew the kids would suffer and she did not want that. She always loved the idea of being an accountant, but now, these kids had her heart.

She sent two letters, before packing up her records books and going into the shower in the last thirty minutes she had before the kids would be up. As she did this, there was a loud bang on the floor. It had come from the building on the left—that was the dormitory for the boys. By the time she got to the place, there was a lot of noise coming from one of the rooms in the dormitory. It was the room of the teenage boys and the boys were now up thirty minutes to their waking time. She could see traces of blood on the floor. She ran in only to see that one of the boys had fallen from the upper bunk. The boys usually slept on double bed and one of the boys had fallen from his sleep. As she rushed to see what had happened, the boys made way for her. It was quite a long room and one of the older teenage boys now had a cloth over the area of the injured boy's lower leg, which was bleeding. On getting there, she realized it was John.

THE EYES OF AN ORPHAN

John, the fighter. John, the trouble maker. The boy that had so much energy and seemed to enjoy just having his nose in people's business.

"*Poor John.*" She thought. She wondered what could have happened to get him in that state yet again.

She needed an ambulance to come into the orphanage soon enough. By now, other staff had gathered around and were now helping to get an ambulance to come pick up the wounded boy. The first aid box was brought around and Miss Janet who had received adequate training gave first aid and helped in stopping the bleeding. However, John was still in pain. He winced and cried before and while he was being given first aid. Some bones in his leg did not align anymore. It seemed like he had suffered a fracture. He had tried to stand on his feet, to no avail. It took a while for the ambulance to get to the orphanage and while they were at it, once his pain had reduced, the mischievous teenager began to explain how he found himself on the floor. He explained that he was having a fight with another boy in his dream. He said the boy had taken an item of his and he had been trying to run after the boy, only to find himself on the floor. While some of the kids found it funny and laughed at his story, the staff members were not having any of his jokes at all. He had fallen very badly. They kept talking among themselves that he could have suffered a brain injury at such a young age.

Despite his naughty character, Julia smiled at him and she told him that she liked how he was not so worried even in the face of trouble. He had landed on his legs and his right leg had suffered either a dislocation or fracture, but there he was, telling them all a story. She told him how she liked his spirit. The truth was that Julia had been troubled about what had happened and had thought about how the extra hospital bills she now had to pay would affect other running expenses of the orphanage. She had been worried, but his little tale had lit up her mood. She hoped he would be less troublesome, but again, children would always be children. Additionally, John had generally been through a lot and a huge deal of condemnation in the moment was going to lead to no good. She was certain about that.

Also, she had realized that there was really nothing she could do about what had happened. They could only give the children precautions for future happenings. For now, she could only hope for the best for the young boy and give him all the emotional support he needed to pull through. She was going to have a long talk with him once he felt better. She realized that even if she decided to have that long talk on the need to be a more composed boy in the moment, it will do the boy in pains no good. Timing was indeed everything in this situation.

Julia had to go with the ambulance to the hospital to be with John and also find out all the necessary procedures to ensure he was in good hands. She was his parent after taking him in legally under her orphanage, so she was the one in the position to know the situation of things with his health. The rest of the day continued with the kids carrying out all their morning routines. As about one hundred kids settled in the dining room to eat breakfast, Miss. Janet went through the trouble of reminding the kids of the precautions they needed to take in the orphanage to avoid falling or getting in any situation that would land them in the hospital. Julia had called the secretary an hour ago, to fill her in on everything going on in the hospital. John had fractured the two bones in his lower leg, his tibia and his fibula. For this reason, he was going to be operated on and also to go through follow-up treatments including physical therapy, to ensure he could walk again. He was going to be in the hospital for at least 8 weeks, from what they could estimate and maybe use crutches following his discharge. This was also going to cost the orphanage a lot of money, but they were left with no choice—he was under their care. The kids nodded in response as his Miss Janet reminded them on how to be safe at all times. They could not afford to roll unnecessarily in bed or fight in their dreams or even have imaginary fight in their sleep. When she announced to the kids that

John would be in the hospital for months, she could see the sad looks on their faces. There were also whispers. John had indeed been troublesome, but he was fun to be with. They kids would definitely miss him, but they hated the hospital and Janet was certain that the sound of staying in the hospital for months did not please the kids. She knew each kid would work to avoid being in such a situation. As the kids moved to their music classes before the school work for the day began, they gathered in groups and talked in low tones and whispers. They also had sad looks on their faces. Janet was also sad at the situation of things. She had seen the worried look on Miss. Julia's face and she had figured that financing an unforeseen circumstance like that could be a cause for worry. She was from Liberia herself and she knew what the importance of what Julia was doing for the community, their county, Bomi and even the country at large. No one else was doing what Julia was doing in the moment and she deeply appreciated everything Julia was doing. Those kids were yet to know what they had, she was sure they would look back and appreciate being picked up from their past horrible situations.

Every evening, Julia stood on the small orphanage field, watching the kids compete against each other. They always waited for the older kids to get back from school each evening, so the kids could continue their practice for the sporting competition. Things were getting even bigger. The kids were practicing and the spirit of competition had been borne in their midst. Hence, they were separated into groups where each of the kids could compete against each other, so general winners for the entire orphanage could come up.

One of those evenings, while watching them, she looked back on how she had started up the orphanage. There was so much to be happy about. Another year had gone by and she had about a hundred kids in total; with all the kids now looking better than when they first came into the orphanage. She had sold everything she had in the United Kingdom and gotten support from everyone she knew. She asked them to consider their gifts to her as her wedding gift and for her friends, the money they would have used to purchase bridesmaid dresses. While family and friends found it really hilarious, they sent her the money anyway.

The kids were truly her source of joy. Each time she looked at the kids, she was grateful that they had all grown better, they looked better and were in better places in terms of the way they saw themselves. John was still in the hospital. He had spent one month there and was still receiving care. She had still not received any financial aid, she still lacked the finances she currently needed to fulfil this project of hers, which was supposed to be a lifelong one. Celine had been kind enough to send some extra money in spite of all the expenses for her wedding that was going to come up in two months. She had a conversation with Celine the last time she sent money and told her to stop sending money since her wedding was just around the corner. However, Celine still did. She was not expecting the favor and was indeed surprised, but the money had been very timely. She could not return it because she actually needed it.

It gave her enough to cover for John's hospital bill and to run the orphanage for the month, but that was about it. From then onwards, she did not know how the kids would survive. She did not know how she was going to pay her workers. Yet, she had so much love in her heart for the kids. Silently, the idea of leaving everything behind and running away had crept into her heart. However, she laughed it off and came to a conclusion that the human mind was indeed capable of thinking all kinds of thoughts. She had to think of something. There was definitely something an orphanage could do to make some income and survive less on the gifts that came in from people and did not exactly have a pattern to it, at least not in a developing nation like Liberia which had just suffered war. The kids were playing innocently and practicing for their sporting competition, not having a worry about where their next meal would come from. That was what she wanted for them, she wanted things to remain that way. She knew her chances were slim with getting help from within the country, but again, she was not new to getting blessings in the most unlikely situations.

She remembered renting an apartment in a desolate area after her friends had returned to the United Kingdom. She had found an amazing girl at the point, Kira, who came as a sign to her that staying back in Liberia had not been a mistake. She remembered falling in love with girl at first sight and just having that kind of love that made her want to do everything to make the girl comfortable in her heart. She remembered how hungry Kira was and how unkempt she had looked. Still, she fell in love with the girl, especially after hearing out her story and how she had followed the group of volunteers. She could see that Kira was resilient and she knew that helping anyone with such spirit does good for the entire world. She was sure of this; she could see the willingness to succeed even in the face of difficulties in Kira's eyes.

Three years down the line, Kira was definitely different. She was acting as the referee on the playground, ensuring that the younger kids stayed safe. Julia had rented an apartment a mile away from the ground where the orphanage currently stood in Bomi county. It was such a poor community and she wondered how if she could make anything of such a place that felt like a dry land. The people were indeed poor and she had a dream she did not know how to materialize. She was starting from zero and there was nothing in sight to achieve her goal. It was a strange place and she was just acclimatizing herself. However, she now had Kira to help. Apart from the fact that this felt like a sign for her, she could not leave because the girl was really an orphan and had no one else in this world to depend on but Julia.

She had remembered having one old neighbor who preferred to stay alone and hardly said a word to anyone. It was such a strange thing. Everything kept being strange for a short while until the woman fell sick. It was the house next to where Julia was staying and so, she had noticed the stench from the house. She had not seen the woman in a few days too. For this reason, she summoned up courage and went into the house to see what was going on and found the woman sick. She was not only sick, but there was also no one to help her. Hence, every single day, she went into the place to care for the woman who could no longer stand. She would wipe her entire body with water and even had a nurse come to check her up, as the old woman was adamant about going to the hospital. The cycle continued for a while, and Julia kept doing her best.

"It is my time." The woman had said one day. "I have nothing to live for. It is about time I left" she had said. Her husband owned the house and had died in the war. The woman complained about losing her neighbors too; she said those that lived in the neighborhood had only taken over houses that did not belong to them. Most of her neighbors were now dead. She now preferred to die and even told Julia how she begged God to take away her life every day. She wanted to be reunited with her family. She felt like she did not appreciate the gifts God gave her in form of sons till she had lost them in the war. She had been too busy being bothered about going about business and making more money. She felt like she did not appreciate her husband enough too.

She had made Julia remember her own mother and write letters to her. Her mother had not been happy about her decision to stay back and had written to her to come home. Julia had written back and stated what she planned to start in Africa. Yet, her mother was not in support of this decision, especially because of the harsh times Julia had just faced health-wise. Julia's neighbor made her now remember to write and just tell her mum (in spite of their disagreement) how much she appreciated her and having her alive. Her mother had suffered a stroke and Julia could not imagine losing her. Her younger siblings were in the United Kingdom to take care of her mother, but she knew she had to appreciate her for sure. She had learnt from her sick neighbor to give people flowers while they were alive and not only when they died. The war had taught the woman the hard way.

The woman appreciated Julia's effort concerning her care. She had stopped caring about everything around her previously, as she was very bereaved about the loss of her young ones. She had not even noticed Julia or Kira all the while; she had been lost in her thoughts all the while. She was glad Julia showed up to help and loved her more by the day. She felt like she did not love the people in her life before and she was not about to make another mistake. The woman had built an entire complex without her husband or children knowing. It was a compound filled with various buildings which could be rented by individuals to do various businesses. Now that her family was gone and she had become terribly sick, it dawned on her that all those possessions of hers actually meant nothing. Hence, she wanted Julia to have the complex. She also wanted Julia to bury her where she currently lived and move to the new building once she was dead, while leaving the one where she currently lived empty.

She just wanted to do good in death even if she couldn't do so fully while she was alive. She begged Julia to put the building to good use. It was a new building. The keys and all the necessary documents were in a hole she had described in her room. The woman had quickly written and signed consent to Julia even before she had started the conversation about giving her the complex. Being a learned person, she knew she had to put it in writing and sign. That she did quickly before she started discussing with Julia, even in her weakness.

Julia did not want to have the property, because it was all strange. However, the woman gave her no time to argue as she gave up the ghost immediately after her description. Julia did exactly as she was told. For her, that woman's act was yet another sign that she was exactly where she was supposed to be. How does someone she only met in about a week dash her an entire complex? The only explanation for that was that she was exactly where she was supposed to be. The act of that woman strengthened Julia's will to stay even more. She knew she might crazy to her family members, but she was definitely on the right path.

As she moved into a building that had been willed to her in writing by its rightful owner, one month after she had decided to stay in Liberia, she came to a conclusion that everything that had happened to her had happened for a reason. She came to an understanding that life was in times and seasons and even the greatest misfortunes could birth the biggest blessings. She began to see the misfortune she encountered when the doctor had announced to her that she had a medical condition that would make her impossible to conceive had happened for a reason. It seemed crazy, but now, she was began to figure out the fact that it had indeed happened for a reason. Here she was, in another season of her life, rejoicing at blessings she never imagined would come her way, yet she had received in the past. She concluded that if such could happen then, once again, another remarkable thing could happen. She believed in miracles, she believed in purpose and she definitely believed in destiny. And she was living in hers; she was living in her destiny.

This was what she was trying to make David understand, but he was hell-bent on having his own way. She did not like that. She did not like the fact that he thought he could come to her and change all her plans at once without even hearing her view on things. He had never understood her outlook on life. He was not sensitive to the fact that her view on many things and her person changed once she knew she could not conceive anymore. She was searching for answers and she had found it in Liberia, Africa.

Yes, he was comfortable and he had all the good things life could provide. Yes, he was also cool with the idea of an adoption. She was not heartless herself, she knew he was a great guy. However, she also knew that she was facing the greatest test of her life and choosing to stay with him or letting him go might go a long way in determining if she fulfilled purpose. Purpose was satisfying. With him, there was a lot of uncertainty about being fulfilled, in spite of the comfort that lied ahead of her if she chose him.

The sun rose in the east that morning, and so did Julia. She grabbed her notepad. How had she never thought of this? She kept writing hard. She ran an orphanage! These kids were stable enough for adoption. Why keep the kids if there were people out there willing to give them all the care in the world they deserved? Additionally, the money realized from adoption would be used to provide holistic care for the kids in the orphanage and to take care of the new kids that came into the orphanage as a safe space. There would also be more spaces to replace the kids that leave when they do.

Then it dawned on her why she had never brought up the adoption conversation with anyone or included it in her emails. An apparent reason was the fact that Liberia had been at war for quite a while and adoption would not naturally come to the mind of any foreigner to Africa, even though it would help enough. However, for Julia, it was more of "a mother never gives away her children" thing. They called her mummy, enough though most of the kids knew that it was just a happy space for kids that did not have parents or adequate parental care. She never just imagined giving them out; naturally. All she could ever think of was how to love and care for the kids even better, but now that she thought of it, she knew she could swing into action.

She began to write to organizations outside Africa, especially in the United States and the United Kingdom, as well as the rest of Europe, specifically to address adoption. She told her story of how she had come to Liberia as a volunteer and ended up staying as a matter of passion and purpose. She also talked about how she had taken in many of the kids and remodeled them into better mental states. She also sent several pictures to these organizations, to show the kids in action. She also included the sporting competitions coming up and how she would love if they could be present or sponsor it. She could only but hope for favorable responses. As she clicked the send buttons for each email, she imagined the kids in various developed countries of the world and imagined them doing even better than they were currently doing. The thought of it gave her goosebumps.

She had a great feeling about the plans she had set into motion. Now, she was not merely soliciting for help, she was showing them the kind of value she offered.

To her surprise, the responses came in faster than she expected. Before evening, she had at least six favorable responses out of fifteen. Five other organizations were yet to respond. To her surprise, some of the organizations were willing to help sponsor the sporting events and a particular organization even promised to send a volunteer to watch the sporting competition. They were highly interested in sponsoring the kids who did best in sports throughout their educational pursuit. Before the end of the week, four out of the other five organizations said that they were interested in the adoption scheme and currently had families looking to adopt kids from war-torn countries. They were reputable agencies. This gave her joy. It was as though she had worked some magic she could not believe herself. She could not wait for the kids to start benefitting from the opportunities. Then, it dawned on her that including the things they had achieved as an orphanage in those mails definitely went a long way in convincing those organizations. After all, some of them had mentioned that they loved her work in their reply. She was encouraged that she was doing a great job and for Julia, it was also huge takeaway, to always remember to tell others what she had achieved with the orphanage and exactly how they could come in to help.

The next week, she went about her day happier, reminding the kids to always be confident about whatever they have achieved, taken a cue from her own life lessons.

She realized that she needed to begin to prepare the kids for living outside the orphanage. Hence, two days later, they did a quick, but painful mental exercise as an organization. It was an exercise that ended up bringing tears of joy to the eyes of the kids. She asked them to look back on themselves and the state of things with them in the last two years, she ask them to make two columns and write five words that described the state of their lives at the point. Then, she went on to tell the kids to write in another column, five words that explained the state of their lives at the moment. The kids did this and she told them to celebrate themselves. That morning, the dining room was filled with the noise of their claps, the kids celebrated themselves and everything they had achieved even as kids.

Seeing the tears in their eyes, Julia knew she had to break a little bit of the news to them, just like she had did to the staff that morning.

"You won't be here forever" she started. "Yes, you, you and you!" she said, turning to make contact with the eyes of as many kids as she could. "As much as I love you, none of you would be here forever."

Sandra rose her hands up to ask a question. "Yes, Sandra."

"Where would we go?" The young girl asked.

"Good question my girl." Julia paused. "Many of you would have families sooner that you can imagine. I do not know who would go first, but all I can tell you is that, it would be for the best. You would all go to happy places. You would be part of really nice families and not have to live within the four walls of this building forever. You would have mums and dads that will love you with all their hearts, just like I do. They would provide for you and also protect you. For now kids, make the best of these moments, love on each other, live happily before your neighbor is gone." She said. "I know you love this place, but I want you to see better places out there. That is how you succeed kids."

CHAPTER
EIGHT

That morning in New York, Amira walked into her office with her head up high. She strode in with her custom-made designer dress, her red bottom heels and a Birkin bag she had bought for herself to celebrate the massive progress she had made with her skin line. Just like she had envisaged, the skin line received massive attention especially with Kira on the forefront as the brand ambassador and also being a business partner. People associated the brand with Kira and that was fine by her. She had only appeared at the launch of the brand and been introduced as the CEO very briefly, just like she had instructed. She wanted Kira to be the focus for the night; not her. That was her strategy for selling. She doubted anyone would remember her name or who the founder was after that night; exactly what she had planned to achieve. She did not want the fame. After working her years through investment banking, saving and investing to the point that she had a huge investment portfolio, she just wanted yet another source of passive income from something she was passionate about. After making all that money, her plan was just to live a quiet and peaceful life away from the press. Coming forward and ensuring that she got seen and associated with her skin line would definitely have sabotaged that for her. Amira was indeed the proof that success meant different things to different people. As for Amira, choosing to become famous when it can be avoided, was no win. As she strode through the premises of the bank in which she worked, she looked forward to sitting on her chair once more like the investment banker she was, and dishing out investment advice to her clients and anyone else that cared for some. She enjoyed creating investment plans and managing the portfolio of her clients. She loved the feeling of seeing money multiply and that was all she really cared about.

There was one more thing no one knew Amira cared about. And there it was, lying on her table. Amira had been pleasantly surprised on seeing the sight on her table. She did not move close enough to smell the roses before she walked out the door of her big office again, to have a conversation with her secretary. She liked the sight, but it had been timely; it came after she launched her line. She was scared that her cover had been blown or perhaps, she was receiving a warning from a competitor; although the latter sounded a bit paranoid.

"Who sent those?" she asked.

Alice, her secretary stood up smiling. Her boss was such a nice person and she definitely loved to see this part of her life bloom, like every other part had. Amira had graduated from finance with a distinction at the age of 23, and because of her hard work, brains and the kind of value she always provided wherever she found herself, at 29, she had gotten to the stage of her career which many people reached at the age of 40. Yet, she never looked down on anyone, not even once. She had an excellent spirit, with humility to go with it; treating everyone as equally as she could. Everyone that worked with her had every reason to love the amazing young woman, and so did Alice, who had been working with her for about three years. She just wanted a simple and luxurious life. She was quite a peaceable person who was also agreeable.

To top it all, she was 5 foot, 6 inches tall with good dentition and a smile that was always sure to reveal her white teeth. She also had the caramel skin of a goddess and had a perfect figure from years of working out, as well as her natural physique. She was 29, but she looked five years younger and each time she spoke, her sweet voice got heads turning.

"There was a delivery man this morning. I tried to ask, but he said the sender was anonymous."

Amira became a bit concerned. She wondered if it was her recent association with Kira had brought her this. She knew celebrity got gifts and some of them also received death threats in flowers. This was another excuse she made in her head for not wanting to be famous.

"Come" she said to Alice. "If this is a time bomb, then I'll be referred to in history as the woman who got blown up with a time bomb that came in form of roses…" She paused "…together with her secretary" she continued.

Before she finished her statement, Alice was already laughing. She laughed even harder when Amira was done talking. That was another great quality Amira had; she was effortlessly funny.

"I am sure this is a good thing ma'am."

"Well, we'll be seeing this together."

They approached the table together and as Amira finally found the courage to lift up the flowers, she realized that there was a note in the middle of it. She could not deny the fact that the roses smelt so nice, but she just had to be sure they were safe, so she took her mind off its wonderful smell and focused on the important thing—their safety. She glanced quickly at Alice to ensure she was still there, then glanced back at the flower. She opened its wrapper and before she even took the flowers to her nose, the amazing smell of the roses filled the air even better than before. Amira became more confident after she quickly took out the note to see it read, "Congratulations on the launch of your new line. I see you." It seemed like a friendly note, and definitely a friendly gift. There was a tone to that short message that made her feel safe. It had to be someone she knew. The smell of the roses also pacified her.

"Alice, you can take your leave." She said, feeling a bit more comfortable.

Alice smiled as she left. She had seem the look in her boss' eyes and had figured out it was probably and admirer.

"Who the hell sent these amazing flowers to me?" she said, once Alice had shut the door behind her. She took in the smell of the roses again. They smelt heavenly, just like roses.

Amira thought the person who sent the roses would call later in the day, probably someone she knew. Instead, she received more flowers every single day, for the rest of the week. Each time, the flowers came with thoughtful notes like, "I was thinking of a way to make you smile", "I hope you are having a great day" and finally on Friday, it came with, "You grew up to become such a beautiful woman, in every way. Can we have dinner next week? I have a place I am sure you would love." There was a number written behind the note this time. She had wondered all week long, but hardly had time to do any findings. She just kept hoping that her anonymous admirer would eventually come out by himself.

By the time she got the flowers on Friday, her smile was so wide. This person, whoever it was, had literally swept her off her feet. It was as though she was the main character in a scene from some movie. Whoever it was had better matched the image of the perfect guy she had in her head; in terms of his looks. She had imagined having someone sweep her off her feet, but definitely not in a detailed manner like this. Apart from the first day the flower had come in, subsequently, the flowers had come in at more strategic times. It could be when she was having such a stressful day or just before lunch. The timing was also thoughtful and perfect. She could not wait to know who it was, but at the same time, she knew that getting too excited early on might just leave her disappointed in the end.

All her friends were other career driven women who were scattered across various cities and were constantly busy with work, so once in a while, they only used to set up vacations to great destinations and catch up on their lives. They never really had the luxury of calling up each other to talk as such during the week, as they were always sure to be occupied with work, just like Amira was. She had thought of calling Kira to ask if she had gotten anything similar, but Kira was a popular model, especially now loved by black people, so she was sure she got those regularly.

Apart from that, Amira got home tired every day from all the brain work she had to do and also came home with a new plan to work on or a presentation to prepare. She strongly believed in making full use of her brain while it still worked at its best, hence her work ethic and her drive to keep pushing for greatness. She really did not have the luxury of time to make a long ass call with Kira, except it was business-related. As for business, before launching the skin line, she had set up a process that could work with or without her presence. She only made sure to get weekly updates every week. However, she could make out time to call whoever had put in so much thought into sweeping her up her feet, even though she was having a crazy week as always. The person deserved that in return. She could make out time on Saturday, when she only got updates on her brands and other investments. She did not concern herself with her day job on Saturday. She figured she could fit in making a call to this anonymous person on the next day, which was Saturday.

Her Sundays were indeed sacred. That was her self-care day, when she put her phone on airplane mode and did the things that made her happy and revitalized her for the week. She had learnt to do this since her last breakup. She had been so attached to that relationship that she did not have the time to do anything else or even have fun activities she loved to do without her partner's presence. She was only invested in her work and her relationship without leaving any time for self-care. She had no time to go to the spa or take care of her skin. Her hair had been in shambles too. She dedicated time only to work and her relationship, with no time for herself. However, now she knew better. Hence, after their breakup, instead of focusing if finding another lover, she worked on creating a life that was now centered on living her dreams and caring for every area of her life. Hence, every Sunday, she put her phone airplane mode and then, went for morning mass. Following this, she would spend a huge chunk of the day in the spa and the rest of the day catching up on her favorite shows with her bottle of champagne and enjoying her own company to the fullest. Loving on herself that way was her greatest decision.

In the last one year, following her breakup, she had people come around and try to woo her, but loving herself had made her see through people and made her realized who truly loved her and who was not putting in enough effort. She would rather be alone than be with someone who did not love her as much as she deserved to be loved. She knew high standards birthed loneliness, but she was willing to wait. However, this one guy, had managed to make her smile all through the week by simple, but meaningful acts. It was not just about the roses, but it was the thoughtfulness in his words. He was definitely someone who saw her, for everything she was—her beauty, her brains, her hard work, and her achievements. She loved it, but again, decided not to get too excited, as life was quite unpredictable. She did not want to set herself up for a disappointment, she'd rather not think too much. However, the words of the man kept ringing in her head. Saying that she had grown to be a beautiful woman in every respect means he had known her as a kid, or maybe she was thinking too much. She tried not to process what she thought it meant, as much as she could. However, it was so hard to stop. Deep within, she felt like this was going to be a special match. She felt like he would be someone who spoke her language and so, they would have no issues. She thought about these things passively as she went about her activities each day. She was in the middle of not taking things too serious, yet not being able to get her mind off him because he could really be that answer to her prayers.

She was scared of sabotaging the whole thing by hearing his voice and then, judging him or jumping into conclusions about who he was. She knew herself to be someone that could do a mini-interview for a man over the phone and cancel him out immediately. She did not want that to be the case. She wanted at least, that one date, she wanted to see this person, who actually knew her before canceling him out. She was Amira and it had taken years of various processes to become the woman she was. Canceling men out was never a big deal; nothing personal. It was always a matter of the fact that things would never work from what she could see. Knowing who she was and how it took little things to turn her off, Amira decided that she would send him a text instead.

"Hey, it's Amira. I loved the flowers, but I'd rather we talk through text messages and see where things go from here."

In about thirty minutes, he responded. *"Hey, I was in a meeting when your text came in. It's good to hear from you, and yeah, I am cool with whatever you want Amira. Have you thought about that date?"*

She smiled. This one seemed like a man who knew exactly what he was doing. However, she tried not to think too much about everything. What if there was one big deal breaker she could not deal with? She thought of the most horrible things—what if this man could not walk? She tried to get her mind off it as she texted back.

"Yes, I thought of it. I would love to see this anonymous man."

Right after then, she picked up her phone. She needed to speak to Kira, even if it was for one minute. Anxiety was killing her and if Kira knew who it was, she had better told her. How did he get her contact? Kira would definitely know. With all the kind gestures he had shown her, she felt like it would be really rude to directly ask how he got her contact. She'd rather just let things move slowly. She was bound to eventually know, so the rush was unnecessary, except she could get the answers she wanted from Kira.

"Pick up the phone, Kira" she said under her breathe as the phone continued to ring.

Amira dolled herself up for the night. She had avoided having conversations with her admirer for the past one week. She had tried, as much as she could. However, this did not stop him from texting her regularly or sending lunch.

There was always an incoming message with "Hey beautiful" either in the morning or at night. And lunch was sure. This one was really doing a good job and Amira had tried as much as possible not to engage him in their phone messages. She would reply his messages with a simple "Thank you for lunch today." Or "My day was great and I am fine." However, she tried as much as possible not to get on with long conversations to avoid disliking the guy or writing him off before actually meeting or knowing him or on the other extreme, getting too attached to him that she could not let go anymore. She hope she had not come off as harsh, but at the same time, she loved his resilience.

She wore a new black custom-made sequin tube dress. It had a high slit just behind, starting a few inches below her bottom and running down to the end of the midi-dress. It was a dress that was sure to put all her curves on display and this made her feel really sexy. Of course, she looked sexy too. She poured her 28 inches bone straight black hair over her shoulder and did a nude make-up with a little of shimmer over her eyelids. She had given her best shot to men who did not treat her half as good as this man was doing, so why not just give in the same energy or even more to someone like him? She looked stunning, she knew it herself and she felt so good in her own body. She sprayed her favorite scent and it left her uplifted and smiling that Sunday evening as she walked up to the rooftop restaurant he had invited her to. He had offered to pick her, but her past had thought her to always meet up first with any anonymous person who was trying to take her on a date, before letting them pick her which was as good as granting them permission to know her house. She did not want anyone showing up at her house and crying for her to take him like she had experienced in the past. The place he picked was quite beautiful. She had heard of it, but had never really thought of trying it. As she walked in, she noticed the glassware, the chandeliers and oh, the ambience. This man definitely had taste and the place itself made her feel even sexier. There were very few people on the rooftop restaurant. It was for really private dinners and you had to make reservations early enough to get a spot. He had promised she would love it and oh yes, she did love it.

Her ugly past dating life came rearing its head up as she had once matched up with a guy from a dating app who took her to a really fancy restaurant, all for her to realize that he was some weirdo. Everything was perfect about this restaurant and she looked perfect too. The only thing now left was a great guy to complete the equation. She had been too busy taking in the beauty of the place, admiring the scenery and maybe thinking about the past that it took her by surprise when she heard "Hi" in a husky yet sexy voice. Yes, she had come to see him, but for some reason she could not place her hand on, she was neither expecting to have him snoop up on her in such a sexy way, nor was she expecting to hear that amazing masculine voice.

"Well…hello." She said, as she looked at the melanin man standing in front of her who was definitely not less than 6 feet and 3 inches. He was wearing a nice tuxedo with a good fit that did not hide the fact that one had to have nice pecs with great abs to get such a fit. He smelled heavenly, oh, Amira could have him for dinner. She needed someone to tell her she was dreaming. No! Good things did not come to people that easily. However, she did not realize that while good things like such a man did not come to people easily, she was now in an elevated position which she did not get to easily either. She had worked her way up there. So, good things now came to her because she had paid her price. She was still staring at him; yet to place the face. She was confused. The statement he had made about her growing up beautifully came to mind again. Where did this man know her from? At that point, the orphanage was the last place on her mind. How could Zeus come from the orphanage—no, never! If he was someone she had admired back then, she would have remembered him. However, she still had absolutely no idea who this man was.

"May I?" he said, offering to lead her to the table they had reserved, making her jolt back to reality. All she had thought off had ran through her mind in less than a minute, the human mind is indeed something. As he took her in, she kept admiring the place. As they sat, he stared at her without saying a word. His eyes were doing things to her. She felt like hiding away from his piercing glance. A million questions were running through her mind and she really wanted to break the ice. He didn't feel much like a stranger, not even after all the acts he had come through with in the last two weeks and now, the fact that he looked so dashing. She decided to treat it like one of those presentations she always had to make. She would look into his eyes and say what needs to be said, and also, ask what needed to be asked. He was good looking, but that was not all that mattered. So, she summoned up courage. She cleared her throat.

"How did you get this place in such a short while?" she asked quickly.

He smiled and then paused for a moment before responding. "I planned a dinner with my wife, but now she's out of town with the kids. So, I thought, why not sweep Amira's feet with the dinner instead?"

As much as she had heard what he said, she did not want it to be correct. What was he saying? The beautiful scenery turned into a dark cloud over her head for a moment and she was lost in it.

"Mission accomplished." He said, bursting out in laughter.

"Oh, that was one expensive joke." she said.

"I am so sorry. I wanted to start the evening with a bit of laughter. You look so dashing, I was getting cold feet, so I decided to throw in some humor. I was wondering if there was anything at all that could shake up a beautiful woman like you." He said.

She chuckled. She was a bit flattered. "So, let's clear the air. Are you married? Ever been married? Do you have kids?"

"Take it easy on a man with cold feet." He said, motioning to her with his hands, to calm down. He called to the waiter and they order appetizers.

"I have a plain record. I have none of those and…no baby-mamas."

She nodded and then, they had a good laugh. "Alright, I guess I am safe then."

The evening continued with lots and lots of laughter and she had hardly remembered that he was a stranger until he called her name and she wanted to call his and remembered that they had not even done a formal introduction.

"My name is John" He said, but it did not ring a bell at all.

"John from Yale?"

"No."

"John…" she muttered, trying to remember where she might have seen him. Perhaps, he was one of the numerous clients she had attended to in the past. She tried hard, but she could really come up with nothing.

Then, came the great reveal out of his mouth. "We grew up together, the orphanage."

She paused, looked at him, and then laughed hard. "Oh no, it couldn't be." she said, laughing. "Stubborn John that caused fights and rolled off the upper bunk only to get his right leg broken. Oh no!" She said, and she stood up to give him a tight hug.

"Damn…it's been ages. Now, I can make sense of the way you almost made my heart jump out of its place with the story of having wife and kids this night. Mischievous as always." She said.

"Not anymore." He laughed. "I am now off to only good. I do not cause mischiefs no more." He laughed.

The evening continued with good food and the stories behind their lives. John was now a footballer and he played for one of the clubs in the United Kingdom. However, his family lived in New York and he had been in touch with Kira after hearing of her own big break. Her fame had helped him reconnect with her and she had invited him for the launch of her skin care line. She also told me that someone I knew was the brain behind it and it only made that someone even more interesting to me. Then I decided to know yet some more about that person.

"Oh, Kira. I should break her neck. She said she knew nothing about no man." Said Amira.

"She did that?" he asked sarcastically.

"That's brilliant; your skincare line." He said.

"You bet!" she said.

"Now, don't blow your trumpet." He chuckled.

"I thought you were in support of that." She laughed. "Trust me, a lot of work went into that."

He had been doing well in his career and was making a killing too. He was such a handsome young man and remained a gentleman all night. Amira liked him already. She liked how he wrapped her up in their hugs too, thanks to his huge stature. They talked about life and recounted their experiences so far. There was so much to talk about; their transitions into various families and how those families had helped in shaping who they ended up becoming. She liked the way he talked and who he had become. He could not stop staring at her. Amira was having the famous butterflies in her belly and she tried to avoid his glance as it made it even worse for her. However, there was not much she could do to avoid his unrelenting look.

When they called it a night and she hugged him, they knew that night was not the end. For John, he was ready for more date nights and he did not fail to tell her that. That night, once she got home, she got on the phone with Kira and called her out on not telling her.

"I did not want to ruin the mystery to your love story." Kira said.

The ladies then spent the rest of their night recounting their times at the orphanage and how troublesome John had been. Amira was so excited to talk about it all that she pushed any thought of work aside for the moment.

"Oh my, he is so handsome now. I wonder how that transformation happened." Said Amira.

"Maybe he had always been handsome, we had just been kids and his troublesome nature did not let us notice how good he looked." Kira thought.

"Maybe."

While Amira imagined that the romantic gestures will be over, John proved her wrong as the random gift boxes did not stop in the coming weeks. There were many spontaneous outings to various shows too and Amira was always up for it. She enjoyed his company and she could not help but say yes each time he offered to pick her up. Amira knew her life was changing and someone else was becoming a part of her life. On some nights, the intensity was too scary for her, but again, she was at peace with everything she was doing. First off, he had been a gentleman and additionally, he was indeed an addition to her life, constantly looking out for her and helping to ensure she was working on things that would help her launch even higher in her career. Love was knocking, and Amira felt like she was about to open.

He had worked his way to the top in his football career too, so they understood each other's struggles. Amira felt loved and appreciated by John. By being in his company, it had dawned on her that what she had been looking for actually existed. She was also sure that she was ready to ride with this man. Now, she had a lot to tell her friends on their next trip. She knew she wouldn't as available as she used to be to them anymore. It was all happening too fast, but it felt right. To top it all, it felt like she was getting romantically involved with someone from her tribe, someone from her roots, someone who understood her struggles and where she was coming from. She had nothing to fear because he was someone that could identify with the life-changing part of her life. He had experienced that too. Hence, gelling with the young man came to her quite easily. John, the troublesome boy, was gradually becoming John, the love of her life and she could not even hold back.

He loved romantic dates and getaways and so did she. They always worked hard at their jobs and would be back together to enjoy some romantic time. He had to practice a lot and she had to work a lot, so they understood each other perfectly. Amira had never really envisaged being in a power couple situation, but it was happening for her, with the best man she ever met, in the most unlikely situation.

CHAPTER
NINE

Every morning, Julia woke up to look at her emails. Seeing the messages of various organizations following up on their promises made her so happy. It made her fulfilled. She was seen that she was indeed making impact. She loved that! At least, those from the side of the world which she came had confirmed this by offering their support.

Julia was indeed living a selfless life, but the price for that life was a huge one. The kids had absolutely no idea. The part of their "mum", Julia, that the kids did not see was the part of her that struggled to get out of bed and motivate the kids on some days. At other times, they did not see the part of her that just did not want to go the hospital, not because she did not love the kid on admission, but because she just wanted some free time when she could rest without thinking of anyone but herself. She did not have a choice, it was the life she had chosen. She had no choice but to keep motivating herself on days when she felt that way. Sometimes, she would peep from her office to see the kids on the playground just to get some motivation from what she had achieved and also to remind herself on why she could not stop pushing.

The kids were pretty much hyperactive. Julia had quickly realized were no breaks from being parents, especially now that she was "mother" to about hundred kids. As much as the staff were always present to do their work and she had employed a few more hands, with kids, you cannot just go to sleep for the whole day. At some point, you would remember that there are kids in your care and you, the adult, is responsible for their lives. It was a huge responsibility to already be responsible for her own life and fulfilling her purpose. And now, for about a hundred kids? While it felt great and fulfilling on some days, on other days, Julia just wanted to be able to live without worries. It took a lot of emotional strength to emotionally cater to each kid and their own peculiar worry. There were kids that had experienced all kinds of situations; rape victims, abandoned kids, stray kids and orphans (whose parents were killed in the war or maybe shot right before their own eyes). John fell in this last category. His story was sad and really peculiar. His parents had been shot before his eyes.

On that fateful afternoon, when the war had been declared over, he had returned from the market with his mother. She had taken the groceries to the kitchen while John stayed in the living room. There was a knock on the door and the young boy innocently went to open the door, only to see a man who begged him for water. He called out to his mum, but she was busy as they just got back from the market and she had one or two things to sort out. The man looked really tired. He pleaded that John went to the table to pour him a glass of water. This, the little boy did and as he turned around to offer the man water, he was met with a sound of gunshot which the man sent into the air. This made the young man startled and he immediately ran for his mother.

"Mummy" He called out, as he ran into the kitchen to find her. He hid behind her skirts shivering, while she wondered what had happened to her son. However, the men did not have time as one of their luxuries. Hence, this applied to John's mother too. She did not have the luxury of time to realize what was going on around her.

Two men came in, armed with guns, and John's mother screamed, asking them to take anything they wanted. However, it seemed like there was so much violence in the hearts of the men. The war had damaged a lot of people, and while taking it out on other people was not right, it was not so surprising. The men tried to bruise the little boy, but his mother stood in between them. This made them direct a blow at her. When John saw this, the young boy fled to the window to call for help. This made them shoot him on his right leg.

"My child!" His mother screamed as she ran to help him and then, the men wasted no time, but went straight for her head. The violence in their hearts had possessed them too. As they realized what had happened, they made for the door before anyone else would realize what they had done. John, whose leg was bleeding could not hardly walk after he landed down from the window of their bungalow. The young boy kept shouting for help. It was the only thing he could do. Unknowingly to him, on their way out, the robbers had encountered his father who also tried to raise an alarm once he suspected that something had happened. The robbers did not think twice about murdering him and leaving him in cold blood. They had taken all the money in the house, but for the violence in their hearts, taking only money was not enough.

John father's dead body attracted people immediately and the neighbors rushed to find John when they heard him crying faintly for help. Luckily, they could save the little boy. However, John had lost a lot of blood and had to receive blood transfusion to be well again. His health was fully restored after a few weeks and a rich neighbor was kind enough to foot the hospital bills. However, when the experience was over, John had no parents.

Over the years, even after therapy, John's distraction had been being in every other child's business, of course, except his own. He couldn't help it. At least, being in their businesses made him laugh.

As Julia looked at the emails that morning, she stood up from her bed with all the positivity left within her. What if John was the child that was going to get the opportunity to travel out? She could not afford to send any staff to randomly check up on him, not after knowing the boy's history. The boy needed to know he was not alone, so she wanted to be there herself, so he could call her mum, just like he had always done. John still had a little pain left in him over the years and it was understandable because watching another person kill your mother in cold blood is not exactly an image one could easily get out of their heads in a little time, even in years. It was not an incidence that would ever leave the memory of a child. It was bound to always be buried somewhere deep down. John had tried to deflect his pain by being that troublesome kid, but it didn't mean the pain was not there.

On getting to the hospital, John almost leaped from his bed as he shouted, "mum". They had to screw his bones into place through a surgery and he had been put in a cast. He was not to attempt walking just yet. He had not seen Julia the day before and he expressed so much joy when he saw her. Julia had been right to come. He really needed to see her.

"Rest son" she said, as she approached his bed and gave him a warm hug.

John was in a hurry to tell Julia all that happened since she was away. However, there was more he had to say. The young boy expressed his displeasure about not being able to practice for the sporting competition that was drawing really close. Especially with the state of his legs, John knew there was almost no way he was going to participate in the sporting competition. It was the same leg that had been affected in the incident that happened with his parents. Julia knew she had to stand by him even though he was not showing signs that he needed all that attention. The smile on his face on seeing her made her realize that he was extremely glad she came. In spite of the fact that it had affected the same leg that was shot years back, the little boy was still optimistic that his leg would be fine again. That was a good quality John had; he was annoyingly optimistic.

Julia did not want to put pressure on the kids concerning their performance in the sporting competition. However, she kept encouraging the kids to keep giving their best into practice every single day as their performance would determine if they got a chance to win a very special gift. She knew that they were kids and bringing in the complex explanation of people coming from other countries to take them to new families in those countries can be scary for some and trigger in anxiety in some other kids. Hence, she decided not to tell the kids what their gifts will specifically be.

The kids kept practicing every evening. Sandra and Joseph were still great friends, ensuring that they maintained the balance between practicing for the sporting competition and studying for their tests, especially arithmetic tests where Joseph once lacked, but had now began to do so well that he and Sandra had started competing for the best grades. The several adages about friends acting alike was becoming true for them. They were both acing their school work, especially arithmetic. The first time they had a tie, Sandra had maintained a distance from Joseph and even confided in Kira, who was like an approachable big sister to most of the kids. She was happy for her friend, yet she could not deny the fact that she was a bit threatened.

Kira had assured Sandra that what she felt was very normal, but she had to move on from feeling that way. In Kira's words, "That is life. And it is okay for him to succeed. His success should not affect yours and yours should not affect his. Rather, as friends, your successes should motivate each the other, to do even better than before."

Sandra took a cue from this and studied even harder for herself. She loved to top the class in arithmetic. She decided to continue studying with Joe, but now, as an equal. She was now more open to hearing his own ideas and seeing how it could help her get better too. She had long been separated from Rhonda, because Rhonda had begun to make other friends that shared her interests too. Hence, once Sandra had found a friend in Joseph, off she went too. Most of her girlfriends; Amira, Kira, Sam, and Martha, were more interested in arts and crafts. They were not interested in sports and did not show up for practice, which usually ate up her time, as well as Joseph's time.

Eddy and Baron also liked sports, but not many of the girls. Rhonda enjoyed just a bit of sports too. One of the teachers had encouraged her to try throwing the discus. Hence, Rhonda threw the discus for kids, but she did not need as much practice as the runners. She grew to love only that part of sports because she became so good at it.

Additionally, when she practiced, she also did so in a different area and did not have time to mix with the runners. The same applied to Angie who participated in both high jump and long jump activities. All these circumstances had further made the gap between her and these other friends of hers wider. However, now, she had missed her friends and hoped that once the sport competition was over, they could reunite. John was supposed to participate in the long jump, but now he had been replaced by another boy, Kelvin. The sports week was also in two weeks. So, she figured that once it was all over, she could be back with her friends. As much as John was such a pain in the ass, all the kids still missed him a lot. There was never a dull moment with the kid who was now popular for many things. They could not wait to have him back.

Two weeks to the sporting competition and the kids were not slowing down with practice. The different groups chose special times, asides the time for general practice to practice on their big play grounds that now had tracks. Now, Sandra practiced with Baron who was on her team. Eddy and Joseph were on the same team, so they woke up earlier than others to practice every morning. The staff in charge of Joseph's team had told them both that if they could be ready to run just after waking up in the morning, then, they would be alert enough to run at every other time of the day.

The day of the competition came and the kids were ready to represent their teams in their various categories. The best from each category would receive prizes and the team that provided the best athletes would also win. The kids dressed beautifully and were excited. There was a match past and the kids watched the various teams presented the match steps they had practiced. As the kids did this, they roared in excitement. While the match past was still on, they received visitors that had the same skin as Miss. Julia. They looked so fresh and used sunshades. Only the staff of the orphanage knew that there were four guests that had been in town for about two days and were coming to grace their sporting event. They had sponsored a huge portion of the event and even donated for the running of the orphanage. From the outfit of the kids, to the decorations, the ribbons the girls used on their heads, to the balloons that were available in abundance, they had all been provided by these organizations. Two of the guest were from an organization in the United States, while the other two were from another organization in the United Kingdom. They looked happy to see the kids. Miss Julia and the other staff also went to usher them to front seats.

The kids were excited to see them and whispered among themselves, as they wondered if the guests were related to Miss. Julia, just like Miss. Celine that had visited them the previous year. Yet, this did not affect their performance. They had been giving their best to their practice and this was the day when they showed their skills. They did not falter on that in any way.

At the end of the competition, for the short distance race, Sandra emerged as the best, based on the timing at which she completed her race. For the 400metres race, Joseph emerged the winner; Kelvin, for the long distance race; Angie, for high and Kelvin for the long jump; Rhonda, was the best at discus. The kids were so happy to see that they had emerged winners. Sandra was happy to see her friends, Rhonda and Joseph as winners. They jubilated and their teams celebrated them too. In the end, the blue team, Joseph's team won the cup, as Joseph and Kelvin were two winners who had come from the team. They had also done really well at their match past performance.

However, the organization only had the opportunity to take two kids each. Hence, they were going to organize a test for the kids—an arithmetic test. The kids were told they were going to take a test and they were to give their best into the test. They still weren't told the purpose of the test. They gave their best anyway. Four of the kids did not know that their lives were indeed about to change.

All the practice over the many months had paid off. As little as Joseph was, he realized that it was the situation that brought a form of shame to him that had made him strive to be more at arithmetic. He wondered what would have happened if he was perhaps an average student in arithmetic and the teachers had absolutely no cause to worry about his grades or ask him to stay back to practice some more sums. That meant that his journey towards becoming a better student of arithmetic was one he would have never embarked on.

Now, he was one of the final four kids that were picked as winners. It was surreal to him that even people who were not his teachers had confirmed (through their results in the arithmetic test) that he was good in the subject. He did not even know what they had won. However, a win was enough reason to celebrate. The fact that he did so well made him proud of all his efforts so far.

"Yes!" he exclaimed, as he jumped for joy that morning at breakfast, when the foreigners that had come to witness their sports competition called out his name. He still had a lot of tension before his name had been called. It was expected that he would have all that tension, especially due to the fact that he had experienced so much failure and disgrace in the past. The kids in class would laugh at him, before the teachers would correct them on how it was wrong to laugh at someone's failure.

He was reminded of all those times he was at the bottom of class in arithmetic tests. Then, the quiet Joseph would wonder to himself why they had to learn how to solve hard arithmetic problems. The teacher had told them that it helped in reasoning and they had to take it seriously, even if they felt like they might not need it in their future interests. The teacher said it helped in reasoning in every area of life and calculations too. All the while, he could not wrap his head around how that was true, but since the teacher had said so, he had no choice but to do better. This was in addition to the fact that he was forced to stay in and work sums while others were on the playground.

Sandra, Kelvin and Rhonda had also made the list. Angie did not make the list, but she was encouraged by their visitors and Miss Julia. The visitors had promised that every year, there would always be such opportunities and probably even more. They were told to report to Miss. Julia's office in the administration building immediately. As they were about to leave, Joseph rubbed shoulders with Sandra, giving that knowing, happy look. He was glad that he allowed her into his space and let her help him. She was indeed a good friend and he was also glad that they both made the final four. Sandra was happy too. She loved winning. She was a competitive child, she literally lived for making wins.

As the kids entered Miss Julia's office, they were offered seats. They sat quietly with smiles on their faces, looking at their mother and the foreigners. They congratulated the kids once more, shaking their hands. The kids felt so proud. However, they were not still sure about what their gifts would be. They looked around, but they did not see presents wrapped in any fancy nylon, like what they had last Christmas. It was one beautiful time of the year the kids could not forget because each kid in the orphanage got something on their wish list. Julia had to pay through her nose for the kids (about 90 of them, at the time) to have the whole Christmas tree and Christmas gift experience. She had that all the time as a kid and could not imagine kids not even getting a chance at that.

"Kids, your reward for doing so well in this competition might be something that would change your lives forever." Julia started, as she stared into each kid's eyes. The kids still wondering how huge the items they would receive would be kept smiling and focused their attention on their mother.

"Perhaps our gifts are so big that they had to put them outside." Rhonda had whispered to Sandra. The thought of it created a picture in Sandra's head that made her giggle. However, she tried her best to be quiet so as not to distract the others.

"Remember what I always told you about some of you going on to become a part of new families?"

"Yes mum." The kids chorused.

"What if I told you that is going to be the reward for doing so well in this sporting competition?" She asked. "What if I told you that having a new family is your reward for doing so well in the sporting competition?"

The kids looked worried, and maybe a bit puzzled. As for Sandra, many things were running through her mind. Did that mean she will be leaving the orphanage forever? Did that mean she would never see her mother anymore? Rhonda worried more about not seeing the friends she had made in the orphanage anymore, she was scared. Joseph did not want to go; the orphanage was his safe place. As for Kelvin, he was indifferent. As far as they could confirm that he would never go hungry, he was fine with whatever life threw at him. He had starved so much at some point in his life and he was just not ready to go through that ever again.

"I don't think I want to leave here." Sandra finally said, with tears welling up in her eyes.

"It's alright baby." Miss Julia said, as she moved to Sandra, helped her up and comforted her.

"Kids, we know the thought of leaving here might sound scary to you. We know this is your home" said Miss. Phillips in such a calm voice. Her English accent was so pleasing to the ears of the children. She tried as much as possible to talk slowly, so they could hear her voice. "We come from organizations that also have orphanages, safe spaces like this. And we have parents that want you children from this place in particular. They want to help cater to kids from war-torn countries. They want to ensure that whatever had happened in your country or to your parents does not stop you from achieving your dreams. They are good humans who want to make you a part of their family and send you to the best schools in the world. They want to buy you nice things and do everything it takes to see you succeed in life."

She paused before she said, "If you move into nice houses with parents that are in a country like the United Kingdom or the United States, you would become a part of great families and even go to great schools, then one day, you could become like your mum here, Miss Julia, and help other kids find safe space. However, you need to be fully prepared in the right way if you would grow up to help other people." No one held on to these particular words as much as Rhonda did. She imagined not having a safe place like the orphanage when her mother died. She wondered where she would be if she had not been brought to the orphanage. She really hoped that one day, she could help children like herself, who had no one in the world to cater for them.

"I would go. I would become part of a new family." She said. "I would like to grow up and help kids with no one to take care of them."

Julia was almost moved to tears. She asked Rhonda to come for a hug. Miss Phillips turned to the other kids.

"Kids, like Miss Julia has prepared your minds, one day, each of you will have to leave this place and become a part of a family. It could be now and it could be later. You just happen to be the first set of kids that would be leaving because you performed especially well in sports and in solving hard arithmetic tasks. And trust me, you would never regret this. However, we cannot force you to come with us. It is up to you. If you do not want to leave the orphanage, it is okay too."

"I would go." Joseph said, staring into space, as if he was imagining a future. And yes, he was imagining a very bright future. He determined in that moment to make good use of the opportunity to become a great person that could help others, just like Miss Phillips had said.

"I would go." Kelvin quickly said.

"I would go" Sandra added, still sobbing.

Miss. Julia asked the kids to come for a hug. She would miss them all for sure. They would leave in two days, two to the United States and the other two to the United Kingdom. A boy and a girl for each country. There was a ballot for the two girls, as well as for the two boys. In the end, while Kelvin and Rhonda chose the United States, Sandra and Joseph were reunited again, as they chose the United Kingdom. They would later leave for the states in the nearest future. However, they did not know this at the time. They were only kids.

Now, the most important for the kids was to prepare to travel. It was surreal, but the process already kick-started. They had to get all the necessary documents. Thanks to the fact that the organizations were notable ones, the processes took very little time. The kids had to prepare to leave in every way and more especially, prepare their minds. Their lives were going to be different from then and henceforth, but it hadn't even dawned on them just yet. At least, not in the way it would have dawned on an adult. Julia stared at them from time to time like a mother hen that was about to have her chicks taken from her. However, she tried not to let them catch her staring. She did not want them to know what she was feeling. It was enough that they were leaving for "strange places". Seeing the way she was looking would only make things worse.

Yes, her kids were about to be taken away from her. That's how she felt. However, the knowledge that it was for the best was what strengthened her and just made her feel better on the overall. Instead of thinking of how she would miss them, she chose to imagine how great they would be in the nearest future. The thought of that made her come alive.

John sobbed on his bed, as his friends turned their back to leave. They were leaving the next day and he knew he would miss them a lot, especially since he did not get to spend their last days in the orphanage with them. He still had at least two more weeks to spend in the hospital. He would not even get the chance to watch them go and he did not have the strength to poke Joseph the way he would have liked just once more.

As his friends turned back, he quickly cleaned his tears.

"Were you just crying?" Joseph asked

"Of course not." John frowned.

Joseph laughed. "Of course, you were crying."

John kept a straight face. He would miss being a pain in the ass to these kids in particular, especially Joseph. He actually liked to disturb Joseph because he liked his quiet nature and he had always wanted him to be his friend.

"I would definitely find my way back to you, Joseph." He said.

The sound of what John had said made Joseph laugh so hard.

"That sounds so creepy. How do you plan to do that?" Joseph chuckled. "I am finally free from your trouble forever." Their conversation was making the other kids laugh. Julia watched from a distance. She remembered how these kids had come in differently, their fights and everything in between. She laughed at the relationships they had developed. She loved it. They were her babies and she would have loved to see them grow up to be young men and women before her eyes. However, a mother always did what was best for her children, so they definitely had to go.

Sandra in particular, had to go say her goodbyes to her mother. Sandra's mother also had to sign some documents. Miss. Julia had spoken to her about the chances of the kind of future her daughter would have. She was in a better place mentally, so she agreed to sign without any troubles. She hugged her daughter, cried and kissed her goodbye. It proved that in the end, as always, every sane mother just wanted the best for her child. Sheila just happened to be sick before. She was now sorry for all the trouble she had caused by her daughter. Her daughter's courage and escape encouraged her too.

John always had the promise he made to Joseph at the back of his mind. He was going to join his friend real soon. He had heard Miss Julia tell the kids while in the hospital that more kids would be able to come to join them in the coming year. The organizations would come to pick highly competitive kids in the next year's competition too. As Joseph left, he was determined as always to develop a competitive spirit in everything and also work better on the sporting activities he loved.

"Always believe in yourself." Miss Julia used to say. He had watched Joseph practice arithmetic hard, and risen to the top in it. He had listened to the whole selection story from his friends and he now knew that the knowledge of arithmetic had helped his friend. He decided that he would take his studies, as well as sports very seriously. He planned to excel and rise to the top at everything he did. The fact that some of his friends had left pushed him to want to do better.

By the time he was fully rehabilitated and leaving the hospital, he was leaving as a new Joseph; one who was charged and ready to do well in everything he had to do. Once he was back at the orphanage, John was no longer that boy who disturbed everyone. He became the focused child who was interested in getting good grades. Sport had been inculcated into school time and the children now had a competitive spirit, especially in sports. Each time the kids had a cause to visit anywhere outside the orphanage or even those like Kira, that were older and now in high schools outside the orphanage, they just stood out. They were different from the regular kids in Liberia and it showed in every single thing they did. They had such a competitive spirit.

Each time they were in the orphanage, lost in their activities, it was almost like they were in a different part of the world. All that happened to them in their past lives felt like it had happened ages ago, because the kids now had so many blissful memories to substitute for the bitter ones.

In months to come, the orphanage began to incorporate football officially into their games. The boys were growing bigger and as they grew, they seemed to have an increased love for football. The games were now officially organized, with different teams, and the boys were sure to always compete to sunset. However, a great academic performance was the prerequisite for joining the football teams. Hence, the boys had no choice but to focus on their studies simultaneously. More activities were introduced every single day and gradually, every child was finding what they had a flair for. While some discovered they loved fashion, others discovered their loves for creating new things. While some kids loved sports and games, others were fine with just focusing on their academics. Whatever the kids were interested in doing, in the orphanage, there was enough room for development.

As for John, he fell in love with football. He also became the captain of his team. He also loved long jumps, but he absolutely loved football. He practiced day and night. He did not know if it would be incorporated into the sports competition, but he loved the game, so he continued playing it for the love of it.

As time went on, many organizations kept reaching out for the adoption of children, especially the babies. Every day, kids left the orphanage for new homes and new kids came into the orphanage too.

When it was time for the next year's competition, to John's surprise, football was listed as one of the games to be played. The representatives from the organizations were going to come yet again. This time it was no secret. John was motivated to practice even more. He did well already, but he had a goal that had carried him all year round and he was not about to joke with it. In the end, it was no surprise when John was on his way to the United Kingdom for being exceptional at playing football. Angie made it to the United Kingdom that year too.

CHAPTER
TEN

I guess it's about time I introduced myself and why I came about the need to narrate these various stories that have summed up to make this book. I'm Olivia, and I became Amira's sister the day mum and dad pronounced her so.

I have always enjoyed the good life. My mother is a descendant of a royal family and my dad comes from old money. As I grew up, all I ever knew was luxury. It was not for the fact that my parents were trying hard to make things so. It was more about the fact that luxury was their normal life; luxury was their standard of living. I did not even know we were living in a luxurious way until I grew older and had some experiences that made me realize that many people did not grow up the way I did or even with a quarter of the things I had growing up and had considered to be normal. However, I can now proudly say that my background and its comparison to the background of others is what has made me the person I am today. And I am proud of the woman I am.

Back to my parents. Well, they always went on several trips; business and fun trips. When I had holidays from my schooling activities (or what my parents referred to as my "formal education", they allowed me come with them. I was only lucky at those times because at other times, they went without me. They always left without remorse. They were bent on enjoying their love and marriage; hence, provided a perfect example of what love should look like to my sister and I. However, they put me in the care of the very best. When Amira became my sister, they were also always sure to leave the both of us in the hands of the very best.

Before high school, I was home-schooled by the finest of teachers, I also had a governess, several maids worked around the house, there was a chef specifically for me and a pantry stocked with my favorite things. My home schooling calendar still ran like the normal school calendar, so do not be surprised about the fact that "the holiday factor" still influenced my travelling. My parents just wanted to have a bit of influence on my most basic education; checking in on what I was learning and also ensuring that I was learning to first be the best version of myself before allowing me mix with others in a school where the concept of competition was usually introduced.

I wonder what else could be termed a better childhood than the one my parents provided for me. I lived a very happy life as a kid; with all the toys, clothes and shoes that were enough for five kids. I woke up to all form of luxurious scents, the helps changed the scent candles in my room from time to time. Ours was a very big house and my parents hid presents all over the place after their trips. It was these presents that made my curious self, wander around the house. I think it was their way of getting me to know everywhere in my big house. Now, I guess you can imagine how big our house is. A house that big was my mum's definition of a dream house and my dad ensured we lived in such a house. Cute, aren't they?

I had always wanted a sibling so bad, but it had always been mum and dad's lifelong plan to birth only one child. Once they had me, they were fine. However, I got lonely and in fact, wanted a sibling as soon as I could get one. My parents listened to me when I talked about it, but I did not see any quick improvement.

And with time, I came to realize that getting a sibling was not like going to the market to purchase a new toy. My parents began to think of adopting a child and they contacted one of the best agencies in the country. The agency my parents were using let us know that it would take quite a while to get a child that fit into what my parents were looking for. As for my parents, they just wanted to make sure that by adopting a child, they were really making a difference in the world. They wanted to adopt me a younger sister, a child whose life they would be changing thoroughly, by adopting her. They also believed it would be perfect as I would have a sister to play with. Truly, they could adopt more than one child if they wanted, but they always wanted to ensure their kids felt special enough. Left to them, having a crowd of kids might have not made this possible. So, going from their decision of one child to two was quite hard for them. Having two kids was quite a huge compromise for them, but they would do anything for me.

I looked forward to having my sibling come to the house soon, but my efforts contributed nothing to the process. All I could really do was get anxious and picture scenarios in which I would be talking or playing with my sister. Documentation had to be detailed, especially due to the fact that the kid my parent fell in love with was in Africa. The plan was to have her come to London and that was another process that promised to be time-consuming.

I had been looking at the picture the agency had given us with so much anxiety. I could not wait for my new sister to come. This explained my behavior the day Amira came to the house. I could not stop touching her, and she seemed confused at my behavior. I was twelve and she was only seven years old, and quite smaller than me in stature. I felt like lifting her up; she didn't understand my excitement. Mum had beckoned on me not to lift her, so she would not feel uncomfortable in any way. This made me draw back, but I wanted to show her around the house so bad. So, we could bond properly, another nice princess-like bed had been made for her in my room. Mum had even created an extra dressing corner. However, Amira still looked at all of us—confused. She looked like she was going to cry and as if she had been thrown into a really strange place and needed rescuing. Honestly, I kept feeling like before the end of the week, Amira would run out of the house. Probably, we would wake up one morning and the girl will be gone. The thought of it made me worried. Silently, I watched her every move. She was just too cute.

However, little me also remembered that the house had security. It would be really hard for Amira to run out. The house was a bit confusing too, as it was quite big, so running would definitely turn out hard for her. This gave me a little satisfaction, because to be honest, Amira was safe with us. There was absolutely no need for her to run. Mum and dad had been preparing to receive her for quite a while and the agency had even come around to see if the house would be welcoming enough for, about one month before her arrival. They also checked and saw all the help we had around the house. There was going to be no hard work for my new little sister to do; all she would know is comfort, just like me. I needed company, and she slept that night, I watched her. She seemed really tired and she had eaten all her pasta. I guessed that at least, those were good signs. I, for one, already knew at my age that food was a component of comfort. That dish was nicely prepared and there was no way she wouldn't feel at home after having it. However, she was still all curled up in her bed, like she was hiding herself from some harm. Finding her sleep in that position was too funny. I can remember laughing that night.

I was quite happy to have a sister and I could only wish she felt the same way about me too. She was warming up to us, smiling every now and then, but still looking at us like strangers. When my governess (who was now "our governess") read a night story to us the next day, I could see how happy she looked. She laughed at the parts of the story that were funny too. I imagined we were making progress, but it was definitely not moving as fast as I wanted it to.

Mum had explained things to me and it was quite understandable. To Amira, it was like she had left her family for people she had never set her eyes on, up until the day before. Mum had asked me to imagine leaving her and dad, and going to stay with another family for life. She said I should imagine that being the case and also imagine how I would feel. I imagined how I would act with my new family and that for me explained the way Amira was definitely feeling. The next day was a Saturday and mum wanted the three of us to go shop for new clothes, especially for Amira. I had so many clothes I had never worn, so I hardly needed clothes. However, none of those clothes would make a perfect fit for Amira. Apart from that, mum wanted her to feel really loved. Well, we already loved her. She didn't just seem to know.

When we got to the clothes store, mum asked Amira to go to the color sections of the clothes she liked and start picking clothes. She looked confused, so mum and I went with her to the colors we thought might look really good on her and were girly too. All the while, Amira had hardly spoken. She only said "Good morning" that morning and "Good evening", the previous day. The remaining of her answers and our discussions with her consisted of "Yes" and "Nos" from her end.

As she took the clothes in and wore them to check their fit, she looked really happy. She smiled each time she came out of the dressing room and looked at the mirror. Mum and I gave each other knowing looks, we were making progress with her.

The next stop was for her hair. Mum did not know much about making black hair look great and the salons around for people of color raised their brows at seeing a black child with a white woman. I did not understand this then, but now I understand why mum did not take her straight up to the salon. She preferred to have my sister do her hair at home. She had asked one of the helps who was black about the products to buy and was ready to pay her extra to make sure my sister's hair looked great at all times. So, off we went, hair shopping. We bought hair products, and then, we bought ribbons too. I could not wait to see my little sister get dolled up. I am sure she did not still understand my excitement because she was still not talking much. I just wanted her to get used to me and let me into her life. She was little, so I doubt she was holding back on purpose. I think she just needed time to get used to her new environment, just like mum had said.

Over the next few days, I noticed that she did not know how to pronounce most things, so she kept quiet most times and just pointed when she needed something. I finally figured the problem, or maybe the additional problem. First off, our accent was different, so our spoken English must have sounded a bit confusing to the little girl. That was probably an extra source of worry for her little mind, but she would not even say it.

I wanted to teach her so bad, but I did not know how to approach her. She seemed to like writing and I stumbled on some things she had written and kept in front of her dressing mirror sometimes. She wrote short stories and they were interesting. She also made some drawings to illustrate her characters. Most of her characters were princess, so I figured she must really love fairy tales. Her English had been properly constructed too. The only thing that was lacking was her pronunciation and she was not quite confident of her spoken English, which was not exactly the best too. Well, by the time she spent a few days, she had cause to speak in sentences and I could notice this. Her accent was totally different too.

Sometimes, I tried to ask her questions, but she was not very confident in replying. I concluded that the fact that she was in London was really a factor. Everyone around the house spoke English very fluently, with an English accent too, which was quite different from her own accent. I did not want my sister to feel any less because she spoke differently than us. I approached mum to tell her what I had noticed, she had noticed it too. She wanted my teacher who coached me on Queen's English at home to school Amira. She would also have our governess explain things around the house, as well as how they are pronounced to her. However, I opted to be the one that helps. I felt like she might end up getting used to the teachers and not need me, her big sister. This might end up separating us from each other to a large extent. I wanted to be close enough to Amira before she gets introduced to the teachers who would also school her at home. However, I did not tell mum all these funny thoughts of mine. I just told her that I wanted to be the one that showed her things around the house and their pronunciation.

I hoped teaching the little I knew would help in getting closer with my new sister, and hopefully, form a bond. I had watched it severally in the movies how sisters would usually cover up for each other with their parents, how younger sisters usually blackmailed their elder sister's for money, so they would not expose what they had been doing with their boyfriends to their parents. I really looked forward to that with Amira. I wanted her to be that little sister that would take my new clothes and would get into silly fights with me. I was young and could not exactly explain it, but I wanted that strong siblings' love so bad. I wanted her to know I had her back too. I wasn't just sure of how everything would play out between us.

In the next few days, with my own knowledge of what I had been thought on Queen's English, I tried to teach my sister. Well, I told mum I would also start with teaching her Queen's English before the teacher would take over; just to bond with her better. I started first with words, then I continued with sentences and speeches, in the coming week. To my surprise, Amira understood and got the concept of everything I thought her faster than a child of her age was expected to. It was surprising for me because at that age, things like that did not usually stick in my own head that quickly. This made me happy and her, more confident. I also took her around the house and called the name of each pastry, each sweet, and all the items in the pantry to let their pronunciations sink in and so she could familiarize herself with everything. It all worked so fast, to my utmost pleasure and she became freer with me, especially after we shared all the ice cream we took, above the limit mum had ordered us for the week. It was no surprise when we both came down sick with diarrhea. Mum thought it was something from one of the lunches the cooks had made when she and dad were absent, seeing that it had affected us both. Only Amira and I knew our little secret, and this was the beginning of the love I share with my little sister.

When Amira announced that she was bringing a young man home, I got on the next plane back to London. I wondered who had stolen my sister's heart and if he really deserved her or I needed to punch him off. Don't ask me where I was when I got that call from Amira. That, I will explain later. Knowing what Amira had gone through with men in the past and her resolution to stay on her own till she got the one that was right for her was enough reason for me to feel overjoyed, but still very cautious. Of course, I wanted my sister to find love, but I wanted her to be safe too. I also knew she usually feel hard, hence my protective side.

Prior to that call, I had begun to think my little sister was not exactly interested in finding love ever again. She had always been a hopeless romantic, but you know what they say about life toughening people. That had been Amira's case. I watched her grow up to love romance series, romantic scenes from movies and everything that had do with romance. I watched her enjoy romantic gestures in her teenage years. However, in adulthood, her love life was not exactly a part of her life in which she was lucky. I always wondered if there was anything I could perhaps do to make things better, but just like I discovered some years back, there are some aspects of your life in which no one could exactly help you fix up perfectly. Those parts of life are always usually determined by a complex interaction of various factors. In such cases, you just had to submit to the journey and hope for the best. Knowing this made me chill out on being that married sister that would try to match-make her sister at every chance. Oh yes, I am married. I would definitely talk more about my husband and my marriage as we progress. No rush guys.

With respect to submitting to her journey, Amira decided to focus on work and truly enjoying the single life till someone who was worth her time decided to show up. She has a good network of friends that helped in making the process easier on her. Although they are not always together, as they are busy career women, they go on luxury trips to cool off from work. And for single people, having such friends was definitely a game-changer that was sure to make your single life more enjoyable. However, by the time six months was gone and there was no man in the picture, I really wondered how she was surviving her singlehood.

Singlehood came with loneliness, especially when you are an adult that lives alone and holds their own. Work can be fulfilling, but it is always more fulfilling to have someone by your side, someone you could celebrate your wins with. There is a level of intimacy that every human craves that can only be found (most times) in a romantic relationship. No matter how successful a human is, most of the time, this always applies to their lives. I guess that explained my concern for my little sister. Well, that is my view on things. I have learnt not to force my opinions down on people as the ultimate truth.

So, once she said there was someone she would love the family to meet over dinner and she was flying in from New York, so this young man could have dinner with family on her sacred Sunday evening, I knew this was a serious situation and I was not about to miss it. I called my husband of two years, Harry, to join us in London for a family dinner. He was in Texas for work, but as we always prioritized family, he promised to join us too.

Dad and mum were always home in London now that they were much older, so they were waiting for all of us to come home for something that was sure to turn into a small family reunion. This was the second time she would invite someone home for dinner. The first one was her very first boyfriend, and as expected, dad wanted to see that high schooler that thought he was worthy of his daughter. Throughout her days in Yale, she was in a few relationships but there were reasons why she was not going to invite any to our home. Amira had quite strict rules for herself and knew that some kind of men did not fit into her persona and her relationship with such men was just to pass time. Hence, she did not see any reason to invite them for dinner with our parents. As we grew and my sister became an adult, I understood to step back when she had drawn a line on a particular subject, as she was an adult and definitely had a right to her own opinions and decisions. I try not to be overbearing, as much as I can. I have learnt to respect my sister's decision.

She had talked to me about John, but I did not want to get too excited like I had done in the past. I did not even commit him to memory, so I would not end up putting ideas in her head about him. Well, we don't exactly make a lot of phone calls, as I am in Africa often, busy with the things I love to myself (okay, I might have just given away an idea of the continent from which I was flying in). She is also usually busy with work and "living" like she would say. However, we always send voice notes back and forth in the middle of going about our lives. That was cheaper than the luxury of time and energy it took to have proper phone conversations. I mean, when we gist, the tea is usually endless, so we would not take the risk of having long ass phone calls when there was a lot of work to be done. Well, you see, my sister and I understand each other and our modes of communication damn well.

The night after she went on her first date with John, she had gone on and on about how great a person he is and how he had even surpassed her standards. Amira had always said that at every point, she would pick personality over looks, but she said that John surpassed what she had hoped for in the area of looks too. To be honest, this made me a bit worried, as I did not want anyone messing with my sister; not anymore. Especially not a guy that looked "that good". However, like I told you, she is an adult and the last thing I want is to make it seem like I am trying to control her life. My sister was so happy after that date and I could only hope she was not trusting too much. She had become more careful after her last relationship, but I now wondered what the basis was for the kind of trust she was giving this man she had just gone on a date with.

Alright, she told me about the flowers and the lunch, but guys in our generation are far different from those in our parent's generation. Amira has done so well for herself and even added another feather to her amazing cap—her skin line. Who knew this young man's real intentions for her? I just felt like she should be a bit more careful, but I decided not to jump straight to giving her advice. It would only let me look like an overprotective elder sister. I did not want her lonely, but more than that, I did not want anyone to screw up her close-to-perfect life. Hence, my plan was to go for that dinner and confirm my hypothesis. Then, I would be able to give her advice with enough information already at hand. He was a footballer, so what? That only told me that he had enough money to be with whoever he chose and many women were sure to flock around him. The women also came with the popularity. So, he definitely had to prove to me somehow, that he was worthy of her because Amira equally had a number of suitors, she was just yet to find a great match for herself.

I told Harry about my plans to notice the young man and then advice my sister, but he asked me to slow it down. You know the thing with men; just never as intuitive as women! Anyway, I took the next available flight for real. I did want the issues with booking flights from my location in Africa (such as cancellations that are uncalled for) to affect my ability to grace the occasion. I might be sounding a little pessimistic to you, but you should know better from the things I have written previously. I am simply a realist, and now, this realist is looking out for her little sister. That is all really.

Harry and I came to dinner one hour earlier. I had gotten in three hours earlier, and he, four hours earlier. We spent some time catching up at our house in London, and then, we were headed for my parent's house. I wanted to witness everything, from the moment John stepped into the house. I really needed to read this guy that my sister seemed to think is worthy, even when it seemed like she had not checked him out that much. Well, it is easy to be blinded by attraction.

From the moment they got off their ride, I was at the window, watching them come into the house.

"Wow! He's really good looking." I said.

Harry gave me a knowing look. "I did not expect him to get accepted this early." He said sarcastically.

"It doesn't mean I have accepted him. People inherit looks, we do little to look the way we look and from what I see, he has not done any surgery." I said, defending myself.

"Uh-un." Harry said, before laughing at my defense line.

Warm hugs and pleasantries were exchanged before dinner. I had not seen my sister in about a year. We came into London sometimes, but our schedules never just fit such that we would be in London at the same time. It just never happened in the past one year, so you can imagine how happy I was to see her.

As for scrutinizing John, I decided to be objective and not pessimistic. First off, I could not help but notice that John was a fine black man with good manners, even at dinner. When our parents began to ask the young man questions over dinner, he spoke impressively, especially about his work. Then, they began to ask where he grew up. It was then that he revealed that he initially grew up in an organization that had a heart foundation and an orphanage. He also added that he was taken up by the organization from Africa for his exceptional skills at football and his studies.

Now, that rang a bell. I sensed that our parents were about to question him further to find out if it he grew up in Liberia and had perhaps known anything about Amira.

"He was one of the kids from my orphanage." Amira quickly added. Up till that time, Amira had decided to keep it away from the family that he was also from her orphanage. She wanted to surprise us and so she did.

"Oh!" I could not help but exclaim. Now the dots connected and I knew why Amira was so comfortable with this man. Now, I knew why she was excited and although humans could be surprising, I could now agree that she was in safe hands, at least, to a large extent. At least, she knew his root to the letter. She had always talked about how the kids from her orphanage had all grown up with the same values. She had told me a little about doing business with Kira and how those values had been highly reflective in the way they worked together.

"Nice to meet you." I continued. I became more comfortable with John, knowing that he was from that orphanage.

"You did well with that surprise." I said, turning to my little sister, clapping my hands together.

I agreed with Amira's philosophy about the orphanage she came from because I have seen this in the kids Miss. Julia is currently raising, even now that she is much older. I have seen the values with which she raised them and how well-behaved and focused the kids are at a tender age. I am usually impressed each time I visit. I can even place a few names around the world to the faces I have seen displayed on the wall of the orphanage. Now, something else was coming to mind. It dawned on me!

"Is he 'THE JOHN'?" I asked.

"Did Miss Julia ever tell you about a stubborn John?" Asked Amira.

"Oh yes!"

By now John was laughing. "The one that broke his bones" I added.

"Well, he now plays football." Said John.

You're probably wondering what is happening here. Well, I volunteer in orphanages around Africa and I am particularly interested in, "THE SAFE PLACE" in Liberia, from which my amazing sister came.

Miss Julia has done well to tell me a little about every kid that passed through the orphanage, but 'THE STUBBORN JOHN'S' story definitely stood out. We all laughed. The joy in the air was now undeniable.

"Well, welcome to the family." My dad said, as everyone was now more comfortable with John, especially seeing how we had bonded in the last few minutes.

CHAPTER
ELEVEN

*O*nce again, my name is Olivia and I am the kind of person you typically say was born into wealth. Being born into wealth is definitely a great privilege. Having seen the situations many people had to go through to get an education, a job or even money makes me realize quite often that the family into which I was born is a huge blessing.

Indeed, living in abundance is all glamorous and something many people look to have in their life. I would not deny this or act like there is nothing special about being wealthy. Living in luxury is how you enjoy life and you cannot do this without money. Growing up, I might not have exactly realized how blessed I was; it was all normal to me. However, going through life made me see things differently. I have travelled far and wide and I have met people from the middle class, and then, those from the lower class. I have also met children that grew up in developing nations and war-torn countries. Indeed, I can say I was quite privileged growing up.

Many of the people I met had to work hard through life, just so they would not go hungry. Thinking of this is crazy. I literally look at people who have gone through situations like this as warriors. They were not born into a house decorated with gold and growing up, they did not feel awkward when the scent candle for their rooms have not been changed in one week. Scents hardly even mattered to them. There were more important things for them to worry about—things like actually getting food to eat and just surviving. Hence, many a time, many of these people, not born into money are highly motivated all through their life. They are motivated because they need to make money to get the basic things in life and perhaps, someday attain wealth.

A friend of mine used to call it the advantage of adversity; when poverty makes someone realize that they actually needed to work to survive. This kind of situation would motivate such a person through school or building a career. The quest to have money determines everything they do (sometimes, even on a subconscious level), right up to the kind of profession or career path they choose in life. First off, whatever career path a person that did not come from wealth chooses has to be one that would guarantee financial security, if not throughout their lifetime, at least for the most part of their lives. This is non-negotiable.

For some born in areas of the world where there were specific problems or communities with specific concerns, they may grow up to want to choose a career path in that area. In the end, every person's environment and living circumstances would have a huge role to play in what their dreams would be. We can conclude that most dreams are centered about money or solving a problem one saw as they grew up. And guess what, that is fine—it is perfect!

However, for me, money was never a problem. Comfort was never a problem. I grew up under controlled living circumstances. I was properly monitored to always get the best things of life. In fact, my parents did everything within their power to ensure that I moved with the best of the bests in every area. I went to the best high school; my friends were also from wealthy families. We never understood the concept of lack at any point and all we knew was abundance. While all these things might have not affected those in my circle and their path in life negatively, for me, it did. Perhaps, "negative" is not particularly the right word, so I would explain what I mean. As

I grew, I was never bothered about what I wanted to do with my life till I was 21. For a child born into an average family, this is not usually the case. The child decides to do something their parents approve of at a tender age. Then, they work to achieve it and even build their lives around achieving it.

Okay, the fact that I did not know what I wanted to do did not mean I was being careless in any way. I was reading the books I needed to read, I was passing my tests and all my examinations like I should. I picked an interest in the sciences and I studied it. I ended choosing a major in psychology not because I wanted to become a psychologist, but simply because I found it interesting. However, the problem for me remained what I wanted to do with my life. I could already afford all the luxuries I wanted in life, I lacked nothing. I had a trust fund and investment portfolios in my name. Hence, unlike many kids I have met on my life's journey, I could not exactly have a dream that was tied to something materialistic. It did not even make sense to do so because I already had everything I needed. For the things I did not have, there was an endless cash flow to always get them whenever I wanted. I could not point out one single problem in my immediate environment. My family had money and influence, so I really had no problems that could not be somehow solved. I understand this is a dream life for many people and that is why I keep saying that I do not taking any of these privileges for granted. I am only pointing to how it influenced my life, my thought process and my future.

While I kept thinking as an adult at the age of 21 and doing a psychology major, I remembered a time in my life when I travelled with my parents and my sister to Africa to do some volunteering. We went to Liberia in particular and the orphanage in which Amira grew up. She was so excited to be back there and to see Miss. Julia, who she always called "mum". Amira was indeed happy and to my surprise, so was I. She ran through the different buildings and looked at the changes that had been made to them with a smile plastered across her face. She looked at the pictures on the wall and even called our attention to the memories.

Mum could not exactly keep up with her and everything she was showing us. She was now sneezing; mum had caught the flu from all the dust and dirt. She had to stay indoors for two days because of how she felt. It was a different experience for me. I had travelled to many places in Europe with mum and dad, but now in Africa, Liberia was just different. Things did not look good for most of the people that lived there at all. Although there were places that looked far better than other rural areas, they still seemed to be far behind based on what was happening around the world. I really felt like I needed to help and perhaps, that was why, despite the fact that I had also caught the flu, I refused to stay indoors. I just wanted to help. Mine was mild though; not as bad as my mum's. She ended up having to see a doctor while we were in Liberia.

Mum had shipped a lot of things from London and they arrived a day after we got to Liberia. We lodged in a hotel that was satisfactory, but it was nothing like home. I trust mum and dad to always pick the best wherever we went and the best there was nothing like our home, but I heard it cost a lot for the people there and only the rich could afford it.

I was 15 at the time, but my ears were all over the place. I was so curious and I kept asking questions from Amira, but she had been too shielded by the safe place orphanage to know too much about the places in the country. Yet, I was excited to be there. I looked at the many things mum had shipped that filled our suite, and I kept wondering if it would be enough to really go round and help the people of the part of Bomi county where we stayed in Liberia.

"As much as we want to, we can't help everyone all at once." Mum had smiled and said, as she dozed off again, thanks to the drug the doctor had prescribed for her use, to reduce her symptoms.

Dad had to call one of the staff to help move the things we had shipped from London to another room, so we could have enough space in our suite. As for me, I was just too excited to experience a different part of the world and it was only the beginning of my many questions for mum, dad and my sister. I did not care to think of if they would know; I kept asking anyway. I just cared too much about this new experience of mine and kept wondering what it felt like to live in Liberia and other areas of the world that were still developing. It was definitely not one experience I would forget soon. Many pictures of the people suffering at the time still lingers in my head till today.

It was my first time of seeing lack at its peak. I heard Miss Julia tell mum of the stories of some of the kids in the orphanage. The stories were so sad to hear and as a child, I felt horrible wondering what those kids had to go through. Above all, I was just thankful that they were now safe. I can even remember shedding tears, but trying to quickly hide it from my mum, who still saw it and gave me a pat. Amira was also really sorry for the kids, but she had been in the orphanage before, so she had an idea of these things. She was not as moved as I was and asked me to cheer up. I could understand that she had grown up with a harsher reality. Miss Julia also told us how the orphanage was now full to the brim, in spite of the expansion that had been done a few months back.

After giving some of the things we had brought to the orphanage, we proceeded to help another set of people. Miss. Julia advised that we could go around and share things to people in certain communities too. She said the orphanage could hardly take more kids, but had been receiving quite a lot on a regular basis, to support the kids already in the orphanage. And so, we could take a lot of the things we had brought for the orphanage into neighboring communities to see how we could help.

She had explained many of those kids who could not get a space in the orphanage were out there without clothes or food, not to even bring in the subject of getting an education. Some of the kids who lived with their parents did not have these basic necessities too. Their parents could not provide those necessities for them. While she emphasized that it was not a problem that could be solved in a day, she was just trying to tell us that they needed help too, maybe now even more than the kids in the orphanage. She told us that she wished more people will have a vision like hers to build and run other orphanages in the community that would even include kids who were with their parents, but were not being properly catered for due to the poverty levels in those communities. Miss Julia made it clear that it was not just about building up orphanages, but the orphanages also had to be run with love right from the very scratch. It was not something one could be forced to do or just do because they had enough money to spare. It was not also a matter of employing people to run it. A head that took the work as a calling was necessary too. I never forgot these words she said, not even for once. However, I did not know that those words would one day be useful as regards what I planned to do with my life.

As we went in the car mum and dad had hired into the town and started sharing things, we had a crowd literally chase after us till we were back in the hotel. It only showed the level of poverty and lack among the people in those communities. I saw kids my age running without clothes on. Miss Julia quickly told us that the fact that they were running without clothes in spite of the harsh weather was not on purpose. Those kids really did not have clothes. They chased to also get the noodles I would typically refuse to eat. Miss Julia also added that it was not as though they liked noodles that much, they were just hungry. My parents had asked what the government was doing, but Miss Julia explained how the poverty level was just too high and it was not a situation that could be curbed all at once.

I could almost not believe that this was happening to human beings that had the same blood running through their veins, like me. I was moved to tears and grateful for my life and my family. I was so grateful for Amira. I tried to imagine her being that child chasing our car just to have clothes on their body or for food, without caring if they would get injured or not. I could not even stand the image I had in my head, so I just closed my eyes and hugged my darling sister. I am sure she must have been wondering what was going on with me. That singular experience just made me view life differently and just made me appreciate my life even more. I never thought of life the same way; not ever again! There were adults on the chase to. They did not even stop the kids. It seemed like everyone naturally fought for survival in that place. The fact that you are a kid does not even count. There was no protection for those kids. It was like having no childhood at all.

Mum and dad had to start throwing money into the air, their currency of course. This did not seem right to do, but the items in our big vehicle had been exhausted and my parents still wanted to do something to help. I think what I have described so far shows the poverty level in those communities.

Even when I got back home in London, the image of those kids did not leave my head. Amira must have been tired of me talking about it. She had seen the situation of things when she was in Liberia howbeit she was not so exposed, at least she had seen these sights. So she was not just as surprised as I was. I talked and talked about it endlessly with my friends who were interested in listening. Many of them were moved to tears to think that people could really be experiencing poverty on that level.

I am simply trying to drive home why looking around me and wondering what I wanted to do with my life at the age of 21 had taken me back to all those happenings. I dawned on me; I wanted to help people, especially in orphanages and maybe outside orphanages too. And of course, in developing countries. However, orphanages were my first targets. It all had to be a step at a time and just like my parents had done when I was a child, if I wanted to help, I had to start from organized orphanages and take it from there.

Once my mind went back to all those happenings, I was sure that I would be sincerely happy lending a helping hand to the less privileged. Perhaps, that was why I was born into such privilege, who knows?

Here's the truth about this book. I have been working hands in hands with safe places since I was 22. At the age of 22, I graduated from college and I knew I was interested to going back to help where my parents had thought to help when I was still a teenager. That was exactly where my heart was glued to and the thought of going there to help enveloped me night and day. I told my sister, Amira, and it sounded like a great idea to her. She emphasized how seeing people from other parts of the world come to the orphanage as a child had boosted her quest to want to thrive in life. She encouraged me by telling me how the kids would be subconsciously encouraged to see that I was interested in them. For her, as a kid who had been born into such an unpleasant circumstance and in fact abandoned by her mother, she had always felt like she was not so important on a subconscious level. However, seeing people from even other parts of the world being interested in the progress of her and the other kids made her feel like she was important to a set of people. It gave her courage to go through life feeling worthy. I had grown up with Amira. I never imagined she would think this way about herself, but because she had grown with me from a tender age, I keep forgetting that she had a life before she came to London. She never really talked about it and maybe it had faded, but the effect of that life still set her apart for me.

It definitely explains why my sister turned out differently career-wise. Well, I would say it is not hard to see. She had history. She had quite a tough childhood and growing up in the orphanage, many things, both the said and unsaid factors had created in her a drive to want to succeed. Oh, my sister had always been so motivated to do so well in life. Right from when we were kids, she had always wondered how there was so much disparity between the rich and the poor. She had come from such a humble place and had come into such a wealthy place. She wondered how some generations, races and cultures had so much money more than others. Then, she wondered how a poor person could become wealthy or if at all there was even a way around it. At some point, she thought it was a mirage; it was impossible for the poor to become wealthy, except they hit a jackpot. The poor was bound to go through life begging from the rich. She had asked me questions about this, but I never had an answer. I mean, all I had ever know was wealth, so it was kind of expected. I thought my sister had given up on this line of questioning until she stumbled on the word, "investment" on the news. Investment, to her, became a way to multiply the money one had. And if the poor could work hard and then, multiply their money, maybe one day, they could meet up with the wealthy. Following this, I would watch my sister take out the parts of the daily times that had to do with investment and finance every single day. She would read it like her life depended on it and would ask our governess for help with the terms she did not understand. In little time, daddy's big oxford dictionary became her companion. She would read with the dictionary by her side. She did not stop focusing on that area ever since and it was not surprising when she choose a career path in it. However, my sister had a motivating factor. Her early childhood was that factor; the suffering she had witnessed firsthand; even subconsciously—each time they journeyed from the orphanage to the city. This factor coupled with the values thought at the orphanage made it hardly surprising that she would turn out that way or be the person she currently is.

Although we grew up together, she was highly competitive in everything she did. Even when we were home schooled, it was as if she always competed with herself. She was always trying to be a better version of herself and it really fueled her passion to do anything and everything. There was this heat around her and trust me, I caught it too. Before she came into my life, I was definitely not that child who believed in doing anything with so much energy or putting in too much work. My life was easy and I treated everything else easily.

However, looking back now, I am glad she came into my life because once I caught that fire of hers, there was no going back. I had vigor too. I just wanted to be the best at everything I laid my hands on. It became an unwritten rule in the house to be the best in everything you lay your hands upon. This was not something laid down by my parents; Amira did that without even knowing it. Just by watching my little sister, just from the time I tried to teach her English and pronunciations, I was changed myself.

I later understood this behavior of hers when I finally visited the safe place as an adult and heard some of the things Miss. Julia had to say about the kids. They had imbibed the spirit of competition in all the kids as they grew and also reminded them that they had the capacity to fulfil all those dreams. And it worked perfectly! I mean, I know Amira, stubborn John and the famous Kira. I already got involved in working with Julia since I was 22, about 12 years ago, and now after meeting John and hearing Kira's exploits of recent, I got really encouraged to roll up my sleeves and continue to be fully be a part of everything Julia was doing.

"Remember me? I came with my parents during summer some seven years ago, to volunteer and share some things in Liberia. I am coming again." I said when I spoke on the phone with Julia. She had remembered me, to my surprise. I later got to realize that the orphanage was her lifelong project and maybe her "life partner" too, as funny as it sounds. She wouldn't miss one thing concerning the details of the orphanage. She could remember every single kid and their adoption circumstances. This was quite surprising. Julia was highly dedicated to the cause and it was inspiring for anyone at all who cared to watch, anyone like me.

The first time I met Julia, she was a lady who was approaching 40 and she hugged me like she had known me for ages. She had been scolding some kids before she noticed a presence and a pair of eyes staring at her. They were my eyes. She immediately turned and asked me to bring in a hug.

"You are all grown!" she said, almost spinning me around. "Your parents must be proud." She had said, looking at me with so much love. Ah! That woman has so much love in her and it is really evident in all she had achieved.

"You should be proud too." I said, with a smile. Now, I had a real smile on. If you know me, you would know that smiles hardly come to me in the situation where they should. I mean, I like to smile, I am a happy person. However, I do not get to smile when I actually want to smile. I smile only when it comes naturally to me. Hence, I do not smile in pictures. Now, you should understand what I mean when I say I had a real smile on. I was thinking about my darling sister as I looked at Miss Julia and that was why I was smiling. She really should be proud to have raised such a child with a culture of excellence.

From what Amira had told me, all the kids in the orphanage were like that. Raising one child with a culture of excellence was great, but Julia was a woman that raised hundreds with that culture. I felt like she really should be proud. She did not carry herself around like she was that woman that had achieved this and that. She had a very humble demeanor, one I had attributed to her youth the first time I saw her. Well, meeting her for the second time, she was still young, but at least old enough to act like she deserved some respect. She had kids that had left her orphanage to different places in the world and were connected to different big families, but she was not one to act like that was a thing of advantage for her. Miss Julia was indeed an angel from God in her own capacity and I could see that.

I hugged her yet again. She had impacted my own life. When my parents told me Amira's story, I could not help but cry. I wondered what would have happened to her if the safe place orphanage was not in existence. That was another life that would probably waste away. Once again, the picture of those kids struggling to have food and clothes came to mind and I wondered what the future of those kids would look like.

Imagine Amira not getting a chance to be educated. Imagine such a bright and promising child having her progress being affected because she was born into an environment that was not enabling. I began to see the reason why I fell in love with what Miss Julia had been doing back then and why I wanted to help even more. People that were doing such good works needed to be supported to do even more.

Julia made me feel like I was on the right path. I had no cause to wonder if she was happy; happiness was written all over her. That day, staring at her with my small bag (which I carried for my two day trip in Liberia) in hand, I had almost wondered if she was happy, but when I saw it written all over her, there was no reason to wonder any more.

For those two days, I helped the staff by relieving them of their duties. I was not particularly used to taking care of younger children, not even myself when I was a kid. So, I opted to teach in the class. I had to tune it down with my accent and try to talk to the kids in their own accent as much as I could. It was so much fun teaching the kids; I found so much joy and happiness doing so. I felt fulfilled too. Seeing the smile on their innocent faces, I could only hope and pray that they got as lucky as my sister, to get adopted into a great family too. When Julia told me some of their stories, I cried and cried. You would never imagine some scenarios until you are told that they are actually some people's reality.

Imagine a baby being found in a bucket because the mother was too poor to afford clean warm clothes. She later came around to say all the clothes she had around her were not clean enough and she did not have the means to make them so or take care of the boy. The bucket had been the only clean place she could put the baby. Such a woman deserves to be arrested, doesn't she? However, looking at the big picture, she was hungry, tired, homeless and hopeless herself. She just wanted something better for her baby. Hence, she had dropped the baby in the bucket in front of the orphanage.

THE EYES OF AN ORPHAN

There was another story of a baby who had marks of being beaten. The father of the child had left the mother in abject poverty. The woman suffered a mental breakdown that made her beat the child. Thanks to neighbors, the child got rescued and was taken to the safe place orphanage, the renowned orphanage were kids were safe. That mother deserved to be arrested, didn't she? However, she had a mental breakdown. What she really needed was to be in a psychiatry home, so Julia had to arrange for that.

Guess what? Life is not perfect for you, but it is by far worse for many people. I could see that Julia was indeed doing a great job and people doing a work like hers, happily at that, deserved to be supported in every way.

So, at age 22, there I was, not only trying to give money to the orphanage, but also giving my entire self, to a good cause. That for me, was purpose. That was what I wanted to do with my life. To volunteer to help the less privileged. At least, if I am privileged to never have cause to work, yet have money in abundance, then I should help those that did not have such an opportunity, to ensure their lives are better than when I met them originally.

CHAPTER
TWELVE

"**Y**ou don't mean you let a man that loved you so much go."

"I had to, and it felt crazy at the time, but now I look back and I see that it was all worth it?" For me, I still could not figure out why exactly she had to let love go. I somehow believed that Julia could have won on both ends, but she did not even seem to be one bit bothered by his actions at all.

"So, where is David now?" I asked intently, wondering if he was somewhere waiting for his Julia.

"Celine says he's now married with kids. She ran into him the last time she visited our mum's graveside in Kent." Julia said casually. She even had an indifferent look on her face as she spoke.

"Oh. And what was he doing there?"

"David did not stop being a son to my mother in spite my own resolution not to get married. They always got along and he did not let the fact that I did not become his wife stop this. We always knew each other as kids. We grew up in the same neighborhood, but he lost his mother early on. My mother took him in like her own son and when he started showing interest in me, she was more than happy to encourage it because you know, David was such a good boy; a perfect gentleman. You know, as kids, he spent a lot of nights in our home because his father travelled a lot and would beg my parents to keep him with them. His father was a busy business man. David spent more time with my own father than he did with his. We graduated from high school together and we went to the same college. We continued being really good friends all the while. When my dad died, he was right there to console me, but I also caught him crying later on, like he had lost his own father." Julia said, smiling.

"He seems like such a nice guy. Don't you feel like you should have just stayed or tried to make it work? You seemed to have loved him. How did you feel when you heard he was married?" I could not help it. I loved romance and I was the kind of person who always looked for happy endings, but Julia was about to disappoint me.

"Maybe I loved him." Julia shrugged. There was a long pause between us before she continued, "Olivia, look around you. Look at this orphanage. Look at the kids. All these wouldn't have been possible if I went with David's plan. For David, it was always all or nothing. And if I had to pay the price I paid to stay here and make all this magic happen, I would pay it again. As for David, I am happy that he moved on, he found love and he had been able to build a family. I am in fact happy for him. I do not feel bad about how things ended between us in any way. In fact, I think it was for the best, since I was not really cool with what he was offering."

I could see it in her eyes. She did not regret anything she had done, but the story Julia had just told me made me have a lot of respect for David. I was also shocked that Julia had gone through that much herself. Her story was almost unbelievable. Although the orphanage was a cause she channeled so well, it looked as if she was one of those people that wanted a charity case so badly, just because they were good people. Yes, Miss Julia is a good person; that is not hard to see. However, she had gone through a lot herself. Everything she had been through had shaped her to become who she was. The orphanage was no charity case to her, it was indeed a calling like she used to say.

At the age of twenty-three, Julia had been diagnosed with ovarian torsion and an immediate surgery had to be done on her, to remove her right ovary, which was first affected. Shortly after, the ovary on the other side became affected too. She lost her ovaries. The doctors said the cause of her ovarian torsion was unknown. The torsions had happened within the space of one year, and while she had tried to take in and deal with the first one, the second one made her breakdown totally. Now, the most vital yet painful part of the story was the fact that she now had no chance at having children at all. It was such a sad and unexpected thing for Julia who had lived her life so well. She had been a nerd in high school and was never a party freak. Her first boyfriend was David, who she agreed to date when she realized they were going to be in the same college. She was literally her mother's pride, not ever making her mother sad or worry at any point. She was every mother's dream girl child; neat, pretty and focused. She would participate in school debates, dramas and contests. She was a star child. I could not begin to imagine what Julia had to go through. She had done absolutely nothing to deserve what had happened to her.

"I sank into depression. I lost myself. I was in my final college year and I just wanted to get out and go into hiding. I shut my family out. I shut my friends out. I wondered what it was that I had ever done to deserve how things had turned out for me. I shut David out. I did not want to see him. To crown it all, following my predicament, he had proposed, probably thinking it would make me feel better. I knew David always loved me, but the fact that the proposal happened immediately following my surgery was just too much. I guess he was trying to prove to me that the whole situation had not changed how he felt about me, but what he did just got me even more pissed. I just wanted to be alone." Julia paused and let out a sob, and then, a smile.

"He must have really loved you." I could not help but say.

"Well, he did everything he could. Looking back now, I can understand that why he chose to propose to me in that moment, even if it was not the best of moments. I guess he was willing to do anything to make me feel better. I did not turn down his proposal to make him look like a joke. I just couldn't at the moment. I was too confused about my life. The future looked really bleak for me. You know, when you have your life planned out and an unforeseen circumstance just changes everything."

"I can imagine." I said.

"My family and friends; they said I should not worry, that they had my back no matter what happened. They told me they loved me over and over. The truth is, in a situation like mine, no one really knew the right things to say, so the things they said to me only hurt me more. I could find faults in everything they said, so I just really wanted everyone out of my space. It did not mean that would help. Having them out of my space only made me realize my pain even more. I kept thinking to myself that I had done nothing to deserve what had happened to me. I wanted to smoke, I wanted to drink to stupor, I wanted to do all the things I had felt I should never do and succumb to the vices I never succumbed to in the past, all just to stay a perfect lady. I wanted to get wild, but when I thought of the fact that it would not change what had happened to me, I sunk into depression again; not eating for days, not taking a shower, not talking to people and not wanting to see anybody." Julia had said. "As for school work, I was in my final year and I was already rounding up my school work. As for everything else apart from research, I simply dragged my way through, still covering my face with face caps and coming out only when it was absolutely required. I did not want to talk to anyone or even make contact with anyone at all."

The next time Julia began to think of life as exciting was when her best friend, Maria, a pretty Hispanic lady, asked that she went to Africa with her, on her volunteering trip. Julia thought it was a nice idea and it ignited a spark in her. That seemed like something new and different from everything she had ever known. She began to think that now, she could at least have a fresh start. She could go see a new place. That spark took her to Africa. For Julia, at that point, it was not about helping people, she just needed a distraction. She needed to escape from her immediate environment, but definitely not in the vacation kind of way, since she was still busy beating herself up. Hence, volunteering just seemed like the perfect reason for her to travel.

While on the trip, she got so happy. She loosened up a bit and was different from who she had been since her surgery. "Looking back, now I realize that Maria must have known that something was off with me. I was just too excited. Hence, she showed a little concern when I was all about a baby crying in the bush. She probably thought I was hearing strange sounds or losing my mind until she eventually heard the cries too."

"Did you ever get to ask her how she really felt back then?"

"Oh yes, I did. She was with me here, two years ago and when she came around, we talked at length about that period of my life. She said my actions that day only finally made sense to her about five years back, in between raising kids and running her company, it's been difficult for her to find time to come. That was why at the slightest chance to come around two years ago, she really came around. Maria confessed to me that she thought I was losing it."

"Oh! Your best friend really thought you were crazy? No, you don't mean that."

"Yes, she did." Julia laughed. "And looking back, it looks like I was really acting crazy. I had never really liked babies before them. I used to refuse to carry babies, I hated their cries. I was usually thinking they would poo on me. I did not want that, so I always avoided them."

"Haha! I get it now. Then, all of sudden, you visit Africa and you of all people is interested in babies. I would have been bothered too, sincerely."

"Yes Olivia. Exactly." She laughed. "This must be the way my friend, Maria thought of it. I now also understand why my mother thought I was crazy too. My decisions seemed absurd, but I really had a plan in mind, the plan you see in fruition today." She said, gesticulating to the orphanage environment.

"I hope you got a chance to visit your mother while she was alive. Of course, I mean after she came here."

"Yes, I did. I visited her every year; after the first two years of running the orphanage. Those first two years were quite tedious and I did not really have the balls to leave Liberia. There were now lives in my hand and I could not take that for granted. Many of the kids that came into the orphanage had been through a lot and it was frankly hard to have them out of sight. Until I had a good system in place after two years and several months had passed, I could not travel back."

"Wow! That is a great deal of sacrifice. What was your mum like whenever you visited?"

"Well, as you can probably imagine, her concerns were for me to get married in the first few years. However, when she began to hear the adoption stories of the kids, I guess she began to see that I was doing good work. She seemed happy at my progress and she supported me. Her resolution changed to how I should do whatever gave me joy to do."

"And that you did."

"That's right baby!"

After Julia told me her story, I spent the rest of my time with her on that particular trip reading journals. By now, it was my fifth trip to Liberia and I liked it there. It was not like the living conditions were perfect, but I was learning to adjust. I always opted to sleep in the hotel I had slept in the time my parents had come to Liberia. Things were not perfect there either, but I had to adjust, for the cause. At least, the place was by far more comfortable.

If Julia could sacrifice so much for the cause, why couldn't I? If I could agree that helping those kids with my resources and my time was what brought fulfilment to me and something I planned to make my lifelong work, I could definitely adjust for them. Of course, they deserved that and even more.

Julia was my inspiration and reading her journals made me respect her even more. She wrote something in the journal every night from the day she came into Liberia as a volunteer. There were several other "volumes" to read, but reading all she had done alone in the first one that night, made me very inspired by her. Her dairy made me get emotional. The woman had done way too much; she had helped way too many people.

Well, well, well; I have something important to tell you, my dear reader. Everything that has been written in this book from the start up to now was borne out of that journal, coupled with interviews with Julia, as well as discussion with some of the orphans that has passed through, "the safe place". I could not reveal to my sister and her new boyfriend that I had read about John and his stubbornness in Julia's journal. That is definitely some privileged information and I am not one to fault on something that personal to Julia. I could also not afford to say or do anything that would affect my relationship with the people I was meeting from the orphanage, thanks to Amira.

After reading the journal, I was just happy to be part of something so great. Julia had been making great moves as a young woman and I wanted to be a part of that too. I really could not wait.

The stories I read inspired me to also think of working with various orphanages in other developing countries of the world. I was sure they needed help and were probably facing some of the challenges that Julia had faced too. I had the resources to do so and like my parents would say to Amira and I, "Let your dream carry you like the wind. Do not be scared of where your dreams would lead you to. Dream as much as you want and never be afraid to move in the path of your dreams. It is usually rewarding to the soul when you look back on your life." Their words really helped me each time I got to a point where I had a dream that I wondered if to plunge into. I already knew what my parents would expect me to do and I never wanted to let them down even in their absence. They have given me a fairy tale life, I owed it to them to be excellent whether they were present or not.

Truly, looking back, I have never for once regretted embarking on my dream; dealing with these orphanages in developing nations. I had the support of my family to back whatever I chose to do in every way; these children in orphanages didn't. Also, not all of them got easily adopted into families. Some adoption plans did not go well too. Hence, I realized that the help that goes to kids in orphanages should never really stop. They need it, yet they can't exactly ask for it.

Hence, I picked up another role. My family had influence and I had never really used it. Well, I did not have any course to use it. I always had everything I wanted. So, I thought to myself, perhaps, this was the time to use that influence of mine. Maybe I could reach out to even more people in the social class of my family, who could help orphanages. There was obviously a gap. While there were many rich people in the developed countries, developing countries had so many children that actually need help. One or two wealthy people from developed countries of the world helping would definitely not solve the issue on ground. However, a collective effort from those in the upper social classes in developed countries was sure to be a huge step forward. If my parents could help, she imagined what about 10 people in the same social class as my parents would be able to do. Whatever the rich community joined hands together to do was sure to be very massive. The thought of this was my drive.

I remembered the smile on the innocent faces of those kids. They knew nothing about life and their predicaments was not in any way their fault. I had gone to several countries in Africa and apart from Liberia that was war torn, there were also several countries with kids suffering from diseases like polio and smallpox, and there was no provision for vaccines to stop the spread of such diseases. The countries were highly populated with no money to cater to all the masses. It was such a horrible sight to also see some children suffer from malnutrition as a result of poverty. I just wanted to tell my rich friends and their families all I had seen and even captured on camera.

Each night when I slept, images of those kids did not leave my mind. Above all, to me, it had also become so important to ensure that these kids make something out of their lives. At least, the more the kids from those areas got opportunities to get an education, the more they would be able to give back to their communities, even if it is only their families they could provide for. Having many kids that had an education and were gainfully employed or owned a business they could use to cater for their family was sure to go a long way in terms of reducing poverty levels. If their next generation is empowered, the cases of unwanted pregnancies and abandoned babies would also drastically reduce. What those countries were facing was a complex interaction of many factors, but money could definitely make everything better.

The world is very big and people could really turn their faces the other way. However, the menace that awaits the world if nothing is done to help kids going through such problems may be one money may be unable to solve. If the kids are empowered to make something out of their lives, then many problems in the world such as terrorism and fraudulent activities can be avoided to a large extent. Although poverty and lack of parental love is not enough to do evil, but let's face the truth, these things happen. A hungry man can be pushed to commit the worst sins if they would put food on the table. However, the real question was, "did the world really have to wait till it got to that before lending a helping hand to people in these poor countries?"

This became the message of my own movement; I became ready to take the future of the world into my hands, in my own little way and I found my purpose in making things better for kids in orphanages. I also became ready to facilitate a movement that helped in building more orphanages that catered to suffering kids. I was indeed ready!

CHAPTER
THIRTEEN

Julia still smiled that evening, as she told the new set of volunteers the story of the orphanage. Working with her always meant buying into the vision she had; "*To help and expect nothing in return. To be of service to humanity.*" That was her vision and she needed each of the new volunteers to fully grasp what that meant. Working in the orphanage was no show at all; it was real work. She wanted to see sincere smiles on the faces of the kids and be glad at what they had been able to achieve. She could have left the staff to pass across the message to the new volunteers, but Julia was not someone who could go for a day without doing some work in relation to the orphanage. As the staff in charge of the orientation was about to begin speaking with the volunteers, Julia came out herself to interrupt. She apologized and cut in; telling the new volunteers about how the orphanage started from almost nothing. She was not doing this in a bid to show off, she just wanted to be sure they understood what was going on and they did not get the wrong idea about the orphanage or the reason for its existence.

However, the volunteers could not see what I was seeing. I wondered if the staff were also seeing that Julia was stressed. I was too sure of this. I had noticed this for many weeks, especially when she took ill. Julia had always been a workaholic. All I had read in her dairy confirmed what I had initially thought. I saw how she had always done everything for years. I saw how she took the orphanage work seriously and hardly gave herself any time off. Throughout the time I read her dairy, I kept waiting to see the point where she would say I took some time off from the orphanage for a vacation. I did not find anything like that. Hence, the fatigue she experienced following her recovery did not come to me as a surprise at all. It had been a long time coming.

Merely looking at how much Julia worked, one would assume Julia would have taken break after these years, but it was shocking to know that since her mother died, she had not left Liberia for even a day. She had taken no holidays. I had never imagined that. It was quite strange to me because as I grew up, I saw my parents take a holiday with every chance they got.

"Life is too short." They would say. Not taking a break for many years was all too strange. When I read through and realized that there was no pint at which she took a break, I approached her to ask.

"This work involves a lot of sacrifice." She said. "I can't leave the kids."

Julia had her way of thinking when it came to the kids and from the way she usually talked and how she kept talking about her sense of duty to them, I knew that convincing her to take a holiday will be no easy task. Hence, I focused my attention on even getting her to rest within the orphanage. I begged her to sleep in on some days as she had enough staff to run the things happening within the organization. She was still adamant.

"This is no serious work for me. This is life to me. Olivia, I am not complaining." She would say. However, I could see it when she was stressed. She was just used to living like that. She could actually catch her breath and relax, but she just wouldn't. She was used to living that way; working and working. Any life outside that did not look like one Julia was looking to embrace. As for trainings, she would rather have virtual ones.

Many of the orphanage kids now all over the world and doing well had asked her to come over as the granny to their kids, but she complained that there were new kids that needed her. That was something no one could exactly argue about with Julia. Trying to argue would only make one look very heartless. The kids truly needed that mother figure. Each time she relaxed, I could see her beating herself up for having the guts to catch her breathe. And she actually deserved to relax. The orphanage kids that had tried and tried in the past had ended up given up. Several tickets had been sent to her from the kids she had raised all over the world to come spend some time with them or to come on a vacation with their families, but she would not budge. It was not unusual to see her on long calls with them, however, at the end of the calls, she would still refuse the offers they had made. They now did the best they could which was send money, jewelry and clothes to her from time to time. However, Julia was not one to wear flashy things. Many of those things were forgotten in her closet and each time she even remembered, she dashed them out to the women that lived around her. It was quite frustrating to constantly see her act that way. I kept thinking of what I could possibly do to make her feel appreciated. I was not just looking to do anything; I wanted it to be something she would actually love and appreciate.

She was proud of the things the kids she had raised had achieved. All the kids constantly called her to let her know of their wins. That seemed to give her satisfaction. Those were the kind of things that really made her happy, but she wouldn't visit when they asked her to come. Many of them were now raising families or at the top of their businesses and careers, such that leaving their base would definitely have a huge impact on them. Julia only saw the fact that the kids were doing well as a source of motivation to raise the next generation of the kids in the orphanage even better. She had of Kira's exploits, everything Joe and Sandra were achieving, the skincare line by Kira and Amira, John's football career, and the numerous professionals that were once kids under her care. In fact, the list was endless.

Julia was too selfless. She was too contented with life to care about whatever I brought each time I came from the UK. I brought the choicest of things; you can trust them I have good eyes (given my background), but Julia would not use any of these things.

Each time I had cause to travel, I brought back luxury things for Julia too, but it all did not matter to her. She appreciated what I had done truly, but those luxury things were not things she was crazy about.

She would say to me, "Olivia, why do I need to carry a Chanel bag? Where would I even carry it to? Around the orphanage?" She would then laugh and ask if it was the kids she was supposed to show off to. She could even hold a quiz that would allow her give expensive pieces of jewelry I brought for her to outstanding teenage girls in the orphanage. Well, she did that often—quizzes, trivia and the likes.

I travelled to the UK from time to time, as well as to several other areas of the world, so I could help in raising funds from my rich friends and giving them to struggling orphanages in Africa. I saw the part of Julia's diary that talked about how they struggled with funding. I could not wrap my heads around the thought of someone who was making so much impact still struggling for funds. I had seen money growing up. I knew wealth and luxury existed in abundance. I knew people who did not even know what to use all the money they had at their disposal for. And here was someone like Julia, using money for a good cause, needing money at some time. How? I could not just be fine with that. Well, things were great in the orphanage now, but I believed that no amount was too much for a cause like that. I volunteered by helping orphanages across Africa, but my major method of volunteering was raising funds; basically transferring funds from the rich to the poor.

I had been in wealth. I grew up around rich family friends that had all the luxury in the world, but did not want to be popular at all.

They did not desire the stress that came with being public figures, so they kept their lives private and even till now, they do. Giving to public platforms is something that gets hard for these people, as they do not want the money to be traced back to them or anyone to blow the trumpet on how they had helped them financially.

Hence, I now stood as a middleman. I got money across to orphanages while protecting the identity of these rich people that I had a personal relationship with. I felt fulfilled doing this.

Anyway, I guess you can now see why I decided to tell Julia's story; because it needs to be told. I wonder if the kids knew what she had been through or how she gave up her life and dedicated it to the orphanage. You know, kids tend to think that everything is fun and games because there is some adult who bears the burden for the good life they have to live.

Julia, as you can see is a source of motivation to anyone who watches her, especially to anyone who knows her entire story. Life is not perfect and as humans, we find ourselves complaining enough, but here was someone who really took the lemons life gave her and made some lemonade. I mean, enough lemonade for literally anyone that cared to drink. She did not go about sobbing about how she would never be able to have kids. Rather, she took her life and her future into her own hands.

It was quite difficult for me to ask about that part of her story. No matter how strong anyone is, some questions are still highly sensitive and must be treated so. Julia exuded joy when she talked about everything she had been through, but I also understood that she had given me access to very privileged information and talking about it with levity would be the worst thing ever to do. She was able to tell me that she had never discussed the health issue that brought her on her beautiful journey to purpose with any of the kids that she had raised from the orphanage. Well, those of them that even knew her as "mummy". Granted, there were many kids that were adopted as babies and probably did not know that they came from an orphanage. Only kids like my sister and her friends at the time actually knew their roots.

She did not want to be pitied. Telling the world her story in that way would definitely get her pity and she was not interested in that. The only reason she had told me was because she wanted to be someone that owned up to her truth. Asides that, she knew I was writing this book to tell her story to the world and the part of her ovarian torsion could never be left out. There was the shocking part where the doctors wondered why it would happen to her other ovary too. As for Julia, at this point, the answer she found was that it was the act of God to make something beautiful out of her life.

I understood Julia perfectly. She did not say it, but I knew for sure that she wanted her story to be told like that of a hero and not a victim. She was no victim; she was indeed a hero. And heroes are usually celebrated. Now, I was back to wondering how I could celebrate this amazing woman; in a way she would love of course. I kept wondering.

"1…2…3…Happy birthday Julia." The lights came on, and we screamed as Julia made her way to the hall. Then John, the troublemaker led us to sing the birthday song.

In that moment, at least I caught the expression on her face and it made me very happy. She was happy. She was very happy. She became even happier as her best friend, Maria came out of the crowd, singing aloud with us. She covered her face and by the time her hands were off it, I could see tears streaming down her cheeks.

"Maria" she called out as they hugged themselves for what seemed like forever. "I never imagined I would see you today. Not even in my wildest dream."

"Well, here I am." Maria smiled.

"Olivia." She called out. I was sure that she wanted to accuse me of deceiving her about where we were coming. Well, what could I do? It was a surprise. Instead of answering her, I hurried from her side and went to hold on tight to my husband, Harry, while I looked at her from a distance, with a big smile plastered across my face. It was a mischievous smile I had on my face.

Julia was now busy, as she was catching up with Maria and she had lots of familiar faces come to say hi to her too.

"Happy birthday mum." Each of them said.

Of course, they were her kids, she could recognize them all. Apart from the fact that they sent her pictures of them on important days of their accomplishments to her and maintained a good relationship with her (as they were free to do that once they were 18), she knew each of them for sure. There was Joseph, Sandra, John, Amira, Kira, Rhonda, and Baron among others. They filled the room and she remembered each of them for sure. She was all smiles as they came around her and gave her warm hugs. She could not believe her eyes. It was like living a dream. There were so many gifts, such that a heap was formed with the gifts. Julia kept covering her mouth, as many the gifts and the people almost made her scream. It was just too much. I was particularly happy that we had successfully made it a case of if Mohammed will not go to the mountain, then the mountain will come to meet Mohammed. At least Julia would experience the love tonight, especially with everything planned out. We really wanted to make it a memory that she would hold dearly in her heart for a long, long time.

After hugging them, her eyes caught mine, still staring at her and taking in the beautiful view of the joy she was feeling in the moment. I was just talking to Harry about how happy I was about how everything had come together. By now, Julia was closing in on us. By the time she was closer, she said, "That must be the famous Harry."

"Nice to meet my wife's boss." Harry said when she was finally with us.

"Ohh, come off it Harry. Your wife has been a solid partner, but right now, I just need her to explain to me how all this came about. I mean, we spend a lot of time together, yet I did not get a clue."

"May I re-introduce you to the queen of surprises?" He said, before we all burst out into laughter.

"Of course. Talk about queens that deserve their crowns."

"There's really not much to say. Please just enjoy tonight. It is your night. The stories can wait for later." I said. Luckily, Joseph came to whisk Julia away, as he led her to Sandra to introduce her to their kids—Erica and Leo. I was happy. That was exactly what she was supposed to be doing; seeing the actual fruits of her labor and not worrying yet again about how this or that came about. She and Maria walked around together to greet her guests. They seemed like young women as they walked together. It was Julia's 40th birthday and Maria had clocked forty earlier in the year. They kept talking as Maria stayed with her all through, acting somewhat like a bridesmaid, while Julia enjoyed her party and was busy with greeting guests. Maria was just trying to ensure that the celebrant lacked absolutely nothing she wanted.

Honestly, planning and bringing everyone to Liberia at the beginning of summer was not easy at all. There were lots of calls, and a lot of stress involved. It was expected. I had a lot of ideas in mind and when it came to planning, my go-getter spirit would not stop till I have achieved the picture in my head. And you can trust that I really achieved that picture. When the planning began, people had made summer plans and now had to move it to mid-summer because of the surprise I was planning. You know, from the beginning of the year, many families plan and start working on their summer budgets, as I had learnt. However, everyone involved was actually very happy to make those adjustments because to be honest, Julia deserved that and even more. They knew this and we all worked in oneness. I can say for a fact that every single one of us (and not just me) in that hall had made a day like that possible. We were about seventy and everything we achieved was the product of collective efforts. I had to check the register for the orphanage, trace contacts and reach out to people, who in turn helped me reach out to other people.

There were chains and chains of communications established. There was also a brief meet up in the United Kingdom. I spearheaded everything from A-Z because trust me, these guys are busy all over the world making big moves. I had no cause to complain. I was enjoying the process of putting everything together and even getting inspired by the fact that I was meeting so many people who Julia's journey had helped to establish in various industries and various countries of the world.

They were warm and excited to hear all the plans I had for her birthday. They expressed their displeasure about how they tried to give back to her personally, but she was never excited about such things. Many of them had been looking for other ways to appreciate her and were now happy that someone had come up with such a plan. I had explained to them that working with her made me realize that what actually gave her utmost joy was seeing all of them doing so well in everything they did. So, having all of them (as many as could come), in the same building as her and seeing who they had grown to become and perhaps, their offspring, would make her happy. I was certain about this, especially from times when she sat down and randomly talked about the things she had achieved. It was not hard to figure out what was actually important to Julia.

Because of work and schooling, we had to move it all to summer when everyone would be available. Luckily, her birthday was in early summer. Hence, what was supposed to be a day of appreciation turned into the idea of a surprise 40th birthday party. Huge donations were made towards the cause without a fuss. I was on the entire process for about six months and I enjoyed it because of the reactions of the people from the orphanage I was contacting. Imagine being so stressed about planning and getting on phone with someone to hear them being genuinely excited about the fact that you were associated with The Safe Place. I mean, I made real friends with great values along the way. I could foresee an amazing future for all of us.

Of course, my sister, Amira and her boyfriend, Joseph were very helpful too, especially at the point where I had to be in contact with lots of people. They knew many of these people, so their presence made my work easier. Thankfully, Amira was on leave from work at that point. So, she was in the United Kingdom with Joseph who had also come to see his family. Hence, we could all meet up in London and they were with me to help for quite a while. I enjoyed myself with them and could tell that they were having an amazing and mature relationship. I got to know Joseph even better too. By now, he came to the house more frequently and we all loved him, especially his sense of humor. He was a great match for Amira and once again, that brought me back to being grateful for the gift of Julia.

Julia was still busy meeting and catching up with "her children". Maria was also there and I could see it in her eyes that she was amazed at all her friend had achieved. She had so many children now. It expanded her view on the subject of marriage and purpose, as she had said before realizing. Harry and I spent a moment with her and she told us how a part of her was still skeptical about Julia's decision not to have a family over the years, but now, she understood that what Julia had was far more than just any small family. There was laughter, smiles and happiness visible all over the room. It was not hard to see at all. When she finally realized that we were in such a big hall that was definitely not far from the orphanage, she came along with Erica, who had fallen in love with Julia and was now tagging along with her everywhere she went. She had questions for me once again. Let me explain. I had brought Julia to the hall in a tinted car, saying my parents were coming for an event one of the politicians in Liberia was having and they would love to see her. I picked out an expensive dress which I had bought from London for her. It was a sequin dress and it made her stand out. I had explained that many politicians were coming to the event and she had to measure up to the way they dressed, if she wanted them to see her as someone was indeed fit to be in their circle. And of course, she knew that being in their circle would benefit the orphanage a lot. She was relaxed and unsuspecting until I brought her into the hall.

So, now, it made sense for her to ask, "Where is this place?" Since, no politician was having a party; this hall that was not so far from the orphanage was whose? It was a short drive from the orphanage and it must have dawned on her that there was no such big hall in this community before. The building itself was really big too and seemed to have other smaller buildings behind and a lot of space in the compound. The space was in fact enough for a field. These were Julia's concerns and as she expressed them to me, I knew the time had come for the big reveal.

"Harry, shall we?" I said, as I gave Harry a knowing smile and instead of answering Julia, the both of us began to clink our glasses. As we did, everyone started coming together. Of course, they knew what was going on, but the celebrant was surprised.

"Maria, what are they up to?" she asked. Maria only smiled. Telling her friend the surprise we had for her was not part of her job description for the night.

John and Amira went upstage to unveil a board that had been covered. As they unveiled it, it revealed the writings, "WELCOME TO THE DEDICATION OF THE SAFE PLACE EXTENSION." Everyone had encircled Julia such that she was in the middle and now facing the stage. She was speechless and just kept sighing the whole time.

"This is too much!" she managed to utter.

"You deserve it and even more." said one of the ladies in the crowd.

Julia was overjoyed. "Thank you! Thank you so much." She kept saying.

"No! This is a token from the kids you helped and raised, to thank you for all your acts. We really hope that this makes you happy, because that is the goal." I said. Everyone cheered in agreement. Then, we sang the famous song, *For she's a jolly good fellow…*"

The buildings in the extension were quite big and spacious. I had seen how Julia complained about wanting to house kids that now came all over Liberia once they heard that there was somewhere they would receive good care in Bomi county. The extension building was only five minutes away from the orphanage and it was built to perfection. The hall was supposed to be a dining and multipurpose hall for the kids and it was a 2000 people capacity hall. There were also housing and classroom facilities on those grounds. We wanted to build a facility that would put an end to all her complains, and that we did.

Immediately we cut the cake, the party continued, but Julia could not stay in anymore. She wanted to inspect the rest of the building. And so she did. It only started as a thought that popped up in my head and the orphanage kids from all over the world helped to achieve the beauty that we built in only six months. Every building on the ground was built and equipped as state-of-the-art facilities. The only gift we were sure that Juliet would take from us had to be perfect.

"Oh my!" Julia said, as she entered each of the building.

"Thank you." She kept saying, and we were sure to keep reminding her that it was only the fruit of her labor. Each time she entered a building on the premises, she did a happy dance. It was fun to watch her. I was finally happy that we could come up with something that truly made her happy. Our efforts had not been in vain. And while at it, we were still making a lot of impact.

Back in the hall, people had a lot of catching up to do and so they did. It was fun to watch people scream as they saw the grown-up versions of each other. I was just sipping my glass of champagne in a corner with the love of my life, as I watched all our plans unfold into the great event we were having. I was experiencing true happiness and I knew I was living in purpose. There were also a lot of children in the hall. Many of the people in attendance had used to the opportunity to come show their roots to their kids and spouses. Happiness was written all over the room. There was also enough to eat and drink. It was a full-course and long-overdue celebration and I was glad that we were able to do it in a way that Julia loved.

When John saw that Julia had gotten back into the building, he signaled to Harry and I. We knew it was time and once again, we started clinking our glasses. This time, others wondered why. They had absolutely no idea about the next surprise. And it was specifically for one person this time. Well, the other one had been for one person too, but now, this one was for a different person.

Harry got his phone out ready to record, as people gathered round. The spotlight then came on Amira, and she turned around wondering what was going on, only to see John down on one knee.

"Amira, I decided it was best to do this here, where we first met. Being with you has been nothing short of amazing. Please, be my wife." He said.

By now, the initially shocked Amira was now smiling.

"You are still yet to ask the question and please open the ring box." She laughed.

Laughter rang across the room and John could not help but laugh too.

"Amira, would you be my wife?"

"Yes." She said, as she brought him up to his feet and he slipped the beautiful ring into her finger.

Finally, my sister was engaged to the man of her dreams. What a happy night!

The surprise party we organized for Julia also doubled as a reunion for the kids from the orphanage. It was a happy time and new connections were forged. In fact, those in attendance were able to network with those within their industries and outside their industries. Following our meeting, business connections were made too. I was not just happy to see this, but I also became one of those that benefitted from the meeting. I met Rhonda and it changed everything. Rhonda was calm, kind and had a beautiful heart that radiated outwards. She was definitely the kind of person I would make friends with.

Her story was quite an interesting one. She narrated that which she was about to be taken to the United States, her motivation was the fact that one of those that came had encouraged her about being able to start up something like what Miss. Julia had started up. Hence, it was her motivation to leave the orphanage, as the promise was that of a better future that would help her give a better future to kids when she eventually had her orphanage. She wanted to grow up to provide shelter, food, education and hope to kids that had no one to take care of them. Along the line, she got busy with life, her career and raising a family. However, connecting back to her roots during Julia's birthday/reunion made her remember what her initial motivation. She had returned to the orphanage and remembered how every story played out. She and Sandra had talked and talked about their childhood and everything that had led them up to where they were. The reunion rekindled lots of memories and she was not the same when it was all over. She knew the time was right and there was no room for procrastination anymore. Because of her dreams, her work was in line with fighting for less privileged kids, but she had been procrastinating on actually starting up an orphanage.

She had lost her parents at a tender age, as I remember from the records of the orphanage. Rhonda valued owning an orphanage for this reason. It meant a lot to her to still be able to have a future in spite of the fact that her parents died so early on. She wanted to start up an orphanage in Kenya, as her husband had been relocated to the area for work. He was going to be an expatriate and she finally saw that this would be a perfect opportunity for her dream to materialize, as she always wanted the orphanage she started to be in Africa, where a lot of kids actually suffered, asides the fact that she was from an African country herself.

"Olivia, I have heard of all your good works and I see how passionate you are about orphanages too. I want to start up an orphanage and I would like for you to be my partner." She said.

Well, I had never thought it was time for me to own an orphanage. She wanted the both of us to partner and startup an orphanage. That meant being highly committed to that orphanage. I wanted my influence to be felt all over the world and not just in one place. Being tied to a spot was just too much for me at the time. However, Rhonda had sounded really sincere. Hence, I decided that only the terms of the commitment had to be reviewed. I knew I could not be available all the time, but I could be a huge partner. Many orphanages all over Africa were benefitting from my work and if I decided to be tied to just one, others would definitely suffer. So, I needed to negotiate my terms of commitment. I also knew that Harry and I would soon start having kids, so I may not be able to travel as much. It turned out that Rhonda just needed a partner that could fire her up when her zeal was not there. She saw my level of commitment to working with orphanages and she saw me as a perfect fit. That was no problem for me, so I jumped on the ship. I only needed to plant the seed with her. She would see to its growth and I only need to bring ideas to the table and fire her up when necessary. That was what she needed from me and it was not a problem.

I was in Kenya for about a month and this time, Harry came with me. We also used the opportunity to tour Kenya for a bit. We purchased a building and we set the ball rolling. Slowly, we built the dream. We targeted areas of Kenya where our work was actually important and that even informed where we bought the orphanage's building. We visited the poor communities and announced that we were there to give all the help we could render to children who were alone or were suffering abuse of any kind. To our surprise, children started coming to the gate of the orphanage to seek help the following day.

Apparently, the kids in that area had been suffering a lot. Rhonda was just as invested in the work as I was and I was glad that I chose to work with her. She was a child right activist and consulted for organizations all over the world, so it was really her field. We felt fulfilled each time a child came to the orphanage. Hence, we started putting structure to things. We had to draw up plans and routines for the kids and having grown up in an orphanage, Rhonda knew the routines that worked. Our work was fun; we found helping people fun.

There were very horrible days even in that first month too. Days when we witnessed orphan girls that had been abused getting raped and then coming to us. Those sights gave us sore eyes. We just wondered why anyone would want to hurt a kid so much. We wondered which animal looks at a kid in a sexual way. Those were heartbreaking moments, but we were still thankful that we could be of help in our own way.

We stocked the orphanage with clothes, food and everything kids would need. I also had some of my childhood friends who were excited about the idea of me actually being one of the partners of a new orphanage. So, they came to visit with a lot of goodies. The kids were really happy and from the look of things, we could see that the adoption rates from the orphanage would be quite high. Some of my rich friends were now looking to adopt. Hence, we had to start working out the whole adoption process earlier than we imagined we would. I was just excited that we were making a huge difference in the world; what I had always wanted to do.

Harry who was on leave also joined us in strategizing for the orphanage. I married the absolute best man. Words fail me when I try to describe him. He may not be everyone's cup of tea, but he is definitely perfect (perhaps tailor-made) for me and I could not be thankful enough for the gift of him. While we looked after the kids together, we realized for sure that it was time for us to make our own babies.

CHAPTER
FOURTEEN

The reunion birthed so much for the orphanage that Julia had not even envisaged. Coming together that way had rekindled a lot of memories and reminded most of the "alumnus" of their roots. They had stayed back for a few days, so there was enough time to run into each other at various spots, catch up and tell stories. There were also opportunities to plan strategic meetups to catch up. Hence, it was not surprising that many great ideas were coming up and being agreed upon.

There were ideas for improvement all over the place. The kids had gone through the orphanage and gone to other parts of the world. Hence, they had begun to see how things were done over there and ways in which the kids in the orphanage could be helped to become better in everything. The old orphanage premises was renovated yet again. We wanted the kids to have water heaters in their bathrooms and air conditioning in every room. It was like having grown up kids who wanted their younger ones to enjoy better than they did when they were kids and it was very beautiful to watch.

In the weeks when the renovations were done, we ensured that Julia did not lift a finger. We got her a standby chef, a nurse and a driver. We just wanted to make sure that she was very comfortable.

We wanted the kids in the orphanage to lack nothing and even enjoy more things compared to the kids in the community that were living with their parents. Following that reunion, the plan was the make the orphanage and the kids there experience world-class standards, such that even if they did not get a chance to be adopted or taken to a more developed country, they would still lack nothing both in terms of informal and formal education.

Different people took on different projects for the orphanage. While a group of two or three of the orphanage's "alumnus" took it upon themselves to get someone that would train the kids in terms of etiquette, another group took it upon themselves to get a taekwondo instructor for the kids. In the next few weeks, it made a huge difference as the kids were not only excited, but also took advantage of the opportunity to become better at those things.

When we saw the progress being made, more people were encouraged to do more. We employed a music instructor from London and an orchestra was formed. The kids learnt out to play instruments in the most standard ways and even had several performances among themselves. They now had a variety night where several of them could come to perform and because of the values of the orphanage which were being continually instilled in them, the kids did not take these opportunities for granted. They kept signing up.

Thanks to the extension, the number of kids in the orphanage continued to increase. Taking them to high school outside the orphanage became quite a huge task. It cost a lot and the process became a bit strenuous. Depending on the time the kids were enrolled, they were in various high schools in Bomi County. Hence, transportation was a huge task too. Keeping track of each kids after school also became a burden. Additionally, one of the alumnus made a point that the standard of education the kids were getting was not as great as that which the kids in developed countries were getting. We decided to look into this quickly.

We realized that we could actually convert one of the buildings on the new premises to a high school. This way, we could employ staff that suited our taste and even send them on trainings to ensure that the kids were getting world class learning opportunities.

Julia was truly happy when the conversion of the building to a high school began. We were all also happy because we had finally found what made her happy after many years. It gave me so much pleasure that I could champion to the cause.

It hit me hard that I was doing something right when Julia randomly turned to me one day and said, "You are a blessing to me. Olivia, you are a blessing to these kids." I hold Julia in high esteem, so I felt on top of the world to have her say that. My one month in Kenya was over at about the time the renovations began. So, I moved to Liberia to oversee things.

I could relate to Julia when she said she was not one to carry kids when she was younger. I used to be like that too, but the kids in the orphanage were changing me. It was hard to watch kids grow and not just fall in love with them and the entire process of their growth.

My dear reader, I guess you have probably watched someone who you really love and wish the best for grow in a while; the process is beautiful, isn't it? To look at someone who knew at a particular level rise far above that level. Well, that is how it felt watching the kids develop in every area of their lives and this is why I wanted to carry them each time I saw them. Children are so innocent. They know absolutely nothing about the evils of the world. Ever looked into the eyes of a child? Trust me, it is calming; probably one of the most calming things on the planet. I loved my work and I loved how much impact I was making. I must have mentioned this before. Oh! I just can't stop talking about how much I love what I do.

The high school process moved quite quickly and with the level of expertise our potential employees had at hand, it was easier to get an approval from the government. We wanted to make the kids in the orphanage the envy of all the kids in the county. Of course, not just for the fun of it. The kids needed to feel loved. We wanted to provide everything that would portray parental love for them.

This is why the idea of constructing a swimming pool came up. Children from all over the world knew how to swim from an early age. We decided that the kids in The Safe Place deserved that too. We started with letting the kids watch swimming competitions. We used that to develop their interest in swimming as we wondered how open they would be to learning how to swim. We infused watching various sports into their routines every Saturday and we ensured swimming was on the top of our list. They also watched soccer, rugby, basketball and baseball competitions. Julia had started off with an excellent standard and we just wanted to ensure that the direction was upward and forwards from then on.

When the kids started looking forward to watching swimming competitions, then we knew it was time to actually construct a pool. The pool construction started in no time and the kids were excited to see it. When it was ready, they enjoyed swimming on Saturdays. As kids, they just wanted to reproduce what they had seen happen on the screens. They had instructors and the kids were also educated on safety rules too. The pool yard had to be on the new premises, as a lot of space was needed for it. It had to be fenced for the safety of the kids.

I was surprised when I saw the kids from the community, trying to peep by standing on tanks close to the fence just to see our kids swim. It was hilarious, but I was more concerned about their safety and the fact that it looked like a luxury to them. Sometimes, I wish I could help every child in developing countries. They looked very amazed to see the kids in the orphanage swim. Our kids were picking up with their swimming quite quickly. Since they were quite a number, we tried to ensure that kids below the age of five did not swim. Kids between the ages of five and seven picked up swimming skills very fast and it was beautiful to watch. However, I could not still wrap my heads around seeing other kids of their age (outside the orphanage), calling their counterparts to come and watch. They even put themselves in danger to see the sight. It was very sad to see them like that. I really wished I could build a swimming pool for the community, but Julia had warned earlier on that if I do not place my focus on what I wanted to achieve in particular, I would end up achieving nothing. In that part of the world, there were really so many people to help. So, if I had focused on orphanages, then my focus should not shift.

Computer literacy was also something the orphanage might have neglected for a while. The kids in high school of course knew how to use computers because of school, but we thought that having every single kid learn from a very young age would be a lot better. There was a lot to do on that level. Importing computers for each kid sounded like a good idea, but we figured that it could also be a distraction. Hence, we decided to have them tutored on computer lessons too. Many of them could grow up to be tech giants, but it would only start if they had a basic love for computer at an early age. They can't love what they do not know.

To this effect, two hours every week, the kids started to learn about computers and how they worked. Some of them seemed intimated at first. You know that feeling of seeing someone driving a car when you have no idea what a brake is; that was the feel they depicted from the look in their eyes. The kids apparently felt like the computer was too complex for them to operate at first. In a first world country, operating a computer was like operating a light bulb. I realized that more than operating a computer or swimming, the mindset of the kids had to be worked on. Well, introducing these basic things seen as luxury for kids in third world countries to them at a young age was sure to definitely work on their minds and make them gradually think like their counterparts in developed countries.

Having a mindset that a thing is not for you because of your environment is quite common. As I moved through life, I began to notice this among humans. However, changing your environment would open one's head to possibilities. Then, it dawned on me that we were doing that; ensuring they had world class musical instruments, a great swimming facility and opportunities for computer literacy was changing the environment of the kids and how they had subconsciously been conditioned to think.

The "That is not for me" mindset does a lot of harm to humans than they ever even realize. Once you think it is not for you, it would never be for you. The concept is really that simple.

Gradually, the kids began to operate computers and operating computers became no big deal. Looking at this progress and every of the kind from time to time constantly reminded me that anything is achievable. I was sure that mindset was gradually being built into their minds too. Even if they got adopted, now I was confident that they would be almost at par with their counterparts in every part of the world. The process was no magic; it was gradual and some kids were picking faster than others. No matter how I chose to think of it, it was still progress.

The reunion changed many other things. It changed people too. One person who was really changed was Maria. She had never grasped the concept of the orphanage until now when she had seen the fruit of her friend's work. She felt like she had to partner with the orphanage in some way; a way that would help keep her friend and the impact she had made in the world close to her own heart.

"I am proud of you." She had said to Julia the next morning, while the three of us were having tea on Julia's kitchen table.

"C'mon…"

"No. For real. Julia, you have done a great job and you should be proud."

"Well, remember this idea came up because you invited me on that volunteers' trip. I definitely have you to thank."

"No! Remember I discouraged you too. It was your brave heart that made you stay. And the kindness in your heart also made you achieve the greatness we now see."

Julia was lost for words. She simply smiled as she took yet another cup of tea.

"Cheers to Julia." I cut in. The women looked at me with surprise as we clinked our tea cups together. It was weird, but I just wanted to make things less awkward, given the conversation they were having. They looked at me with surprise because they had actually forgotten I was there. I knew this too, but I had not a worry. You know how old friends can be with each other; well, I know.

Later that afternoon, a child in the orphanage, Juliet had a crisis. She was a sickle cell disease patient and she had crisis quite frequently. Juliet had been in the orphanage for about a year. She was abandoned at the gate of the orphanage by her stepmother, after her father died. She was just five years old at the time. Surprisingly, prior to this child, Juliet, the orphanage had never housed a sickle cell disease patient. In the past one year, the orphanage had ensured she had the best living conditions and had also given her the best possible medical treatment in the County. It cost the orphanage a lot of money, but Julia did not mind. She had a philosophy she still carried around; that the life of every child there was under her care and their bright future could be jeopardized if she did not take care of each of them properly. For this reason, the bills were never too much for Julia's health.

When Julia initially came into the orphanage, there were marks that showed her child had been constantly physically abused all over her body. She was old enough to narrate how her stepmother beat her whenever she hawked and did not make the target amount. Well, she hawked fruits for her stepmother. The beatings triggered her crisis sometimes and her stepmother would feed her herbs. Her dad had been sick all the while, and her stepmother usually complained about how she could not cater for both a sick father and daughter.

When her crisis became very regular and she could no longer hawk, her stepmother decided that it was time to get rid of her. The best plan she could come up with was abandoning her in front of the orphanage. She had tricked the girl saying she wanted to purchase something nearby and would be back in a bit. Juliet waited and waited. It was the rain started that the security guard noticed her and gave her a place to sit. Her stepmother did not show up again. Julia came around and once the girl narrated her story, she understood what had happened. Julia talked about being sick frequently, hence a special attention was paid to her routine tests (a series of tests usually ran on all the kids in the orphanage at the point where they got accepted into the orphanage). They ran the tests and it was discovered that she had sickle cell anemia.

From then and onwards, special attention was paid to Juliet. At this point again, her crisis was back and she had to be rushed to the hospital for medical care. We figured that it was as a result of the increase in her normal activity level. She had developed at interest from swimming and the instructor allowed her to practice more frequently, because she pleaded to be allowed.

We knew she would be admitted for days, but Julia was really tired. She did not say so, but she was not hard to read. So, Maria and I figured it out. Additionally, it was a no-brainer. She was the celebrant, just the previous day. She was bound to be stressed.

"I would stay with her." Said Maria. It was a welcome idea, as I had other things to see to, being the chief planner of the birthday and reunion.

Julia tried to interrupt, but I reminded her that she really needed to rest. Luckily for me, she agreed easily. I think she trusted Maria, especially for the fact that she was also a mother. Of course, Maria's motherly instincts now took over and was all over the place in the next few days following Juliet's admission. Then, I started noticing an attachment she was beginning to have with the girl. She was around for the next one week and she had Juliet sleep in her room when she was back from the hospital, three days after her admission. I sensed something special, but I tried not to jump into conclusions until Maria said she wanted to adopt the girl the night before leaving. She had two grown up boys (twins), who had just gone to college. She always wanted a girl child and she had fallen in love with Juliet. She mentioned that adopting a child from the orphanage would help keep her best friend close to her heart. She promised to be back to pick Juliet in the next month. So, there was about one month to do all the necessary paperwork. It sounded crazy that she wanted a child with sickle cell and not any other child, but that was what she wanted.

"There are better facilities to take care of her condition in the state. It is not a problem." She had said. Apparently, she had a friend with a daughter that had the ailment. Although, caring for the child was quite some work, she saw how it was the love for the child that really mattered.

"Trust me, I am ready to care for the girl." She had said. And of course, she was back the next month to be Juliet's new mum. Juliet also loved her, so it was a win for everyone.

"Mum, that's Miss. Kira on that advert."

"Yes, my darling. She is picking you up this weekend, isn't she?"

"Yes, she is mummy. I cannot wait to see what it is like to work as a model."

"Kira lives a busy life. You should be happy she has a shoot in our city."

"She promised to always create time for me." Said Erica.

"Of course, she did." Her mother giggled.

Another amazing relationship that had blossomed from the reunion was the love that Kira and Erica had for each other. She had been glad to meet Sandra and Joseph's highly outspoken daughter and she loved her guts!

Kira loved outspoken black women and the fact that Erica was so young thrilled her even more. Climbing to the top of her career was no child's play. She had to speak and ensure she was not just seen but also heard. That formed an important part of her story. Hence, she loved it when young black girls were encouraged to speak.

"Are those not Louboutin shoes?" Erica had asked at the party.

She caught Kira's attention, so Kira bent down to meet halfway with the little girl that seemed to know so much. She knew the child must be really sharp to not only know those, but also say it to a total stranger with confidence. She saw great social skills brewing.

"What's your name?" she asked. "And you look like someone I know. I can't just place the face." Kira raised her head, looking around and trying to figure out whose daughter the girl was.

"My name is Erica."

It was then her mother came. "Oh, I have been looking for her all over the place." Sandra said.

"Oh, she's your daughter. Sandra, she's a bright one." Kira said as she stood up.

"Oh, I know this lady from the television." She said.

"Oh, is that so? Do you watch modeling shows?"

"All the time." Her mother quickly cut in. "We have even enrolled her at an academy. She just goes on some weekends, because of school and other activities."

"Oh, that is interesting." Kira said.

"You are quite popular ma'am. I would like to be on billboards too when I'm all grown."

"That's interesting. I love your daughter already." She said, turning to Sandra.

"You can just take her with you." Sandra laughed.

"I am coming to the states and to your city for a shoot."

"I'd like to watch you ma'am."

"Exactly why I want to take you away." Said Kira.

"You can come by and pick her up." Sandra said.

That Saturday, Kira came to pick Erica for a real life experience of the life of a model."

Erica was excited. They first went for ice cream before they were on their way to the shoot. Kira took no ice cream, telling Erica that what worked for her was not having anything before shoots. Every model needed to know what worked for them.

They went to the studio and Erica only fell more in love as she watched Kira stand out from the other models, because of her skin color. She watched them doll up all the models and how they were professional and did not say anything throughout their makeup session. They had learnt to perfectly pose the exact way their respective makeup artiste needed them to, for perfection to be achieved. Erica stayed quiet in a corner and was just taking in the view.

She watched the photo session and how it took hours to get the results they wanted. She was surprised that it took serious work. She had thought one only needed to be beautiful and pose randomly in front of a camera. Her experience that day made her realize that modeling actually required skill. At the academy, they had only done a few lessons on fashion and were yet to start the classes on modeling, so she had no idea what real modeling actually entailed till that day.

As Kira drove them home, she looked at her and said, "Miss Kira, you must be really tired."

"No baby. I am used to this. It is my work. It is as good as saying you are tired of schooling, yet you want to remain a student."

"Wow! Modeling is real work" said Erica. However, she still loved modeling to the core.

"Has your mind changed?"

"No. I still want to model."

"Oh, that is great. Then, you always have me to call anytime you want to find out about anything."

"Thank you Aunty." Erica hugged her, as Kira walked her to the front door of her house.

Sandra and Joseph asked Kira to stay for dinner and all night, they talked about how they had an entire community based on the ugly circumstances that had brought them to the orphanage. They were just grateful that they had each other and Kira was even playing a great role in the life of their child.

"I had fun today." Erica said at dinner. "…but modeling is no child's play."

"I bet you learnt a lot from your aunty Kira."

"Yes, I did dad."

"Thank you so much Kira." Said Sandra.

"You are family. There's nothing to thank me for."

It was all bliss between Kira and Erica from then and moving forward.

By the time he saw his sister take her modeling academy more seriously, Leo began to remember seeing a popular footballer at the reunion in Liberia.

"Dad, was Uncle John your friend back at the orphanage."

Joseph laughed. He remembered the kind of relationship he had with John when they were kids and he had even more cause to laugh. John had truly found his way back to him in the following year, just like he had promised. Sandra and Joseph were initially in the United Kingdom, with the organization that had taken them out of Liberia, until after college when they decided to get married before going to school in the United States.

Sandra started having kids shortly and they both combined raising a family together with schooling. The crux of the matter is the fact that John had also found his way to the United Kingdom the following year by playing soccer exceptionally well. He had asked for Joseph's contact before leaving Liberia and once he landed in the UK, he called Joseph to tell him that he had achieved exactly what he said he would. Joseph usually remembered that night when he was told that he had a call by the governess who they had put in charge of him, Sandra and some other kids. By the time he held the phone in his hand, he realized that it was John…their troublesome John.

"Yes, he was my good friend." He turned and said to Leo with a smile.

"What are you not telling me dad?"

"Well, you already know he's a great footballer."

"Okay, can you please help talk to him about the whole basketball thing? I think I might be ready."

"Oh, that is good news."

"I guess."

The next day, his dad put him on a long call with John who had enough time on his hands for the week.

"Do you love the sport?" asked John.

"Yes, I love it. I watch it all the time. To be honest, I am just too intimidated to start. I keep thinking I would never be as good as all those high flyers I watch play."

"No, son. You cannot afford to think like that. That kind of thinking would get you nowhere. Let me tell you a short story: Your father was my favorite pal at the orphanage and the fact that I would probably never see him again made me give my best to football. You see, your dad was a goal-getter. He did not have good grades at first, but with the help of your mum, he did not stop practicing arithmetic or studying till he got to the top. Now, I am telling you this because I know you have that spirit of theirs in you. I have heard of your grades too and I know that you are a high flyer. Now, I want you to bring that energy you use to work for your grades into basketball. Look at scoring like an important grade you need to make. You are your own competition. Leo, when it comes to sports, there are no full stops. There are no limits. You just need to keep competing with yourself each day. The fact that you did well the previous day does not mean you would have the luxury of slacking the next day. You have that spirit in you; the one that never stops competing. Your father has told me this about you and that is why you would do well in sports. Kids that are not half as smart or determined as you are doing well at basketball, so why not you?"

"But they practice a lot."

"Then practice a lot too."

"But they're tall."

"You may think I do not know you, but trust me, your parents share pictures with me all the time and I can see you are far taller than you were last year. Leo, I think you are ready for the court. Don't chicken out. It is time for you to get started. You would still have to start someday, but if you say that day is not today, then you would have made some time go to waste."

"I do not want to waste time."

"Then, start."

The next day, John was around to take Leo to the field for his first play. John was a footballer, but he played basketball as a hobby. So, he knew a lot about the sport too. While they played, Joseph was outside the court, cheering them on. Leo was totally enjoying his first time in the court, thanks to John who made it all easy for him to understand, every step of the way. John and Leo were creating a strong bond.

If there was one thing I could pick from the acts of Kira and John towards Erica and Leo respectively, it was the fact that they were selfless. This act of selflessness reflected in the lives of everyone who passed through The Safe Place orphanage. The only explanation I could come up with was that people are a reflection of whatever they have received from life and the way they had received it. Those who received favors without much stress were generally more generous, as that was the way of life they understood.

On the other hand, those who had experienced a rough life and never got favors from anyone or hardly got anything easily had a tougher approach to life. I found them to be generally not as kind to others and also very hard on themselves and others.

The kids Julia had raised, who were now adults, had a very kind outlook towards life. They fell in the first category and had received so much kindness for being in that orphanage at that time of their lives that they were so used to being kind to others. They had received kindness that they did nothing to earn and they could never repay, so why not?

CHAPTER
FIFTEEN

If someone had told me there was a special reason for us being in Kenya, apart from housing kids that simply needed help, I would have laughed. I had worked with orphanages in Nigeria, Gambia, Ghana and many other countries in Africa, helping them raise funds, looking into their structure and management (based on the experience and expertise I had been gathering) and that was it for me. It was the kind of work that made me fulfilled. The joy in my heart each time I did an act of service for these orphanages was literally unexplainable.

Establishing an orphanage in Kenya was for me was just like building something that was now for me while doing the kind of good work I had been doing all along anyway. There was supposedly nothing new to me about working in the orphanage setting. I had seen it all and it was no different from everything I had been doing all along. Well, in my eyes.

One evening while in Kenya and more precisely, in a meeting with Rhonda on developing our structure properly and obtaining all the necessary documents from the government, someone began to hit the gate of the orphanage very hard. With the intensity, we knew it was definitely not a child doing this. It was a little scary, but from the look of things, it seemed the person was in some trouble. We wondered what was going on, but we thought the security guard will sort it out. So, we continued our meeting, but the hittling of the gate would not stop.

She spoke in her native language (Swahili), so we could not really understand what she was saying. She went on and on, but instead of answering her immediately, the security guard came to alert Rhonda and I before attempting to open the gate since it looked like a matter that needed some application of caution. I could understand his fear.

"Peep through the small hole before opening the gate" I said.

"I have done that. She has one child on her back and she was holding another. However, some parts of her clothes look burnt." He said.

"Oh, is that so? You said she had children with her, right?"

"Yes." He replied Rhonda.

"Then, let them in quickly." She said.

By the time the woman came in, although she could not communicate with us in English, but what she was describing seemed like a fire situation and we got an idea what she was saying thanks to her burnt clothes and the kids who were crying. We quickly gave the kids who were toddlers to a member of the staff as we followed the woman who was beckoning on us to come with her. She was pointing at the bus we had gotten, but had no cause to use so far. It was obvious that she wanted us to use the bus to wherever she was leading us to. Hence, we had our driver drive us all in the bus down to the next community, taking turns as she described. It was late in the evening and the woman was in a lot of distress. She could not stop sobbing, so we could see that the situation must have been really serious. I tried to hold her hands and calm her down, but she started weeping even more and kept trying to explain a situation we could not understand. We could not understand because this woman could not speak in English. However, we kept following her directions. It was really the best we could do at the time. She would not take some juice or drink some water. She was wailing uncontrollably and only tried to keep herself in check so she could direct us accordingly. All along, we did not even think to get a translator, especially with the level of urgency the situation seemed to have.

On getting to the spot to which she was leading us, we realized what was happening—a house was on fire! There were so many children and some adults in front of the house wailing. The fire service was there, but so much damage had been done. We wondered why there were lots of kids in front of the building; toddlers, young children and teenagers alike. It took a minute to figure out that the big building was an orphanage. It was a three-storey building. It took some extra time for us to also notice that there was fire coming from a smaller building behind. However, we could hear from the conversations that the people around us were having that three buildings were behind and were all burning to ashes. We could also hear them say that some kids who were sleeping when the fire started had been hurt and were rushed to the hospital. However, no life was lost. That was the part that really made us heave a sigh of relief. The staff had done a good job when the fire started, ensuring that they woke as many kids as they could and rushed them out of the building. It was a matter of life and death. None of the staff took the situation for granted, as they were so used to the kids. It was expected. When you work in an orphanage, you grow to love the kids as your own.

However, it was still crazy to watch kids that had already been through a lot in life (knowing that many of the kids in orphanages have actually lost their family) go through even more hurt. It was very sad to see where you live burn to ashes for even adults, how much more children. I could not help but wonder how the owner of the orphanage was feeling. Apparently, there was some fault with the electrical work in the house and it had sparked a fire which kept spreading till it affected all the buildings, which were quite close to each other. Also, the electrical wiring for the buildings were similar, so the trouble kicked off quite easily.

It was hard to watch this and as much as we wanted to rescue the kids from the site in front of them quickly, by taking them into our bus, we knew that protocol had to be observed and respected. The woman who had brought us was now talking to another woman who looked well-off. She had been talking to the woman since we got there. We wondered what she was telling her, but all we could do was wait and see how it all played out. Now we were sure that the woman who had come to us wanted us to take the kids in our bus, to our orphanage, but we had to be careful and be sure it was authorized. It did not work like that with kids. The person in charge needed to give us permission and sign some documents at our orphanage too. So, we waited for the go-ahead from the appropriate authorities.

In about fifteen minutes, the woman who seemed well-off walked up to us.

"Hello." She said, waving to us. The first thing I noticed was that she was very beautiful and seemed to have been crying for quite a while. Her eyes were red and swollen.

"My name is Akello and this is my orphanage." Tears dropped from her eyes as she continued to speak. I was dumbfounded and I was not ready for the tears that came from my own eyes. I had worked with orphanages and I knew the efforts it required to own and run one. Hence, I could understand her pain. Rhonda quickly held her hands, before hugging her tight. Apparently, the woman that came to call us was a cook that worked in the orphanage. The cook had moved from our community to the one where Akello's orphanage was situated just recently and had been working with them. She knew of our own orphanage and when it started out. Once the fire had started, she had told Akello about the new orphanage where she had come from and how they could beg us to keep the kids safe till they could get on track again. She had given the cook, Almasi, the go-ahead to ask us for help from wherever she deemed fit, as she had been confused herself. The kids Almasi had brought with her were asthmatic. Almasi had noticed how those kids coughed each time they came near the kitchen fire. So, even though she did not know what asthma was, she knew that there were certain people that just could not stand smoke. She figured that those kids were one of such people. Hence, she had remembered to carry them while coming to us.

She was surprised that we answered so quickly and was very grateful for our response. We were grateful to help too. I am a strong believer in purpose, so at that point, I began to connect dots on how the purpose of our own presence in that community was probably for a time as that. Akello wanted the kids to stay with us for a while till she could figure out a way forward, even though she did not know how exactly she would go about that.

"We are here with you and for you." I assured her. I could see that her heart and her intentions were pure and I wanted to help her henceforth, in every way I could. Since she had given the go-ahead, together with Almasi, we started letting the kids into the bus. We also used the services of their own bus to take the kids to the orphanage, as our own bus was not enough for their numbers. They were about two hundred kids and since we were just starting up ourselves, we had enough space to accommodate all of them. That night, I felt fulfilled, I was glad we could make impact. That was the core of my living—making impact. That night, we had Akello sign the necessary documents, as a matter of protocol.

Gradually, we started getting accustomed to each of the kids. They were amazing kids, all 200 of them. In the next one week, Akello was a bit calm as we had pulled every string we could; financially, in terms of insurance and therapy for her. As for the kids, there was group therapy for them, as they had whispered a very bad incident that we did not want to affect their childhood or their growth in any way.

Once Akello was calmer, we learnt more about her and why she started the orphanage. She was an orphan herself and was only lucky to get a scholarship to study in England that changed her life. She made it her lifelong project to ensure that she could give kids the same kind of opportunity. Hence, she started up the orphanage. She was unmarried, planned to start a family later on, but preferably with someone who understood her vision and truly bought into it. She also told us the interesting story of some of the kids, about their journey and their growth.

We had a lot to share with her to. It was a time of learning. There was so much to learn, unlearn and relearn. We ended up deciding that renovating her orphanage and moving the kids back there could affect their psychology on the long run. Hence, instead, thanks to the funds we could pull from my small organization that worked on the side to get funds for orphanages, we could get a new building. I was happy that this was possible.

However, the plan was not to move the kids to the new building. Having kids move like that in a short while could still affect them psychologically. We had decided to partner together and work as a unit. We had used up our own orphanage to full capacity with the additional two hundred kids we brought in (including those who were still receiving treatment in the hospital and were yet to join us). Hence, partnering together meant that we would all be joint owners and could bring in children as they came. After all, we were fighting for the same cause. The new building was in her own community and she was back to managing that. We had purchased it and renovation only took two months. We could not find one as big as the former, but it was a good start and we planned to even buy another once the sale of the first one. We easily retained the staff from her orphanage, but made sure to rebrand it for a fresh start. The magic of new beginnings are undeniable. As for Almasi, the brave cook that quickly thought up a great idea in a time of trouble like that, we decided to send her for a six-month training in England, where she not only learnt to speak English, but also learnt the in and out of managing an orphanage. It was obvious that she had potential to do far better than her current situation. We could see that the future was bright and we were ready to invest in whatever it took for that future to materialize for sure.

"That night after the other boys had gone to sleep, he asked me to come over to his quarters. He promised to teach me a prayer I had faulted in. I was happy because I had been punished the previous day for not reciting the prayers correctly, so I went. He began to touch me in a way I felt was wrong, but he could have not been wrong. He was my teacher and he always told us that it was bad to sin against God. So, I thought I was wrong. So, I let him….and after that…"

Moses could not keep going again. He burst into tears. He had ran away from his boarding school. He was tired of being constantly abused by his house master. There was no one to report to. He had tried reporting to the principal, but narrated that on the day he tried to do that, the house master had also come to see the principal. The man had threatened to tell the principal that he had caught Moses stealing the personal effects of other boys in the hostel. It was a missionary school; stealing was a grave offence over there far more than any random school. It was not just any missionary school. It was also one in Africa and punishing a child that had faulted in the way you deemed fit was no offence. The punishment for stealing was cutting a tree into two with an axe. It could take weeks, but you had to do it. He did not want to do that. He could not imagine missing his classes.

His parents had passed away and his uncle had put him in the school on the condition that he would keep getting good grades. Having a drop in his performance was sure to make his uncle forget about his schooling. He did not want to lose the opportunity to go to school. It was a hugely complicated situation. For this reason, he continued to abide by the dirty rules of his house master. He became withdrawn from his close friends, as he did not ever want to open his mouth and expose the house master. He knew the price he would have to pay for doing that and he was not ready to pay that price. Hence, he continued, but the young boy was getting frustrated. The pain he got from doing the nasty things the house master had him do was unexplainable. One day, he was tired and frustrated, so he sneaked out of the school while the security guard went to pee. He had not been thinking of it prior to that but an opportunity had shown up and it was more like a ship to freedom for him. So, not thinking of the housemaster, his uncle or anyone else, he rescued himself by running away. He did not bother to think of the consequences. The 10-year-old was just tired of everything. He was not exactly receiving any love from his uncle either. His uncle was only taking care of him as a matter of duty and never bothered to know how he felt about his parents' death.

Moses had a lot of unresolved emotions. It was as though the young boy was running from his situation, but it was far more than that. He was running from that life. He wanted to leave that life behind. It was enough that his parents had died in accident that he witnessed. He was in the car. He was the only one that survived the accident. His uncle saw him as an evil child for this reason. Having always benefitted from Moses father, he was only angry that his benefactor was dead. Moses had heard him say many nasty things that portrayed how he really failed about his father's death. So, he knew his uncle's way of thinking. After all, the man did not hide them from the boy.

He had learnt about orphanages the week before in his social studies class. Hence, he knew in his subconscious that there were places kids could go if their parents died. Hence, when the opportunity presented itself, he put all the two's together and his young mind knew that running away and leaving this life behind was not the worst thing that could happen to him. The worst thing that could actually happen to him was not finding an orphanage was he was out of the school. And the universe somehow helped him. Rhonda found him.

He had been hiding for about a week and it was Rhonda that spotted him when she had gone to get some essentials for herself earlier in the day. She looked at the boy and she wondered how any child would look that dirty and unkempt. She had initially been wondering how any mother would leave their child in such a state. However, another thought that occurred to her was the fact that he could have no parents. She had dealt with a lot of kids without parents, so it was not surprising that this would occur to her. Pity overrode her disgust. She looked at him walking with his head bowed to the ground. The young boy seemed to be deep in thoughts. He was also conscious about the way he walked. It was as if he was being careful, so no one would catch him.

She drove up to him and said. "Hey!"

The young boy tried to run once she called out to him.

"C'mon, she shouted from a distance. I have some food over here." She said, holding up some snacks she had bought to munch on. Moses stopped. He looked back and seemed to realize that she was really with food. So, he began to walk up to her slowly. By the time, he got back to her, he just lowered his head.

"Get into the car. You can sit and eat."

"No ma'am. I would just take the food and go please."

"Then, I can't give you the food Rhonda teased."

"Please ma'am. I have not eaten in three days." He had some money in his pocket when he was leaving the school, so he had been able to eat once a day for four days. Now, the boy was left with nothing.

Rhonda tried to touch him, but he stepped backwards.

"I am not trying to harm you. I just want to help." She said.

Moses looked down and said nothing, still trying to draw back.

"Where are your parents? I'll take you home."

"I don't want to go home" He cried.

At this point, Rhonda bent over to wipe his tears and handed the food over to him.

"I am looking for an orphanage that can take me in. Do you know of any ma'am?"

"Have you lost your parents?" Rhonda asked, surprised.

Moses only nodded.

"I know an orphanage. Come with me." She said.

Moses stared at her for a moment before getting into the passenger's seat.

"Can you see that I don't bite?" she asked as they drove. The boy still said nothing.

Then she passed him her iPad as they drove. She wanted him to see pictures and videos of the kids in the orphanage during their parties. She wanted him to see that he was truly safe with her and had nothing to worry about.

"I own and run and orphanage." She said. "I want to take you in, but you have to tell me everything." She could tell there was more to this boy.

"Everything?" he asked.

"Yes, everything."

He said nothing for the rest of the drive. Once he got to the orphanage, he talked about his parents and his uncle, but would not talk about why he ran out of his school. Rhonda had met him wearing his uniform. It was a popular missionary school and she knew the school. However, she did not want to force the boy to talk.

"You can talk to me once you are ready." She said. "I need to know everything, so I can really know how to help." She said. He still would not say a word.

A thorough routine medical examination was done on Moses, as was done on every new child that came into the orphanage. While at it, the doctor noticed the blisters in his anus and around his private areas, so he began to question Moses. After much persuasion, he told the doctor and Rhonda what had been happening to him at school, with his housemaster.

First off, Rhonda reminded him that none of all that had happened was his fault and they were going to make sure the man got arrested, so he was free to tell them everything in details.

"I don't want to cause any trouble at school. I do not want him to be arrested. Other boys would also make fun of me."

"You won't be causing any trouble Moses. Whether your friends know it or not, you would be their hero, as you would be protecting other kids from going through what has happened to you." Said Rhonda.

"Would you want your friends to also be forced to do things like this?" The doctor asked.

"Never." Said Moses.

"Great. Then, you have to tell us everything. We would see to the root of the matter. And after this, we could get your uncle to sign for you to be here permanently, if that is what you want. And from what you have told me about him, I think he may just agree."

Moses nodded. "I am only scared."

"Don't worry. We're going to see to this.

First off, Moses got all the necessary medical treatments and his injuries were also treated appropriately. Once he felt better, Rhonda took the test result to the school. The school called his uncle, who said he was a cursed child and he was willing to wash his hands off him. Rhonda was right there with all the necessary documents to accept the child. She was happy at their win. Moses was happy too.

To their surprise, many other boys also began to come forward to talk about how the house master had done the same to them. It had been going on for years and many of the boys had been scared to talk because of the different types of threats the man usually issued. No one made fun of Moses. He was seen as the brave boy he was, as he had given others the room to speak up. The house master was the only culprit and he was appropriately dealt with as one. He lost his job, any hope for pension and he was also arrested.

As a kid, if someone had told me that one day, I would save kids from a den of kidnappers, somewhere in Africa, I would have taken that person for a clown. That is for sure.

Five months after the start of the orphanage in Kenya, in the middle of a rainy night, there was noise at the gate. Harry was in Kenya with me this time, so we were in our hotel room. The security guard being used to such noises, went to the gate. He thought he heard the voices of children.

"Help!" they shouted. The security guard, Chege managed to rise up from his bed to see what was going on outside. There were three boys at the gate. It was about 1.a.m and he was more bothered about the safety of all the kids inside, who he was supposed to guide. His best bet was to go call Rhonda.

Rhonda was confused, so she called me.

"There are kids at the gate. What if it is a trap?"

After going back and forth with our deliberations, we decided to let Chege go out through the back gate to snoop on if there was anyone else with the kids and on confirmaing, signal to Rhonda to open the gate. It did not exactly guarantee the safety, but it was the best move we could come up with at the time.

The mission was successful. The kids were in and we could see marks all over their bodies. They had been kidnapped and maltreated in many ways. However, being our imperfect selves, we thought the important thing was to clean them up and allow them have a good night rest and we would all wake up in the morning to discuss the details. We had a stressful day, so Rhonda could understand that all the staff were tired.

The boys were tired too, but began to talk about their other friends that were still in the den of kidnappers. They were going to sell them in another country, as they had overheard the kidnappers say while they were trying to escape. I did not like the sound of that. No one else did. Our sleep was over for that night. We began to make calls to everyone we knew; the police, security experts and everyone else we thought could help. I was particularly anxious. The boys had said they were about 50 kids that had been kidnapped from a faraway district. Apparently, the people that saw them when they escaped wanted nothing to do with them as they knew about the kidnappers den all the while. They also knew not to mess with the kidnappers for the safety of them and their children. So, as opposed to hiding the boys, they directed them to the orphanage. We knew that safety was definitely the first concern in this case. The thought of the kidnappers tracing the boys to the orphanage scared me. There were so many kids in the orphanage. We could not afford to take chances.

The boys had heard them also say they would sell the kids the next day. That was what gave them the motivation to run. They knew that if they did not make it out of that place on that particular night, then they would never set their foot on the soil of their fatherland again. They had heard of human trafficking and how they made young boys become slaves, even sex slaves. They just had to take a chance at escaping and also trying to save the other kids who had given up.

Luckily, the police and secret service force responded by guarding the orphanage first off. Then, taking the boys to lead them to the den of the kidnappers. The police had said Harry and I had no expertise to escort them on mission, so there was no need for us to come around. It was a hard pill to swallow, but it was the truth. I had been hoping that they would come escort us to the orphanage to stay with the kids, but there was really nothing we could do.

Well, the kids were eventually rescued and there we were, on television, the next day, as the heroes alongside the young boys that came to cry for help. I had rushed to the orphanage earlier in the day. The kids were also on television, so their parents could identify them. However, they were transported by the police force to their district, so their parents could easily pick them up. This particular incidence gave the orphanage publicity we never solicited for. Following this, we had a lot of calls from people that either wanted to donate or knew a kid that needed shelter. Well, we were happy in all instances. We were grateful for the little good things that we did not plan; Rhonda and I.

The fact about the orphanage in Kenya was that it was the most dramatic I had experienced so far. It brought out every emotion in me. One day, I could be happy and excited about our progress. The next day, I could be scared for the kids or another set of kids. It always had to do with extremes—a total rollercoaster.

I talked to Julia often on phone about the happenings in the orphanage. She only laughed. Hers had been worse in her time. She basically faced most of the things Rhonda and I were facing in addition to lack of funds to do the things she wanted to do. She had also been seen as an outcast and had no mentor to put her through, unlike in my case. She had literally started from nothing. I even had the support from a partner in my case.

Harry was just perfect for me. He was always supportive; totally present every step of the way. Not for once did I look back and not find the solid support system who is my husband, standing right behind me.

CHAPTER
SIXTEEN

N ow, talking about parents, I had begun to play the role of parents in the lives of many of the kids. It had been three years since I started volunteering for orphanages in my own way. So, watching the kids grow both in The Safe Place and the orphanage Rhonda and I had established (Safe Haven orphanage), created some form of attachment. I could not stand watching those kids do anything that was likely to harm them. Holding a sharp instrument or running around in a way that was dangerous always made me bothered about the kids. I did not just want them getting in harm's way even in the slightest way. I guess there is a responsibility that came with being a parent and I began to exhibit that in all the orphanages, even those in Ghana, Nigeria, Gambia and other countries across Africa.

"Olivia, you remind me of my younger self." Julia had said one day, on seeing my reaction in terms of protecting the kids. I think I was finally understanding why Julia could not leave the kids or take a vacation. She was that attached to them and she could really not be blamed. In my case, I used to travel and come to the orphanage to stay for some time, but she was always with the kids, responsible for them every day, so I understood better now. The kids across various orphanages were my life's project. I had made my career helping them. I think that further explains the attachment. In Julia's case, they were her everything; they were her children, her family, career and purpose. So, she was not crazy all the times she would not leave them. It is just what naturally comes to you when you start caring for the kids.

Looking at how I felt about the kids, I wondered how I would feel with my own kids. I wonder how protective Harry would be. Protective like my father? As a child, he did everything to ensure I was safe. He kept my governess, the security and everyone on their toes. When Amira came, the energy doubled. My parents even employed extra staff. I can also remember the time when Amira and I ate too much ice cream and got diarrhea. My parents were bothered that it had to do with something about the hygiene in the house. It was sad to see the staff do extra cleaning because of us. Mum also made sure they paid utmost attention to cleanliness while cooking. Well, we did not have the nerve to confess. The good thing still, was that my parents were always lenient with their staff, but they could not just afford to take things with levity when it comes to my sister and I. I guess that is it about parents. It should not be surprising or annoying to any child when their folks try to stick out their necks for them.

And oh Harry's parents. They are literally the best. They not only treat me like their own, but also like a queen, all the time. Their love was usually overwhelming, but they had only extended the love they gave Harry to me. Well, I could not wait to see how Harry would act as a father. I knew he would make a great father for sure, because of his good nature. I was more than grateful for the fact that we had parents that thought us the basic things about building a family, just by the way they acted.

Hence, I was not surprised when my parents started getting concerns about my stay in Africa and the fact that I was travelling from one country to another. I was staying in the best hotels and their most expensive suits, but that was not enough for them. They were bothered about my safety, as the security in some African countries were now being threatened by terrorists. My dad offered to send a private jet to be on standby for all my travels. However, I thought that would be too much. Also, I did not want to get my purpose for being there mixed up or my focus to be redirected to luxury. I think I was doing just fine, so I had to turn the private jet offer down. My parents were still worried, so I called them more often. We spoke on video calls every day and I travelled to London at least once in two months. I usually used the opportunity to just relax and also see my doctors for an all-round check-up, like my parents had even suggested since Harry and I were trying to start a family.

In the past, as I grew up, I wanted my parents less involved in my life. They had such a strong influence in my life during my younger years, always wanting to give me a picture perfect kind of life, but I started resisting it at some point. Now, being with kids myself and getting attached to them, I understood my parents a lot better and why they were always looking out for me. It was simply out of love. Here's the thing: no matter how old a child grows, they would still be their parent's child, the age gap would remain there and there is nothing you can do about it. They knew you since you were born, they have been with you through life and they were wiser. Hence, you are one of their life's project and as annoying as that sounds, there is nothing, absolutely nothing you can do about it.

Well, the good part is that they are always sincere and do everything they do out of true love and care for you. If there is anyone's advice or judgment for your life that you can trust, it is definitely that from your parents (all things being equal). So, dear reader, it is time to pay more attention to understanding your parents.

I remember the reunion and the way Julia looked at the kids that had passed through her. I could see the look in her eyes. No matter how much they had grown or how far they had gone in life, they were still very much her children. And that's on period.

A part of the reunion period I later got to discover was that Sandra went to see her mum. It had been ages since she got out of rehab and Julia had set her up in a nice place. Julia had told Sandra about how her mum was now out. To this effect, Sandra and Joseph did everything within their power to make sure she was comfortable. She was now a food vendor in her community and she would also bring food to the orphanage from time to time. It seemed to be something she enjoyed doing—the cooking. However, they could not bring her to the states yet because Sandra realized that she had not fully healed from everything her mother had done. She still had some paranoia about how something could come up some day. She also did not want the kids confused about their grandmother. She wanted to be sure that the time was ripe before introducing her to the kids, as she and Joseph had generally always ignored questions about their parents for a long time. First off, they did not want to lie to the kids. Yet, they felt like the kids could not handle all that information just yet. So, they had waited for that long.

Sandra had been going for therapy before their trip to Liberia. She felt a lot better and had dealt with so many issues by the time she was set to travel. When she became a mother, she also had to go for therapy because of everything she had gone through in the hands of her own mother. She also had to deal with the issue of rape and the fact that she was a bit overprotective with her children. She went to therapy for all that.

Sheila, her mother, was now a new person. She was part of her church's women group, actively involved in everything they did and how they gave back to the community. She was also very committed to her business and seemed to love everything she did. Since I was writing a book for Julia, it was only normal that she would tell me of the crazy day Sheila had come to the gate of the orphanage, almost ready to in fact kill her own daughter if she would not hand her the money she made from peddling drugs for her in a petty manner, on the streets. She had told me about that day, but when I finally saw Sheila in person, she was nothing like the personality in the story Julia had told. She was now different and a proof that lives could be changed with the proper level of care and attention. She had come to render community service to the orphanage, courtesy of the church where she worshipped. They helped in cleaning the orphanage for the day. Additionally, she had brought food and all sorts of snacks for the kids. She seemed very happy to help and now had quite a bond with Julia. I could see them talking and laughing in a distance, probably about old time or perhaps, recent happenings. Any way, it was a beautiful site.

Sandra and Joseph had stayed the whole week around the reunion period. Sandra had now healed to a large extent, so they went to visit granny Sheila, first as a couple. She apologized to Sandra over again and even Sandra could see that the woman was a lot different. There was now little or no cause to worry about what she would do or if she would harm the kids. Judging from the time I saw her in the orphanage, I don't think there was any cause for alarm at all. To my best knowledge, Joseph and Sandra (especially) had nothing to worry about.

Later on, they went with the kids. Sheila had cried at the site of her grand kids. I was told that Erica did not understand why she was crying and even joined her to cry.

"Stop crying grandma. Mum, dad, why is granny crying?" she had asked. Children would always be innocent, right? The entire family bonded and then, they kept coming to spend more time with Sheila each day, so the kids could familiarize themselves with her. When they were leaving, they promised that very soon, Sheila would come spend some time with them in the United States. I love to see happy endings!

Joseph's parents had died many years ago, so the best the family could do was visit their grave. Joseph still cried once he got to their graveside. Visiting their grave side was like rekindling the memories of all that had happened. Their death was a moment that changed his childhood forever. The kids did not understand why he was crying, but they cried too any way. However, the story of their death was too much of a story to tell the kids. They were too young to hear of such evils that were possible in the world.

As for John, he finally had the courage to tell Mira about why he was a stubborn child while they were younger. As a matter of fact, he was not really stubborn, he was only a troubled child who needed an outlet. His attitude towards others was only his way of venting. Mira could understand, knowing that the kids in the orphanage had gone through various tough situations that brought them to the orphanage. Up until then, John had avoided telling her the story, but being in Liberia, he had an urge to tell her, he felt the time was now right. She had not forced him to tell her a thing earlier, as she had the basic knowledge that how much a person had healed played a factor in how much of their story they would be willing to tell.

He started by making them visit the grave side of his father together. The man had died in prison and in spite of how much he had hurt John by killing his mother, John still cried. That was the thing about family, you could love them but still dislike them. That explained John's plight. Your father is still your father no matter what; so is your mother. You cannot run away from family totally (well, except in very extreme cases). John's case seemed to be extreme, but he still cried when he received reports from Liberia that the man was dead many years ago. He had been very sick and had lost his life. When they visited the grave side, the young man still cried. There and then, he told Mira everything he needed to tell her about his childhood and the battles he had to fight. He told her about how beautiful and kind his mother had been and how she would not speak up. He also told her about his dream of starting various campaigns on domestic abuse for women, and perhaps, a non-governmental organization that would help women as time went on.

Before then, John and Joseph had never discussed what happened to their parents. The reunion week and spending time over drinks, just talking during the reunion, gave them the liberty to pour out their hearts about everything that had happened to them from their past. It was indeed a time of healing for both men. The bond of their friendship turned into brotherhood.

After the reunion, plans for Mira and John's wedding started up fully. I was excited to see that Mira was going to get married soon. Like I had mentioned earlier, Mira used to be very much a hopeless romantic and that part of her was back again. She always had an idea of how her dress would look, how the decorations would be and the way she would recite her vows. All that was on ground before life hardened up my girl. Well, there was nothing we could do about that part. However, I was glad that someone who she could trust was back to bring back that part of her.

It turned out John was a hopeless romantic, just like she was, so they had been going on several romantic getaways. It is not as though they never had their own differences, but they were just two highly mature people who had come together to ensure that they had a relationship that worked. Being romantics, they knew exactly how to appeal to each other's love languages. That played a huge role in ensuring that their relationship really worked out.

The wedding plans started and you could trust that I would take charge of things to a large extent. I could not help it, I loved the thought of putting things together and making them work. Now, it even involved flowers, decorations, wine, cakes and everything weddings remind you about. That was a part of life I liked—whatever depicted beauty. Growing up, while Mira was busy, reading all those parts of the newspapers that involved investment banking, I was the child that went out with mum to shop for flowers and decorations, just because I loved to. I must have took after my mother in that area. She was such a lady! To blow off steam, she would go shop for furniture, fine china or flowers. And I absolutely loved to follow her.

Now that this event even happened to be for two people I held very close to my heart, I was more than ready to throw in myself and ensure that the event planners did their best to make the day a memorable one. Mira cared only about work to a large extent; for her, it was always a cycle of working and relaxing. So, she left me to make choices for her and just send her two options to do the final picking. It was no burden for me, it was something I loved to do, so trust me, no complains.

I saw it as a way to blow off steam, just like my mother. You know, I just love to see beautiful things. And the wedding day was indeed filled with beautiful things. My favorite couple decided to make it a destination wedding. The parents were fine with whatever made them happy. So, off we went to Seychelles, to enjoy our time with the bride and groom. Harry and I saw it as a time to even rekindle our love, as we were very much travelers (but for work), who found it hard to travel to romantic destination. We took the four days we spent in Seychelles as another time for a honeymoon. Everything was set, so I had little or no reason to worry about what was going on with the planning. I wanted to spend time with my lover, so I left things for our planners to sort out.

The wedding day finally came and my girl looked so pretty in her Vera Wang dress. Everyone that was dear to our hearts (especially from the orphanage) were in attendance. Mira had told our parents that she wanted her very intimate wedding, so there was no need to invite all the dignitaries my parents would have loved to invite. However, Julia finally agreed to travel this time. What a miracle! We were happy to have her there.

As dad walked Mira down the aisle, I held hands with Harry and mum, as my mind took me down the memory lane. I was just grateful for the gift of her, everything she had achieved and the fact that she had now found happiness. As they said their vows, I could not hold back my tears of joy. Oh my! My sister was really getting married to the love of her life. I had seen her dream of this since we were kids. Dreams really come true in the end; trust me!

After the wedding, Harry and I stayed back in Seychelles. We wanted to have our own time out, as a couple. The new couple had gonc to thc city of love, Paris for their honeymoon. It was such a fun time in Seychelles. After two weeks of enjoying our time there, we were back to our house in London. Work had pulled us apart to a large extent, so we decided to make it up to each other by just spending some time at home, doing nothing but loving on each other. It was in that period that I realized that I was pregnant. I had been sick for about a week and our time travelling around had made it super hard for me to keep track of my menstrual cycle.

I went to the hospital and after a blood test, it was confirmed that I was pregnant. I was even happier to discover later on, that I was carrying a set of twins. Harry had to stop me from travelling once he knew I was pregnant. He just wanted the best for me and our babies. He was also home more often. I was bothered about work, so I decided to form a team. They would carry on the work I had been doing in the last few years. They would do all the travelling and report to me. Using an HR firm, I was able to get the best hands for the job. I sent mails to notify all the orphanages I worked with about the new development. The most important thing to everyone was that work did not stop. I could not bear to see the good work we were doing stop too. So, there was no problem at all from my end.

In my third trimester, Julia confessed that she missed me and all our tea evenings. For this reason, she came to London to stay for a while. I was just happy that she was finally learning how to relax a bit and also delegate. In my time working in orphanages, I realized that there was a time to the work solely by yourself. There was also a time to delegate. Perhaps for Julia, her own time to do the work was for an extended period because her calling was far greater than that of most of us. I wonder what life would be for me if Julia did not run after her purpose. This is what made me realize that her own calling was higher. I cannot even begin to imagine not getting the opportunity to meet all the amazing people that had passed through her and were in great positions.

Her presence brought so much joy to me, she had become like a second mother to me. It was almost impossible for me not to feel that way. Julia's motherly instincts were quite strong and there was just enough of her to go round for everybody. I guess that is why many great many and women could come from her. As much as she hated to admit it, I knew I had a special place in her heart. Julia, who would hardly ever leave the orphanage to travel to even another country in Africa, came to London to stay with me for a while when I was in my third trimester. That would sound like a miracle to many of the kids from the orphanage.

She was in London with me all through my third trimester. We had lots and lots of good times together. She told me about how she felt like she did not enjoy her youth in the UK. She did not travel to fun places as a young adult when her friends were doing that. When she was supposed to do that was the same time she had gone to Liberia to start up a good cause. I reminded her that she had not had all that fun for a good reason; she had every right to be proud of what she was doing at that age. I also told her that it was not too late to do all the things she had not done. It was not too late to visit all the places she wanted to visit. After all, she had been away from Liberia in three months and things were going on smoothly. So, she really had no cause to be always there. She could oversee things and always travel whenever she liked. She had planted and it was time for her to harvest. It seemed like the scenery in London made her agree with me very easily. She did not argue for a moment. She agreed that she should now travel often, especially now that she had overcome her initial fear of how the orphanage would be run if she was not around. I was happy about this, but I think her change of heart had started a lot earlier—precisely the time when we did her surprise birthday/reunion. Attending Mira and John's wedding probably sparked up something in her too. Anyway, I decided not to dwell on the "why".

I finally had my twins and they were beautiful to watch. I was surrounded by family at the time of the birth. John and Mira who had their home in New York had come to London, my parents were present, Julia was present, Harry's parents were present and of course, my darling Harry, the father of my twins was present and there to support me. I felt blessed to have them all in my life. I could not imagine life without them.

The next few years were focused on spending more time with my husband and raising my kids. About parenting, well, I had been literally parenting for quite a while, in the orphanages I worked with. It was a bit similar to what I felt for the kids in the orphanage. However, it was stronger since I carried my kids in my womb and had monitored them since inception. There is an attachment motherhood comes with that can never be explained. I knew my feelings for the kids in the orphanages would be a bit more intense once I was back to work, because I was now a mother. While I bothered that this feeling I got from motherhood was something Julia did not get a chance to feel, I was comforted by the fact that she had true joy from walking in purpose and she had made far more impact than several people who were mothers to their own children would ever make, even with their kids.

And oh, did I mention that I had a boy and a girl? I would save their names for later. Well, that is Harry's take, but I may be willing to reveal that and a thing or two about them in my next book.

On the overall, working with orphanages really opened up my eyes to the real meaning of life. I keep imagining what things would be or which story I would have told if Julia did not take the crazy, but bold step she had taken. She is indeed a hero and the fruit of her work just keeps speaking. She is not just a mentor to me, but also my mother.

You may not have money to give orphanages, but if you try volunteering in an orphanage, you would see life very differently. If you are at a point in your life where you are looking to find purpose or you are looking for a deeper meaning to life, I am encouraging you to go volunteer for any orphanage. Giving your time and your skills would go a long way. If you are a nurse or health practitioner, you could volunteer to provide free services to the kids for a weekend. If you are a teacher, you could volunteer to teach a class for a day.

Even if you have no skills to offer and all you have is food, you can go give whatever you have. You have no idea who you would be saving by doing so. There are many people that are destined to be "Julia's" in our world. When the call comes upon you, please remember Julia's story and don't turn down the call to fulfil purpose. Please take inspiration from her story.

You see, life is not supposed to strictly go in one particular way. There are many ways around achieving success and fulfilling purpose. So, don't be caught up in the web of trying to do things in a particular way. If your life's direction is towards an unfamiliar road, do not begin to think that it is an impossible path. Many people, just like Julia, have gone through seemingly impossible paths. However, those stories are not told that often. More of the stories told are usually about how someone made a particular amount of money from doing this or that.

Of course, I come from money, so I am not one to tell you that money is not important. Money is important to make even orphanage work progress. However, there are some impacts that change the world that chasing money would have never helped in achieving.

Looking around and seeing so many kids all over the world and the quality of life they could give to their family because they were motivated by a woman who they called their mother in an orphanage after their parents died is amazing. I have seen it first hand, so for me, Julia's existence would always be a joy. She is probably one of those angels that were sent on our way to make this harsh world a bit better than what it would have been without them.

Printed in Great Britain
by Amazon